THE
KEPT
SECRET

kept \ˈkept\ *vb:* to refrain from revealing

secret \ˈsee-kret\ *n:* something shared only
                              confidentially with a few

THE
KEPT
SECRET

STAN WILCZEK JR.

GATEWAY PRESS
UTICA, NEW YORK

Printed in the United States of America

First printing: May 2006
10 9 8 7 6 5 4 3 2 1

Library of Congress Cataloging-in-Publication Data

Wilczek Jr., Stan
The Kept Secret / Stan Wilczek Jr.
p. cm.
ISBN 0-9701516-2-4
1. Terrorism-Fiction I. Title

2006923403

Gateway Press
Utica, New York

For Rose

... my day is not complete without
a glimpse of your intoxicating smile.

ACKNOWLEDGMENTS

Although this book is a product of my often too vivid imagination, none of what I have written would have been possible without all of you, past and present, who have in some way touched and influenced my life. Thank you for letting me be a part of yours. That said, some of you may think that you see yourself, or possibly others, described in this book. Let me assure you, you do not.

Many thanks to my cadre of would-be book reviewers: Bill D'Angelo, Dave Gentile, Robin Lundy, and Ray Pasternak. Your insights and input were invaluable in shaping the finer details of this book. A thanks also to Dan Dupee for finding, several times as I recall, my manuscript lost somewhere in the depths of that humming gray box on the floor next to my desk. A special thanks to my lifelong friend Larry Britt for his technical input on the intricacies of the law enforcement investigative processes.

A very special thanks to the editorial staff at Gateway Press, specifically Sheila Orlin, Jennifer Rotundo, and Jerry Dischiavo. You never know how much you don't know until you talk to a real expert. Thank you for your guidance and input, but especially for your patience. At times this seemed like too much fun, which of course is the way it should be.

Finally, I thank you, the reader, for taking a risk on an unknown, first-time author. My fantasy is that this book will be permanently clutched in your hands for the next several days and you find yourself sneaking a read when you know you should be doing something else.

As a final note, any and all mistakes contained herein are mine.

THE
KEPT
SECRET

PROLOGUE

The morning paper rattled in his hands as he read, for the third time, the bold black headline. His pounding heart finally broke the trance. Mouth wide open, he inhaled a huge gulp of air. The pounding got worse.

"Tell me I am going to outlive them all."

The wispy words barely flowed from his parched mouth. His face whitened just as it had following the death of the others.

"Or am I next?"

His right hand instinctively reached to his left breast shirt pocket for the well-worn, gold wire-rimmed reading glasses he always kept there. It took both hands to put the spectacles to his face. Seconds later the headlines blurred and the fine print came into focus.

Pravda, 13 September 1971 — The Central Committee of the Communist Party and the USSR Council of Ministers announce, with regret, the death on 11 September 1971, after a protracted, painful illness, of the former First Secretary of the Central Committee of the Communist Party and the Chairman of the USSR Council of Ministers, Nikita Sergeevich

1

Khrushchev, at the age of 78.

"He died of a heart attack?"

His loud words filled the room and seemed to calm him. He no longer felt the pounding in his chest. His hands stopped shaking.

For almost ten years, Aleksandr Popov lived with the constant fear of his own death. He knew others, perhaps scores, were murdered to assure the secret would be kept. They were all expendable. But he also knew, of the five left entrusted with the secret, he was the next most expendable. Yet, in less than ten years, two of the five were murdered, and now a third, Khrushchev, died of natural causes. He wasn't sure if he should feel relieved, or even more fearful.

Aleksandr leaned back in the over-stuffed leather chair. It wasn't long before he felt his body go limp. A slight smirk settled on his face.

"Why should I be afraid . . . to the rest of humanity, I am already dead."

1

Even with his back facing the doorway to his office, Jack could feel her eyes wandering over his body. The thought alone made him shiver. As he swiveled his chair around, his heart rate picked up. He drew in a slow deep breath through his nose to try to disguise his excitement. His eyes locked onto hers in a long gaze. He didn't blink. Neither did she.

"You decided to stop in after all." Jack was the first to break the silence, although his comment was followed by another bout of voiceless stares. "I take it the presentation did not go well."

"Well? Let's just say it died a slow death as I was making it."

"Sit down and tell me about it. It's probably not as bad as it seems."

"Oh yes it is."

Dyan slid her tall, thin, twentysomething body into the chair in front of Jack's desk, the same one she sat in so often over the past year. Just being back on her own turf, in familiar surroundings, was enough to alleviate at least some of the stress she was feeling. She took in a deep breath and closed her eyes.

"Low-tech, low-cost terrorist acts aren't sexy enough for the

Bureau," she said with her eyes closed. "They don't even think they're credible." Then she sat up, eyes wide open. "Mine was the only presentation that didn't have the word biological, chemical, radiological, or nuclear in the title. I was the last speaker of the day standing in front of a roomful of mostly male FBI jocks, mouths already salivating for their first happy hour drink. A wimpy female presenting a bunch of wimpy ideas. Terrorists who might use gasoline instead of uranium, or feces instead of anthrax."

Dyan lowered her head. "I didn't even get one question. Not one goddamn question."

"I know how much time and effort you put into . . . "

"It's not that," Dyan interrupted. "I felt honored to be picked for this task force. I knew I was the youngest, least qualified person assigned to it. I just thought people would be more open. Now I know how the Phoenix agent felt before 9/11 when he tried to warn us about bin Laden sending students to U.S. aviation schools.

"Just because we haven't had a terrorist attack on U.S. soil since 9/11, doesn't mean it's never going to happen again. It's just a matter of time. We all know there are terrorist cells in this country. It's only a matter of time before . . . "

There was a long silence before Jack spoke up. "Dyan, everyone is doing the best job they can to make sure the next time doesn't happen. But you know, and I know, we aren't perfect. These guys are smart. And very patient. No matter what we do, there is still probably going to be a next time. Hopefully, what we are doing will lessen the impact and severity of it. Don't let the system get you down."

Dyan looked up at Jack. She was glad that she stopped in to see him before going home. His words were exactly what she hoped she would hear from him. Their eyes locked again. Jack Nelson is wickedly handsome, she thought to herself. It didn't matter that he was black and she was white. In fact, it probably

4

heightened the sexual tension between them. The fact that she just spent four nights away from her husband of three months, the first time she had gone without sex for more than twenty-four hours since her honeymoon, also contributed to the tingling she was feeling in various parts of her body as she tried not to squirm in her seat.

This time Dyan broke the silence. "Don't worry . . . I'm not giving up." She stood up, turned, and walked toward the doorway. Two steps later, she stopped and looked back over her shoulder at Jack. "I think I'll go home, open a bottle of wine, get naked, and wait for my husband to come home and play with me."

Jack's face went hot. He knew if he was white, he'd now be red. Then he felt other parts of his body go hot. He watched as Dyan turned her head away and started for the door.

"Oh, you are still here," the out-of-breath secretary said, as she almost ran head-on into Dyan in the doorway of Jack's office. "You have a phone call from the director."

"The director of what?"

"FBI Director Blackman."

"Blackman?"

"Yes. He wants a copy of your report that you gave earlier today at the task force meeting."

"His assistant was there. He can get a copy from him."

"His assistant has misplaced his copy."

"Right. I bet the SOB never took a copy."

"He also wants you back in Washington first thing in the morning."

"Tomorrow's Saturday," Jack interrupted, as he stood up from his desk.

"Did he say why he wanted me there?"

"Haven't you guys heard what happened? Fifteen minutes ago, several tunnels were blown up in Boston. They think it was a terrorist attack."

5

2

"Cocamo. Great name. Have you been to the island?"

"Yes. We spent a few days there."

"Sylvan Beach, New York. Isn't that on Oneida Lake? The Erie Canal goes through it, right?"

"Yes it does." Mozat forced himself to act politely to the tall, slightly overweight, sixtyish-looking man standing on the dock with one bare foot resting on the inflatable boat that was mounted on the swim platform to the aft of his boat. "Sylvan Beach is on the eastern end of the lake, just after you leave the canal." He then turned and responded to the voice he pretended was coming from the hatch below. "I will be down in a minute."

"We will pass right by it on our way home." The man continued to carry on the conversation, oblivious to Mozat's inattentiveness. "Our boat is about ten slips down, the My Island. We're doing the Great Circle Route. Left South Haven, Michigan, that's our home port, last summer. Spent the winter mostly in the Keys, although we did take a side trip to the Bahamas during the holidays. Kids flew down for a week and met us there. It was great. Have you ever been to the Bahamas?"

"No . . . we have not."

"If you get a chance, you've got to go there. And don't believe everything you hear about modern-day pirates in and around the islands. Most of the rumors are probably driven by the drug-related activities in the region. There were hundreds, maybe thousands of snowbird boaters in the islands. I didn't hear of anyone having any trouble. So, did you come down here in the fall and are you headed back up the Intracoastal Waterway?"

Mozat stood motionless, staring at the man. He never saw anyone breathe and talk at the same time as the man in front of him appeared to be doing.

"Actually, we arrived down here just before the holidays." Mozat noticed the puzzled look on the man's face. "Not by boat, but by car." The puzzled look disappeared. "We purchased this boat in Miami late last year, and spent the rest of the winter and spring in the Keys relaxing."

"I know what you mean. So are you on your way back up to Sylvan Beach?"

"That is our plan."

"Honey, who are you talking to?" A tall, slender, dark-haired woman, in her early forties, yet younger-looking, especially when she stood next to Mozat, who was twenty years older, stepped out of the hatchway onto the rear deck area of the boat wearing a loose-fitting Hawaiian print sun dress. "Oh, hello."

"Hi."

Remembering the coaching he received regarding the demeanor of the average boat person, friendly but not overly friendly, the latter describing the man standing on the dock, Mozat spoke up, though he would have rather cut off the conversation there. "This is my wife, Ziara."

"Hello. Dave Lawson. Nice to meet you."

"Very nice to meet you." Ziara knew how to play her part well.

"Mo," Mozat said with the wave of his hand, as Lawson turned his sights to him. "Dave is from Michigan and is doing the Great Circle Route."

"Oh, how wonderful. Have you been through New York State yet?" Although Ziara knew from her coaching that the Great Circle Route — a circumnavigation around the eastern third of North America, down the Mississippi River, across the Gulf of Mexico, up the east coast along the Intracoastal Waterway, across New York State via the Hudson River and Erie Canal, then into the Great Lakes — was almost always cruised in a counterclockwise direction to take advantage of the southerly flow of the Mississippi, she did not want to appear too knowledgeable on the subject.

"No. We are headed north, up the Intracoastal Waterway," Lawson replied.

"So are we." Ziara felt Mozat's fingers, from his arm wrapped around her waist, dig into her ribs. "Perhaps we could travel together?" Another dig. "When are you leaving Sailfish Marina?"

"We're heading out first thing in the morning. We'd love the company up the waterway."

"Oh, that is unfortunate," Mozat chimed in, sounding overly apologetic, as he gazed from Ziara to Lawson. "We are not leaving for another week. We have decided to spend some time in the North Palm Beach area."

Lawson's face went long. "We'd love to stay a few more days ourselves, but we need to continue heading north, otherwise we won't make it back to South Haven by the end of September. It can get mighty cold crossing the Great Lakes any time beyond that."

"We know what you mean," Ziara replied, her arm now around Mozat's waist, her fingers digging into his ribs. "I was just going to mix up a batch of rum swizzles. Could we interest you in one?"

"Sure. Let me go get my wife."

They both watched Lawson turn and head down the dock toward his boat. Mozat was the first to speak up. "I thought the odds were against him accepting the drink offer?"

"They were. At least that is what they told us anyway."

Mozat looked at Ziara. "It will not hurt to be seen with another couple sitting on the back of the boat. We will blend in all that much more."

Blending in was something the couple was desperately trying to do. They were less than 200 miles into their journey, with almost 2,000 more to go before they reached their final destination by August. So far everything was going according to their plan. In fact, the most daring part of the cruise, leaving the continental United States and traveling to Rum Runner Cay, a small island located in Crooked Island Passage, at the southern tip of The Exumas in the Bahamas, and returning to the United States without clearing Customs in either direction, went as smooth as they planned. With the most difficult part of the cruise over, they just needed to blend in with the thousands of other snowbird boaters heading north along the Intracoastal Waterway for the summer.

"Ziara, Mo, this is my wife Anne."

"Nice to meet you, and welcome aboard the Cocamo."

3

"Hurry up and wait," Dyan mumbled as she sat by herself in the large, black, high-backed leather chair at the forty foot-long mahogany table that looked like it was custom made to fit in the conference room lined with flat-screened monitors instead of windows. She arrived at the Washington, D.C., FBI headquarters building at 8:45 A.M., fifteen minutes before the scheduled 9:00 A.M. start time for the meeting, only to find out that it was moved to 10:00 A.M.

She thought she'd use the free time to call her husband. She instead spoke with their answering machine. He was probably at work himself, using a Saturday without her to catch up on his own backlog, she thought. Or golfing. She knew he understood that she might be in Washington for an indefinite period. Nevertheless, tensions between them ran high yesterday when, after four days of being apart, their much-anticipated Friday night encounter was reduced to a farewell airport kiss as Dyan caught an evening flight back to D.C. so she could be on time for the Saturday morning meeting. Although she needed to focus on the upcoming meeting, her mind kept wandering to what should have happened the night before. She wondered if what she was feeling now, after three months of marriage, would last forever. Though she hoped it would, she guessed it wouldn't.

Dyan joined the FBI five years ago as a research analyst after graduating from the State University of New York at Buffalo with a degree in Information Technology. Envisioned to improve the efficiency of the Bureau in the new information age, the newly created analyst positions proved difficult to staff due to private sector demands associated with Y2K, vague job descriptions, and a lack of qualified candidates. To entice applicants, the Bureau offered unlimited job location flexibility. Being a native of central New York, Dyan accepted a position in the Syracuse, New York, FBI Field Office.

Her analytical capabilities and fresh out-of-the-box thinking quickly became a sought-after commodity in an agency built on long standing, archaic work practices. Unfortunately, the biggest boost to her short career came post 9/11 when the true importance of her skills were noticed. As part of the Bureau's effort to improve its effectiveness following 9/11, an interagency task force was formed to assess future domestic terrorist threats. Dyan was its youngest member.

She worked for almost six months on her hypothesis regarding the direction terrorist organizations, such as al Qaeda, might head in the future. While most experts focused on future terrorist scenarios that used sophisticated nuclear, chemical, radiological, or biological technologies, Dyan believed there was a much higher probability that lower tech, lower cost options were available to the terrorists that could produce the same physiological impact on the public. Although a nuclear or biological attack might produce a high level of sensationalism, the cost to achieve such an attack would likely be in the tens of millions of dollars and involve highly technically skilled individuals. Contrast that with 9/11, which cost less than half a million dollars to execute, and was carried out by two dozen mostly uneducated individuals who brought nothing into this country but themselves. Few in the Bureau agreed with her hypothesis, until yesterday.

Dyan glanced at her watch. 9:55 A.M. and she was still the only one seated at the large table. Just as she was beginning to wonder if she was at the right location, a stream of mostly elderly — at least when compared to Dyan — males, dressed in dark suits — not cheap ones, but not expensive ones either — filled the room to capacity. As Dyan took the initiative to introduce herself to the gentleman to her left, who was ignoring her, the room went silent when Director Blackman, at six-three and pushing two-fifty, entered the room and sat at the center of the table in the one remaining seat obviously earmarked for him, almost directly across from her.

"There should be no doubt in anyone's mind that the war on terror continues," Blackman began. "Since 9/11, almost three years ago, I feel we have been successful in thwarting attempts by our enemies to inflict damage on our homeland. We have had repeated warnings of imminent attacks, all of which did not materialize, until the attack yesterday. In an obviously well-planned, well-coordinated mission, the enemy has broken their three years of silence.

"I would like Ryan Reynolds to review what we know so far from our investigation. Ryan."

At age thirty-five, Ryan Reynolds was the youngest assistant director in the Bureau. Mentored and fast-tracked by Blackman, he was appropriately nicknamed the "fair-haired boy." Although he was smart and ambitious, his meteoric rise had gone to his head. You learned very quickly to watch your back around Ryan Reynolds.

"At exactly 4:45 P.M. Eastern Standard Time, on Friday, June 4, 2004, explosions occurred in three tunnels of Boston's recently completed Central Artery and Tunnel Project, known as The Big Dig. As of 6:00 A.M. this morning, the death toll stands at just over a thousand people. Based on the number injured, somewhere in the range of two thousand, mostly from burns and smoke inhalation, we can expect at least several hundred more fatalities, which would make this the second most deadly attack by terrorists on American soil.

"Our preliminary investigation shows the terrorists poured gasoline, somewhere in the range of one hundred to two hundred gallons, mid-way through the tunnels and then remotely detonated the mixture several minutes later after a significant portion of the gasoline evaporated, which created a highly explosive mixture.

"Based on a review of the video tapes, we believe the terrorists used three minivans to transport and dump the gasoline. Two of the three vehicles have since been reported stolen from Logan Airport parking lots. We are still tracking down the owner of the other minivan, but expect similar findings. It appears the terrorists stole the vehicles early Friday morning and retrofitted them in time to carry out their afternoon attack. We have not found any of the stolen vehicles."

"Don't these tunnels have emergency ventilation systems to handle an event like this?" Blackman asked.

"They have massive ventilation systems, but they were designed to handle fires from a single bus, or truck, or a flammable fuel spill no bigger than what would cover the floor of a two-stall family garage. Once these fires propagated, hundreds of cars were engulfed in flames."

"Why gasoline?" Blackman interrupted.

"It's readily available, effective, and cheap." Dyan couldn't resist blurting out the canned response she gave to anyone who asked that question.

"It's not cheap where I buy it," someone spoke up, to which several in the room laughed, but only for a second or two.

Blackman, not amused, asked, "I'm sorry, you are?"

"This is agent Dyan Galloway from our Syracuse Field

Office," Reynolds spoke up before Dyan could answer. "She is a member of our interagency task force on future terrorist threats and author of . . . "

"Low-Tech, Low-Cost Terrorist Acts: The Next Wave," Blackman interrupted. "I read your report last night. When was the report officially presented to the Bureau?"

"Coincidentally, it was presented near the closing of our task force meeting early yesterday afternoon . . . "

"If you don't mind Ryan, I think Ms. Galloway can speak for herself."

"Friday afternoon, sir. I have been working on the hypothesis for several months, but last week's meeting was the first time I presented it to the rest of the task force."

For the next minute the only sound in the room was made by Blackman's large fingers as he noisily squeezed each page of the report, which was open in front of him, spending no more than a few seconds on each page before slowly flipping to the next. Although Dyan was on the other side of the table, a distance of more than ten feet, she recognized the report as hers.

"I want to make sure the chronology regarding the development of this report is well documented. We have been criticized enough over the past three years by all the Monday morning quarterbacks for not acting on information that surfaced within the Bureau. I do not want this to become another example of that." Blackman then looked directly at Dyan. "I would like a written report summarizing the chronology of your work on this report on my desk by the end of the day."

Before Dyan could respond, Blackman placed the report on the bottom of the three-inch stack of documents in front of him and moved on to the next agenda item.

Dyan sat motionless, staring at Blackman, only half-listening to the rest of the presentations and discussions. She could not believe the only thing anyone appeared to be worried about was protecting their asses.

4

"Can I help you?" The receptionist's steely voice matched the rest of her profile, like that of a female prison guard, tall and slim, yet tight and muscular. Her short cropped, bleached blonde hair added to her masculine look. Even her name tag, Ms. Rock, was intimidating. She was a woman even a man would not want to tangle with.

"Director Blackman wanted this by the end of the day." Dyan held the envelope out, but the receptionist did not reach for it.

"Please have a seat, Ms. Galloway. The director will be with you shortly."

Dyan gave the woman a look anyone would give a stranger who knew your name without asking for it. As she turned and walked toward the chairs along the wall, she first saw the key card reader near the elevator door, then her key card security badge hanging from the lanyard around her neck. The prison guard knew who she was before she even got off the elevator, Dyan thought.

Before she could sit down, a door at the far end of the reception area flew back and Blackman stepped through the opening.

His suit jacket and tie from this morning's meeting were gone and his shirtsleeves were rolled up to his elbows. "Ms. Galloway, please come in." Without waiting for her to get to the door, he turned and disappeared through the opening.

As she stepped through the doorway, she saw Blackman walking down a long, dimly lit hall. The only sound came from their shoes against the carpet. She could almost feel the tension building as they approached the door to his office. He disappeared through the opening. She followed.

Once inside the cavernous, dark oak paneled room, Blackman suddenly turned, which caused Dyan to instinctively stop in her tracks. She looked into his eyes. His large pupils looked like glowing embers. As if on cue, she blinked and he started to speak.

"Ms. Galloway . . . Bill Blackman." A smile formed on his face as he extended his right hand out to her.

"Dyan Galloway," Dyan said, her voice cracking, as she placed her hand into the giant one in front of her.

He motioned her to one of the six chairs surrounding the hexagon-shaped wooden table in the corner of the office. As she sat down, she saw a copy of her report laying on the table along with a red expandable folder stuffed with a three-inch stack of papers.

He pulled out the chair next to her and sat down. Their eyes locked again. "First . . . I'd like to commend you on your report. It's the kind of out-of-the-box thinking we are trying to foster in the Bureau."

There was a long silence before Dyan spoke up. "Thank you, but . . . "

"No," Blackman interrupted. "Let me say what I think is on your mind. If it wasn't for yesterday's terrorist attack, no one, including me, would have even paid attention to this." His large thick index finger made a loud thud as he tapped the report in front of him. "And I'll be honest with you. Maybe you're right.

But whether we would have taken it seriously or not, we still wouldn't have known when or where they were going to hit us."

"But we might have known how," Dyan shot back, then suddenly remembered who she was talking to, although Blackman sat as composed as ever.

"Sometimes you have to hit someone over the head with a two-by-four before you get their attention. 9/11 was a wake-up call for all of us, just like Pearl Harbor was a wake-up call for the previous generation of Americans. Although all the warning signs were there, we chose to ignore them. For almost three years we were successful in fending off any more attacks. I think we all hoped the killing in Afghanistan and Iraq would somehow substitute for any bloodshed on American soil. But deep down inside, many of us knew it would come sooner or later."

The room went silent. Dyan could see beads of sweat forming on Blackman's forehead.

"Dyan . . . I'd like you to work on a special assignment for me." Blackman put his right hand on the red folder and slid it in front of Dyan. "We believe there are about a dozen terrorist cells operating in this country. We've never gone public with that fact. We believe each cell is probably comprised of between two to ten people. So far we have positively identified — and have under twenty-four hour surveillance — three of the cells. We also have intelligence, you'll find it all documented in here, that indicates al Qaeda is planning a number of terrorist attacks over the next several months across the U.S. We believe their attacks are a prelude to a massive attack planned for either the upcoming anniversary of 9/11, or perhaps the November elections.

"You will have high-level security access to this file, which is code-named Domino. I'd like you to go through this data. Look at it from an outsider's perspective. See if you can come up with a how, when, and where these guys are going to hit us next, based on your theory."

Dyan's heart was pounding, not from what Blackman was asking her to do, but from what he just told her about the terrorist cells. "We are aware of three cells and haven't arrested them?"

"That's correct."

"Were any of them involved in . . . "

"No, they weren't involved in yesterday's explosions. If they had been, we certainly would have intercepted them before they had a chance to hit those tunnels."

"But why not pick them up? Why take the chance?"

"We were lucky we found the first cell. It was well over a year ago. Through our surveillance, we have been able to uncover the two additional cells. Though they don't do it often, periodically they do communicate with one another. Our hope is to eventually get them all."

"How certain are we of there being a dozen cells?"

"We estimate a fifty percent probability."

"How certain are we these smaller terrorist acts are leading up to a massive attack?"

Blackman paused, then responded with a low muted voice. "Very certain."

5

"But I don't even know the man," Iullia repeated again. It was the fourth time she said it in the past thirty minutes, and she didn't understand why the obviously well-educated elderly man, sitting on the opposite side of the desk in front of her, wasn't grasping the significance of what she was saying.

The letter she pulled from her mailbox three days ago caught her eye immediately. Although business letter-sized, the texture of the off-white envelope told her it was expensive. That, along with the embossed return address of Randal B. Chapman, Attorney-at-Law, State Tower Building, Syracuse, New York. She double-checked to make sure the envelope had been put in the correct mailbox, but typed in block letters across the front was her name, Dr. Iullia Zola.

After reading the enclosed letter, it too typed on expensive bond paper, her initial reaction was to toss it in the pile with the rest of the junk mail she received that day. After all, to be named as the beneficiary in a will for someone she didn't even know was surely some scam. Probably a marketing ploy to get her to write her own will, which at forty-two, a full-time professor of Russian Studies at Syracuse University, single, and with no known relatives, she saw little need for. Throw it away and you'll never hear from them again, she thought. So she did.

The forgotten letter came back to life less than twenty-four hours later when the phone rang. Then came the frantic search through the recycle bin already out by the curb, just minutes away from being picked up. The letter was not a marketing ploy. Randal B. Chapman was not looking for new business. He was carrying out the wishes of his client. He needed to meet with her.

Iullia read the three-page will for the third time. It was clearly her name, almost impossible to mix up with any other, and her address, 321 Comstock Avenue, Syracuse, New York, typed out on the pages. But no matter how long she stared at the pages, the name Richard Williams did not jog one neuron.

She listened even more carefully the second time Mr. Chapman told her what he knew of his deceased client. Williams was seventy-eight years old when he passed away two weeks ago, of natural causes, so said the coroner's report. He lived alone in a cabin just north of Old Forge, New York, a small town located in the Adirondack Mountains, about a two-hour drive from Syracuse, and taught English, Spanish, and French at the local Adirondack high school for thirty years, retiring in 1993. He previously confided to Chapman that he had no living relatives. He bequeathed $100,000 to the high school he taught at for the establishment of a college scholarship fund. The remainder of his estate went to Iullia. Chapman indicated that he was still in the process of determining its value, although he already concluded it was into the high six figures.

"It still doesn't make sense to me," Iullia said as she looked up from the will that was resting on her lap. "The only thing we appear to have in common is teaching."

"The only suggestion I have for you is that you visit his cabin. It now belongs to you. Maybe there is something there that will answer why you were in his will. You need to visit his place anyway to let me know if you want me to sell the cabin and its contents." Chapman handed her an envelope which contained a key and a map showing the location of the cabin.

Iullia started to reach for the envelope, then pulled back her hand. "I don't even know the man and you want me to rummage through his cabin?"

"Your cabin, Dr. Zola. Technically, it belongs to you."

Iullia reached for the envelope. "Mr. Chapman, how long have you known Mr. Williams?"

"Mr. Williams came to see me for the first time in the fall of 1971. He asked me to draw up his first will for him. The only time I have ever dealt with him over the past thirty-plus years was when he made revisions to his will. Maybe a half a dozen times or so."

"And when did he add my name to his will?"

"Add? My dear, you were in his original will."

6

Dyan sat in her windowless office, if that's what you could call it, staring at the bare white wall in front of her. The ten-foot by ten-foot room, which she concluded must have initially been a storage closet, was her work space for the past two weeks. In her short five-year career, she was always able to glance to the outside world at any time during the workday. Until the past two weeks, she didn't realize how important it was for her to know if it was sunny or dark, blue sky or gray, calm or windy or rainy out.

Cooped up in her "prison cell," as she jokingly nicknamed the office, she lost all track of time. Two nights ago she was startled by a banging on the door, which was always kept closed because of the material she was reviewing. At first she thought it was odd that the cleaning staff was vacuuming the outside hall during normal working hours, until first the pain in her bladder, then the glance at her watch told her it was 10:17 P.M. She hadn't moved from her chair in hours. She then realized why solitary confinement was such an effective tool in breaking a human being's psyche.

She was escorted to the prison cell by Blackman following

their initial meeting in his office almost two weeks ago. Starting early the next morning, a Sunday, and for every day since, she found herself confined to her cell for no less than fourteen hours a day. Her plan to take last weekend off and return to Syracuse and her new husband, who by that time she hadn't slept with for almost two weeks, was derailed when Osama bin Laden's top lieutenant, Ayman al Zawahiri, appeared on a new video aired on Qatar's al-Jazeera news network on Thursday morning and took credit for the previous week's tunnel attack. He also warned that al Qaeda was planning more strikes in the U.S., and that it would spread disease throughout the land. When Blackman paid her a visit later that morning to check on how she was doing, the first time he'd even spoken to her since the previous Saturday, she knew there would be no escaping from her cell for the weekend.

Now, a week later, she had completed reviewing all of the top secret intelligence files on the suspected terrorist cells in the U.S. and started to piece together her theories on what she thought their next moves might be. Confident she would be able to complete her report by her self-imposed deadline of next week, she decided to quit early, although it was already after six, and head back to her hotel room where she would treat herself to a glass — or two or three — of wine, and a bubble bath.

As she walked through the lobby of the Crystal City Marriott, dreaming of the warm bubbly froth caressing her naked body, and the cold tart liquid cooling her taste buds, she almost didn't hear, let alone recognize, the voice of the man walking toward her from the right.

"Dyan."

She turned and stared in almost disbelief. "What are you doing here?"

"Thanks a lot. I thought you'd be glad to see me," Jack responded.

Dyan stood there staring at him. "No. I mean . . . I am. I am glad to see you. But what are you doing here?"

"Last-minute meeting got scheduled for tomorrow at headquarters. One of the cases I'm working on. Anyway, I was just coming to check to see if you were back in your room. I've been at the bar. Come on. Let me buy you a drink." Jack put his hand on the small of Dyan's back and motioned her into the noisy, crowded, dimly lit bar area. But Dyan remained frozen.

"What?"

"Nothing. I guess I'm in shock. I can't believe you're standing here talking to me face-to-face."

"Well, I am. So come on."

"Wait. Let me put this up in my room," Dyan said as she held her black leather briefcase in front of her.

"Sure . . . I'll walk up with you."

Before Dyan could say anything, Jack headed for the bank of elevators. She gazed up and down Jack's body as he walked in front of her. She still couldn't believe that it was actually him. She also couldn't believe that she was following him up to her room.

"What floor?" Jack asked as they stepped into the elevator.

"Ninth."

Seconds after Jack pushed the ninth-floor button, the elevator doors closed, sealing the two of them within its small space. Neither noticed the start of the slow ascent.

Dyan's heart was pounding so loudly, she was sure Jack could hear it in the silence of the elevator. She felt her body going hot and her face flushing as the memories, almost a year into her past, but as vivid as yesterday's, raced through her brain triggering the right combinations of hormones into her bloodstream.

"Do you remember?" Jack finally broke the silence.

"Yes."

"Are you sorry we did it?"

Before Dyan could answer, the voices they heard outside the elevator grew louder as the doors opened. They both exited the elevator, walked silently down the hall, and without hesitation, Jack followed her into her room.

"Your message light is on." Jack pointed to the annoying red light that was flashing on the phone next to the bed, and then to the one on the phone on the desk at the far end of the room.

Dyan picked up the phone, pressed the message button and listened.

"You have one message. Message one. 'Hi honey. You are not going to believe this, but I'm at the airport waiting to get on a plane to Washington. I'm looking forward to a hot, sleepless night with you.'"

Dyan again felt her face go flush, then quickly turned around as she remembered Jack was standing just feet from her in her hotel room.

7

The thick forest of long-needled Austrian pines, carefully planted years ago, formed an opening just wide enough for the single-lane dirt road to weave through. The tree branches screeched as they rubbed against the roof and both sides of the new Chevy Trail Blazer SUV. A low-hanging branch bent back the radio antenna and sent it springing with a metallic twang, just before it scraped its way up the windshield. Although it was just past three in the afternoon on a cloudless mid-June day, the headlights automatically switched on, illuminating the dark cave formed by the overhead pines.

The opening ahead looked like it was getting smaller, Iullia thought to herself, but as the car inched ahead she saw that the cave snaked its way to the right. At first she wasn't sure she turned into the right driveway off of South Shore Road, even though it was the only one with a numberless mailbox, just as the directions Chapman gave her indicated. But as soon as she entered the pine tree cave, another landmark noted in the directions, she knew she was on the right track.

The dirt road curved a second time to the right, then suddenly the surrounding pine trees disappeared and the car was bathed in light, although it was still a shaded one due to the tall hardwoods, mostly large-leafed maples, that now surrounded the road. Within seconds, the dark brown log cabin with a covered porch running along its entire exterior appeared from nowhere.

As Iullia stood next to her car staring at the cabin, the almost spooky quietness, broken only by an occasional chirping bird, sent a shiver through her body. "There's no one around for miles," she mumbled, then shivered again, not sure if the thought should make her feel more comfortable or more ill at ease. As she stood there she noticed a swarm of black flies, whose nasty bite usually left you bleeding, starting to form around her head.

She ducked under the swarm and headed for the steps leading to the porch. She took the well-worn key from her pocket and placed it into the only lock on the heavy, thick-wooded, windowless door. She took a deep breath, turned the handle, pushed on the door and stepped inside.

Instinctively she reached to her left, feeling for, then lifting the three light switches on the wall. The soft glow of several lamps cast dozens of shadows throughout the open expanse of the cabin. In contrast to the dark brown-stained exterior logs, the interior logs were left their natural light pine hue. That, together with the knotty pine-covered cathedral ceiling and raised loft area, created an open air feeling. The scent of a burnt-out wood fire added to the rustic atmosphere of the room.

For the next several hours Iullia lost herself, exploring every nook and cranny of the clean, well-maintained cabin. The place was filled with years of memories. From books by Tolstoy, Follett and Emerson, to a bear rug, and more than a dozen stuffed animal heads, among them a red fox and a mountain lion, the place spoke of and defined the man who lived there. Yet for all her searching, Iullia did not find one clue linking Williams to her. He was still as he was when she walked into the cabin, a total stranger.

By early evening Iullia's stomach told her how hungry it was. She fought her way through the bug-laden air to the car to retrieve the cooler she brought. The smells of the homemade beef stew brewing on the stove quickly filled the interior of the cabin. As darkness fell, the clouds rolled in, and as predicted, thunderstorms echoed through the mountains. The wind-driven showers spattered against the windows and Iullia felt a chill streak through her body. Within minutes, a fire was crackling in the large, floor-to-ceiling stone fireplace, and it wasn't long before the entire cabin was flooded with its heat and light. Exhausted, she turned off the lights, laid down on the couch only feet from the stone mantle, and dozed off.

Suddenly something, a sound, broke the steady whir of the rainfall. She jumped as a blast of thunder, loud enough to shake the windows, echoed over the cabin. There was still enough light from the fire to illuminate the face of her watch. 11:15 P.M. Seconds later, she heard it again, this time clearly above the whir of the rain. Footsteps. Someone or something was on the porch.

She slowly got up and tiptoed to one of the windows that overlooked the porch. As she moved her face closer to the glass, her eyes were suddenly blinded by a flash of lightning that filled the night outside with a fluorescent white light. But before her eyes instinctively closed shut, she swore she saw the outline of a rain-soaked human standing on the porch, just inches from the window, staring back at her.

8

"Well hello there, young lady." The gangly looking man, standing just over six feet, but weighing no more than 165 pounds fully-clothed, including his size twelve wing tips, slipped through the narrow opening in the curtain surrounding the bed without causing it to flutter. "I hear that your baby hasn't been feeling well." Leaning over the bed, the man took his stethoscope from around his neck, placed the earpieces in his ears, then placed the metal bowl-shaped bell hanging on the end of the long black rubber tube onto the chest of the doll clutched by the tired-looking five-year-old. "Mmmmmm . . . she doesn't sound like she's sick to me." The man lifted his head and looked into the eyes of the little girl.

"She's not sick. I'm the one who is sick," the little girl said in a very mature-sounding, motherly tone, then moved the doll, which was laying on her chest, along the left side of her, away from the doctor.

As the man stood up he reached for the metal chart and stared at it. "Isn't your baby's name Jessica?"

"No, my name's Jessica."

"Oh, your name's Jessica. Then what's her name?"

"Her name is Monica."

"Monica . . . and Monica is feeling okay today?"

"Yes, she is fine."

"So, if you are Jessica, I guess I should be listening to your heart."

"That's what I've been trying to tell you!"

At 7:00 A.M., the normal starting time for most of the hospital staff, Dr. Cantor was finishing up a twenty-four hour shift in the emergency room, his second in the past sixty hours. Despite the fact that there were written guidelines in place to preclude the hospital from taking advantage of first-year residents, it was the unwritten ones that guided the way things were really done. He knew his current state of jovial attentiveness was being driven by both caffeine, and knowing that if things went smoothly, in less than thirty minutes he'd be in bed, sleeping away the first six hours of a well-deserved three days off.

"Are you Jessica's mom?" Cantor extended his hand across the bed to the woman standing on the other side.

"Yes. Deb McNeill."

"So what seems to be the problem Mrs. McNeill?" Dr. Cantor asked as he leaned over and placed the stethoscope on Jessica's chest.

"It started three days ago. She was fine when I put her on the bus. She goes to morning kindergarten. An hour later I got a call from the school. Jessica was throwing up and complaining of a stomachache. So I went and picked her up from school. She slept the rest of the day. I got her up for dinner, but she didn't eat much. A bowl of chicken soup."

"And oyster crackers," Jessica interrupted.

"And oyster crackers. Then she went back to bed and slept through the night. The next morning she said she felt okay, so I sent her off to school. I didn't realize there was an end-of-the-year party planned for that day. It was probably the reason why she forced herself to go to school. When she got home, she was

30

exhausted and went straight to bed. Since then, that's just about where she's been. She hasn't eaten much, most of what she has eaten has come up on her, and she says her stomach hurts."

"Any diarrhea or fever?"

"No, I don't think so. Do you think it could be something she ate?"

"I don't think so. It sounds like the flu to me. There's not much we can do for her. It just has to run its course. Make sure she gets plenty of liquids and lots of rest. Children's Tylenol should take care of the pain. Keep an eye on her temperature. If she does develop a fever that lasts more than twenty-four hours, give us a call. But I'm guessing she'll feel better in a day or two."

"Thank you doctor," Mrs. McNeill extended her hand to Cantor.

"You're welcome. And you make sure you take care of Monica."

"I will." Jessica extended her hand to Cantor.

Cantor slipped back out through the slit in the curtain. As he glanced at his watch, he felt his head bob and his eyelids go heavy. I've got to get to bed, he thought. He briefed the emergency room nurse on his last patient, handed her the metal chart holder, and exited the room. Exhausted, he decided to skip his usual end-of-the-shift shower, and head straight for home.

9

It was as if he only lived for forty years. Of course that was impossible, she thought. His death certificate indicated that he was seventy-eight years old. The only problem was, after almost a week of searching, Iullia could not find any evidence to indicate Richard Williams ever existed before 1963.

After last Thursday night's thunder and lightning storm, which at least for a split second revealed the outline of someone standing on the covered porch, the imagined ghost became real during the early daylight hours the next day when Iullia found the almost washed-away mud-painted boot imprints just below the window. Even though she couldn't be sure if they were made hours, days, or even weeks before, she was certain they were not Williams's, as the boots she found in the cabin storage closet were at least two inches longer than the muddy imprints on the porch.

Undaunted, Iullia continued her search to find out why she was named the beneficiary of Williams's will. She started at the Adirondack Public School District offices. Although Williams retired from teaching over ten years earlier, he was still remembered by several of the more elderly staff in the office. Iullia was shocked by their openness, as they volunteered Williams's personnel files for her perusal. As she would learn over the next few days, the small upstate New York community had few policies when it came to the protection of confidential information. This was especially so if the person in question was dead.

However free they were with the information, the school district files provided little help to her. She learned that Williams came to the district in September 1963. He was one of several teachers hired that year to deal with the growing baby boomer student population that even small towns like Old Forge were experiencing. He initially taught Spanish, French, and English, although as time went on, and the school district continued to grow, he eventually migrated to Spanish and French, and then just French.

Even though his file was crammed with documentation from his teaching years, such as awards, citations, commendations, and parent and student praises, there was nothing, not even a resumé, to document his background and experience prior to the date he came to the district. This was especially odd considering he started teaching there when he was thirty-seven years old. When questioned, the staff concluded some documents must have been misplaced over the years.

The staff also provided her with the names and addresses of over a dozen retired teachers who still lived in and around the Old Forge area, and taught during the same time period as Williams. Iullia spent the rest of the week tracking each of them down. In their seventies, and either living alone or with a spouse with whom they long ago ran out of things to talk to about, her visits with them turned into half-day affairs complete with coffee, iced tea, lemonade, and cookies, mostly molasses, as each of them was glad to reminisce about the "good ol' days." While she now felt she knew more about Richard Williams than she did about any other person she knew, she still did not have an answer as to why he bestowed his estate on her.

As she exited the dark pine tree cave and eyed the now familiar cabin, she thought she saw someone run across the porch, and disappear around the corner. She stopped the car. As the wind blew the tree branches overhead, their shadows danced along the front of the porch. Iullia drew in a slow long breath through her nose, and quickly exhaled through her open mouth.

Even though the daytime temperatures increased during the past few days, the black flies were still as vicious as ever as she fought her way from the car to the cabin. Iullia already sported several of the nasty red bite marks on her wrists and neck, but they were wounds she picked up on her early morning hikes through the woods.

"Teaching," she said aloud, as she dropped onto the soft sofa, careful not to spill her freshly poured glass of wine. "And hiking," she added. They were the only two things she appeared to have in common with Williams. The teaching connection she learned from Chapman. The hiking link came from her week of interviews. Everyone she spoke with told her about Williams's passion for hiking the mountains and trails of the Adirondacks. It was ironic that she shared that same passion. As she again flipped through the pages of pictures neatly filed in their individual albums, she now knew why they looked so familiar to her a few days ago. She visited many of the same mountain peaks herself.

Iullia jumped as the solitude of the afternoon was broken by three knocks on the door. She turned and looked at the big wooden door. A second round of knocks vibrated into the room. She got up and walked toward the windows. Her car was the only one parked in front of the cabin. As she leaned close to the glass to see if she could see who was in front of the door, three more knocks brought the door to life again.

She slowly walked toward the door and opened it.

"Dr. Iullia Zola?" the short, slim, elderly woman asked as

she looked into Iullia's eyes and extended her right hand. "My name is Barbara Davis. I was a friend of Richard's."

Iullia shook hands with the woman, trying to recall why her face looked so familiar.

10

"You may go right in Ms. Galloway. The director is waiting for you."

Dyan wasn't even out of the elevator before Ms. Rock was barking her orders. She wondered how he could be waiting, since she was five minutes early for their meeting. As she walked past the short-haired bleached blond, Dyan thought she either had to be a dominatrix, or a dyke. No . . . a man.

"Come in Dyan. Sit down." Blackman spoke up as soon as he saw Dyan standing in the doorway to his office. "Thanks for changing your travel plans. Were you able to get on another flight?"

"Yes. There's a flight that leaves a little past seven."

Blackman glanced at his watch. "From Reagan?"

"Yes."

"Great. We'll get you there in plenty of time. I only have a few things I want to cover with you."

"It's not a problem. I can always take the early morning flight tomorrow."

Of course, she was lying. It was a problem. Dyan had been in Washington for three weeks straight. Almost four, if you count the task force meeting she attended prior to this latest stint, when she flew back to Syracuse, only to return to Washington hours later. The close quarters of her hotel room, coupled with the even closer quarters of her windowless prison cell were driving her batty. Add to that consecutive fourteen-plus-hour days, not-so-healthy restaurant meals, and a long for-gotten exercise routine, Dyan fully understood why she looked and felt like shit. And if that weren't enough, this weekend was her four-month wedding anniversary. Except for last weekend's surprise conjugal visit, during which she got absolutely no sleep, she hadn't touched, tasted, or smelled her husband for a month. It dawned on her this morning that for one quarter of her young marriage, she slept in a strange bed, alone. No wonder her private nighttime fantasies, something she hadn't needed since first sleeping with her husband, were getting more fre-quent and more erotic. They were even beginning to involve Jack again.

"First, you again did an excellent job summarizing your thoughts and ideas."

Dyan didn't like Blackman's opening line. Although subtle, it felt like he just used that two-by-four on her. To her it meant one thing. She was not convincing enough in her report. Damn it. Why don't they see it, she thought.

"You don't agree with my conclusions, do you?" Maybe it was the lack of sleep. Or the lousy food. The lack of exercise. The way she looked. The way she felt. Hell, maybe it was even her sexless love life. For whatever reason, her emotions, like some outside, uncontrollable force, were taking over her mind.

"I think some of your ideas certainly have merit."

"You mean like using an inexpensive, readily available sub-stance, like gasoline, to blow up a bunch of tunnels."

Blackman peered into Dyan's eyes. It was the first time she ever saw him speechless. Perhaps she stooped too low. After all, over thirteen hundred people were dead, and thousands more were still suffering in the hospital. Some of them, too, would not survive. No, damn it. She needed to pull out all the stops. Go for broke. She knew it was now or never.

"Dyan, I know how much time and effort . . . "

"You think the tunnels was a lucky guess on my part, don't you?"

"No. I believe . . . "

"A one in a million long shot that came in. Score one for the young, inexperienced broad."

Dyan dropped her head, but continued silently tapping her fingers on the table. Blackman, obviously experienced in handling difficult situations, used time, silent time, to let emotions dissolve.

"I apologize."

"There is no need to apologize."

"Maybe you're right. I happened to get lucky. The whole idea is crazy."

"Dyan, I don't think your idea is crazy. If I had, I wouldn't have made you spend the past three weeks putting together this report."

"Then what. Why can't I get people to listen?"

"Because you're too far out of the box that everyone else is sitting in. Dyan, most of your ideas do not result in anything spectacular happening. At least nothing spectacular, like the thousands of deaths, and the billions of dollars in damage caused by 9/11. Your tunnels theory was probably the most significant terrorist attack described in here. The Boston tunnel bombing has resulted in over thirteen hundred deaths and unknown damage to a fifteen-billion-dollar project. Except for how it was carried out, others have warned for years about something like this happening. Starting forest fires out west will certainly cause a lot of damage, and it might kill a few people. I'm just not convinced yet that it's al Qaeda's modus operandi. They are into car bombings and suicide bombings."

"But don't you see. Those tactics rely on two things they don't have in this country; a supply of explosives, usually things left over from years of wars, like C-4 and artillery shells, and a supply of expendable people, hundreds of people, who are willing to commit suicide. Without these resources, unless al Qaeda is willing to settle for one spectacular event every three or four years, they will need to change their tactics. One forest fire might not be spectacular, but how about fifty, or a hundred, all going at once. It's something ten men could do in a single night with gasoline and a book of matches. And those ten men walk away to commit their next deed. And the next, and the next.

"It won't take long to break America's will when you start to hit us everywhere in the country, and not just our big cities."

"Even if you are right Dyan, your report does an excellent job with the what part of the equation, but it doesn't answer the where and when."

"You're right. And that's why I believe these tactics will become al Qaeda's new modus operandi. With their attacks to date, we could answer the what and to some degree the where portion of the equation. Hijackings, airports. Airplanes as missiles, tall buildings. Car bombs, large populated buildings near streets. Chemical weapons, large groups of people, like subways or sports stadiums. With these new tactics, we only know the what. Gasoline, a common virus, propane. The where part of the equation turns into almost anyplace in the country, not just in big cities where the tall buildings are, and the when is anytime because the time needed to plan for these new tactics can be measured in days, not years like 9/11. That will make it more difficult for anyone to discover what they are planning, so it makes it that much more appealing to al Qaeda."

"Look Dyan, I'll say it again. I think you've done a fine job here. But, I need more meat. Dig some more. See if you can uncover anything from the Domino files. I'd also like you back here next Wednesday to attend the Broken Arrow task force meeting.

"But first, I want to make sure you get on that plane this evening." Blackman stood up, so Dyan did too. He extended his hand to her. "Take a few days off and I'll see you next week."

Blackman sat at his desk reading Dyan's report. Over the past twenty-four hours he read the forty-two page document no less than three times, and each time he did, he grew more concerned over the potential threats it implied. He also wondered why no one else came up with these scenarios, and prayed that al Qaeda wouldn't either.

11

The man jumped to his feet when the electronic ring of the cell phone filled the dark, quiet, but sticky-warm room of the small three-bedroom apartment. Although the phone was kept on, and plugged into its charger on the kitchen counter, it rarely rang for incoming calls, and was used even less for outgoing ones. The fast walk to the kitchen was no more than ten feet, but when covered in seconds from a sleeping-on-the-couch starting position, it was enough to cause even a well-trained athlete, which the man wasn't, to breathe heavily. The man picked up the cheap plastic phone, unplugged the dangling wire from the charger, pressed the oddly shaped green button, placed the phone to his ear, looked at his watch, and waited. Exactly one minute later, the silent phone began speaking.

"C-one?"

"Yes."

"This is D-one."

"Yes."

"Has the cold surfaced there yet?"

"No, nothing."

"It has been twenty-eight days. Should we continue?"

"Yes. We are to continue until the symptoms surface, which we expect any day now. If we are lucky we may take in another holiday weekend. Have there been any problems?"

"No problems. But I will need more material."

"I will meet you tomorrow morning at ten. Same place."

The phone went silent.

The man pushed the oddly shaped red button, plugged the black charger wire back into the bottom of the cell phone, placed it on the counter, strolled back to the couch, and lay back down. Within minutes, he was sleeping.

12

"I can't believe how much it cools down at nighttime. I've made a fire every night to take the chill out of the air." Iullia handed Barbara the glass of red wine, and sat on the couch across from her.

"Even though it's the end of June, believe it or not, you can still find some snow in a few of the steep mountain gorges, where fifty or sixty feet drifted in during the winter, and the sun hasn't touched. If you'd like, we can hike to one tomorrow."

From their conversation, it was hard to believe that just a few short hours ago, Iullia and Barbara Davis were total strangers. Although Iullia still could not recall where she had seen the woman before, her initial uneasiness quickly faded as Barbara told her what she knew about Williams.

"I met Richard a little over twenty years ago, twenty-two to be exact. It was Veterans Day, 1982. My husband passed away that spring. A heart attack at the ripe old age of fifty-five. I always told him his job was gonna kill him. He didn't heed my call to stop and smell the roses. Goddamn corporate America." She took a long sip of the room temperature wine from her glass. "We lived a very comfortable life — apartment in

Manhattan, time-share in Jamaica, the cottage up here in the Adirondacks."

"Any kids?"

"No. I . . . I couldn't. Probably good that we didn't anyway. I can only imagine the additional complications that would have put on our lives. Doesn't matter, the bastard went and died on me. There I was, a fifty-year-old widow, without a financial care in the world, and no one to grow old with. What good was all that money."

She took another sip from her glass.

"So I decided to slow down. I vowed not to let the same thing happen to me. I quit my job. Resigned from all my char- ities. Sold everything, except the cottage, and moved up here. I took up hiking. By the fall, I was in the best physical shape I'd been in in years. So I started hiking some of the Adirondack peaks. That's when I ran into Richard.

"It was warm, in the sixties, when I started the hike up Blue Mountain that day. It's only a two-mile hike up the mountain, and only about a fifteen-hundred-foot vertical rise, but if you take it at a good clip, you get pretty warm, so I left my wind- breaker in the car. Two-thirds of the way up the mountain, water started flowing down the trail, and a few minutes later there was snow on the ground. Only a dusting at first, then the entire ground was covered, then it was inches deep. By the time I got to the top, the temperature was in the lower forties.

"The view was spectacular that day. You could see forever. The sky was cloudless, and the sun felt good as I started to cool down from the hike. I laid back on a huge rock outcrop on the southern face, where the snow had melted away, and let the sun warm my body. I don't know how long he'd been standing there. I didn't even hear him come up the path. But I opened my eyes and there he was, looking off into the distance through a pair of binoculars, not ten feet away.

"I can still remember him jumping when I spoke up and

asked him how the view was. I must have scared him out of his wits. Who'd expect to hear a voice out of the blue like that, on the top of a mountain, up in god's country."

She took another long sip of the wine.

"Who knew that day would be the start of a lifetime friendship. It turned out our cottages were less than two miles away from each other. If you take the trail that runs north, along the base of the mountain to the rear of the cabin, it will lead right to my cottage. It's the most well-worn trail back there. You can't miss it."

It was obvious to Iullia that it was more than a friendship that the woman was describing. Although she was curious, she knew she had no right to ask how deep the relationship really was. But she did ask Barbara to share what she knew about Williams, and after almost three hours Iullia realized the woman told her little more than what she already learned during the past week from the dozens of other people she spoke with.

"Do you know anything about his past? About before he moved here in 1963?"

"We rarely spoke about our pasts. I guess he wasn't much interested in mine, and I wasn't interested in his. As far as I knew, he lived here forever, and I'm sure he thought the same about me."

"Up until last week, I didn't even know the man. Do you have any idea why he would leave all of this to me?"

Barbara remained silent and held her head down, her eyes locked on the glass of wine, which she was moving in a circular motion.

"No . . . no I don't," she finally responded, as she raised her head, placing the glass to her lips.

For the first time in their three-hour conversation, Iullia felt an uneasy chill jolt through her body. Was it the darkness that was descending over the cabin, chilling the damp mountain air flowing through the open windows, or was Barbara lying to her?

"Oh my lord, look how dark it's getting. I've got to be on my way," Barbara said, as she started to get up from the couch.

"Where did you park your car?"

"Car? My dear, I haven't driven a car to this cabin in years. I took the back trail."

"But it's getting dark out. Please, let me drive you home."

"Nonsense, I'll be fine." Barbara first stared at her wrist-watch, then out the window. "It's a clear night and I should be back to my cottage just as darkness falls. Besides, I could walk this trail with my eyes closed, there's a full moon out tonight, and if all else fails, I have this."

Iullia felt her body jerk and her heart thump as the silhouette of the woman in front of her was illuminated by the bright white light of the flashlight. In the dark interior of the cabin, it looked like a flash of lightning.

As Iullia watched Barbara disappear into the dark shadows of the trail, she suddenly felt the urge to call to her. Questions, ones she didn't have even moments ago, kept popping into her head. Like how did she know her name earlier and why was she standing on her porch in the middle of the night last week?

13

"Three days off and it feels like I never left the place," Dr. Cantor mumbled to himself as he stood in the doorway leading to the emergency room area. He glanced at his watch. Of all the shifts he worked, he hated the 7:00 P.M. Sunday night one the worst, even more than the Friday and Saturday night tours. At least on those nights there was the occasional bar fight cut, gunshot wound, or grizzly car accident. Patients who were a challenge. Patients who would test your doctoring skills. Get your blood rushing. Push you to your limits. To Cantor, that's what made his job fun, and interesting.

Unfortunately the Sunday night shift was none of that. Most of the patients there were either weekend jocks with broken bones, scrapes, scratches and bruises, or sick kids who kept their aches and pains hidden until the very end of the weekend.

Cantor grabbed the first chart, glanced over it as he walked toward Station Number Four, then abruptly stopped in front of the curtain surrounding the bed, the leather sole of his size twelve wing tip shoe slapping the hard linoleum floor. "Have I really been away for the weekend?" he said under his breath.

He took a deep breath and slipped through the curtain.

"Jessica and Monica, have you been here all weekend?" he asked, with an obvious smile in his voice, when he saw the doll clutched in the little girl's arms. As his eyes rose up to Jessica's face, it didn't take long for his smile to disappear. If it wasn't for the chart with the name that he recalled, and Monica, he would not have recognized Jessica as the same five-year-old that he saw early Thursday morning, just a little over three days ago.

Jessica lay there almost lifeless in the bed, the only movement being the slight rising and falling of her chest as she took in shallow breaths of air. Her eyes were closed. Her face, arms, and hands almost glowed a pale yellow hue. Cantor thought he remembered a rounder, fuller face. As he glanced back through the charts, he did the simple math in his head. In just over three days, the girl lost six pounds, or ten percent of her body weight.

It took several hours, but the blood tests Cantor ordered confirmed his earlier preliminary diagnosis of hepatitis A.

"Hepatitis? But where would she get that from?" Mrs. McNeill asked.

"Hepatitis A is a highly communicable, or contagious disease."

"Disease?"

"It's actually a virus. It's transmitted by the fecal-oral route."

"Fecal-oral?"

"Most people contact hepatitis by eating food contaminated with the virus. The food preparer or cook is the individual most often the person contaminating the food. The virus itself can survive up to a month at room temperature."

"What's going to happen to my baby?"

"Jessica has already developed jaundice, that's the yellow discoloration of the skin and eyes. That usually means that her body's normal defenses are destroying the virus. There isn't much we can do for a patient with hepatitis A. Jessica is dehydrated, so I've ordered two pints of intravenous saline solution. We will keep her in the hospital overnight. Other than that, she'll need plenty of rest. A diet high in protein will help get the liver back to normal. I'll get you a list of the foods she should be eating. It's going to be several more weeks before she's feeling normal, and there is a chance the symptoms could last longer."

"I still don't understand where she got this. How common is this?"

"More common than you might think. About 50,000 cases occur annually in the U.S. You might recall the outbreak in Pennsylvania last year that infected 600 people."

"Is there any permanent damage?"

"Only very rarely, and mostly in the elderly. In fact, for most children, we never even know they get the disease. They find out years later from blood tests that they have the antibodies in their blood indicating they had hepatitis A sometime earlier in their lives."

"But . . . "

"Don't worry Mrs. McNeill, Jessica is going to be fine."

"Thank you doctor."

"Oh, one other thing. We are going to want to test you and the rest of your family, and anyone else Jessica was in close contact with over the past two weeks, to make sure no one else has contracted the virus. Also, I need to report Jessica's case to the state Department of Health. They will no doubt be contacting you to try to determine the source of the infection."

14

NEW YORK STATE DEPARTMENT OF HEALTH ISSUES
NATIONWIDE HEPATITIS A ADVISORY FOR PATRONS OF
THRUWAY TRAVEL PLAZA

*ALBANY, NY, June 28 — The New York State Department of Health
today issued a nationwide hepatitis A advisory to people who may
have eaten at the Pattersonville Travel Plaza, located twenty miles
west of Albany, New York, on the westbound lane of the New York
State Thruway, from Memorial Day weekend through the month of
June. The travel plaza is located between Interchange 26,
Schenectady, and Interchange 27, Amsterdam.*

*The Department of Health was notified that more than three dozen
employees at the travel plaza's six restaurants have been confirmed
to have hepatitis A, also known as Infectious Hepatitis. Although
unconfirmed, more than fifty patrons are believed to have contracted the disease.*

*The nationwide alert is being coordinated with the National
Centers for Disease Control and Prevention (CDC) because of the*

significant number of out-of-state residents that utilize the inter-state highway. The CDC would not confirm if there were any cases identified outside of New York State.

The hepatitis A virus is found in the stool of people with hepatitis A. It is easily spread from person to person by orally ingesting any-thing that has been contaminated with the stool, such as food items handled by an infected worker, that are not subsequently cooked.

Approximately 50,000 people in the U.S. are infected with the ill-ness annually, and most recover without complications. Symptoms include fever, tiredness, weakness, loss of appetite, nausea, vomit-ing, abdominal pain, and jaundice. People who are experiencing symptoms or who feel they are at risk should contact their family physician.

Physicians are reminded that confirmation of hepatitis A is a reportable condition. The New York State Department of Health number is 1-800-NY HEALTH.

15

"The eleventh, and I might add, the last broken arrow, was lost off the coast of Tybee, Georgia, on February 5, 1958."

Broken arrow? Why can't they just call it what it is, Dyan thought to herself. No, not the Department of Defense. They have to have a code name for everything. After sitting for the past three hours listening to the presentation, she wanted to stand up and yell at the top of her lungs, it's not a broken arrow; it's a nuclear bomb! One that you lost, though she felt the adjective was more appropriate for your car keys, not a nuclear bomb. On top of that, we can't find it. How moronic.

"Number 47782 is a MARK 15, MOD 0 thermonuclear device, which is one of the earliest designs."

Thermonuclear device? It's a goddamn hydrogen bomb!

"The device is a bullet-shaped, aluminum cylinder, approximately eleven feet long, with a snub nose and four stubby fins. It has a yield of two thousand kilotons, or about a hundred times more powerful than the Hiroshima bomb."

Two thousand kilotons? It'll level the bottom half of Florida. How could we have produced such a weapon?

"Since the plane was on a training mission at the time, the

detonation capsule was removed from the device to prevent it from accidentally activating."

Exploding, she wanted to yell. It prevented the lost hydrogen bomb from exploding!

"In summary, in each of the eleven broken arrow cases, a considerable amount of effort went into trying to retrieve the device. As I indicated, each of the geographic areas is under a periodic surveillance by our network of spy satellites. We feel the probability of a terrorist organization, such as al Qaeda, or even a rogue nation, obtaining any of these weapons is close to zero."

Dyan wanted to ask what they calculated the probability was of loosing a nuclear bomb, before they lost the first one, but again she refrained.

"My god. I can't decide what's worse. Sitting in that meeting this morning, or sitting here." With the door to her prison cell always closed, Dyan noticed that she had developed a habit of talking out loud to herself. It reminded her of the increasing number of people she saw in the grocery store, talking on their cell phones. She was constantly turning around to see if someone was talking to her. "I've gotta stop doing this," she said aloud, then smiled.

She was still trying to figure out why Blackman insisted she attend this morning's Broken Arrow Task Force meeting. She knew there was credible intelligence that indicated al Qaeda tried for ten years to acquire or make nuclear weapons. Bin Laden himself considered the acquisition of a nuclear device to be a "religious obligation."

Dyan did not take this threat lightly. The consequences of al Qaeda acquiring, then using a nuclear device, would be catastrophic. On the other hand, she felt the probability that they could obtain such a device was extremely low. Her conclusion was not based on conviction. It was based on a rigorous analysis of the subject. She had conducted a considerable amount of research to try to understand what options were available to anyone who wanted to obtain a nuclear bomb. She concluded there were only two. Either build one, or acquire one already made.

The only practical way a terrorist organization could build a bomb is if they had access to weapons-grade uranium or plutonium. The resources required, both technically and monetarily, to manufacture the material themselves — after all it originally took the U.S. government a multi-billion dollar Manhattan Project to do so — made it prohibitive. Unfortunately, vast quantities of weapons-grade material did exist. The most likely source for a terrorist bent on getting some would be to steal it from Russia, which inherited the material from the former Soviet Union, and in some cases keeps it stored in unsecured, unprotected facilities.

Even if they had access to the pure uranium or plutonium, which Dyan learned only needed to be the quantity required to fill a sphere about the size of an orange, they would still need to construct a working device. Unfortunately again, the plans to do so are also readily available. Dyan read a top secret FBI report about a Princeton student who, in 1977, used publicly available information to demonstrate how to construct a small nuclear device. She wondered why the FBI report was top secret, since it contained no more information than the student's thesis, which was readily available, along with all the others at Princeton. Since the student got an A, she concluded the plans were technically accurate.

Even with the right materials and technical know-how, although constructing a nuclear device was doable, Dyan felt it would still be far too difficult for even the most competent terrorist organization to pull off. Therefore, acquiring an intact weapon was the more probable scenario. Again, the most likely source for such a weapon, one small enough to easily smuggle into the U.S., as well as detonate in the right location, was Russia, with its thousands of Cold War Soviet warheads. Couple that with a government rife with graft and corruption, and you have the ideal storefront for weapons sales.

But these two scenarios were still less probable than the third nuclear threat she came across, which was the use of a conventional explosive to disperse radioactive debris. Unlike warheads designed to kill and destroy through a huge nuclear blast and heat, the radiological dispersal device, or dirty bomb, would rely on conventional explosives to blow radioactive material over say, a city, and potentially make it uninhabitable for years. She came across several intelligence reports indicating al Qaeda may have acquired radioactive isotopes, ideal dirty bomb ingredients, from the Taliban.

Ironically, it was the dirty bomb scenario that eventually led Dyan to formulate her thesis on why al Qaeda would use low-cost, low-tech approaches to terrorism in the U.S. She found that the most likely weapon of mass destruction, the dirty bomb, would probably kill only those people within the initial blast radius of the conventional bomb. But the radioactive material involved would be so dilute after the blast as to make any radiation doses non-fatal. It was unlikely a dirty bomb could produce the kinds of mass causalities that we saw on 9/11. The damage would be economic, from the cost to decontaminate, to potentially abandoning an area for some period of time.

However, Dyan felt a dirty bomb attack could produce a psychological effect that would far outweigh any physical destruction it might cause. Threats of these attacks alone petrify their targets. And even a small dirty bomb blast, requiring any kind of immediate evacuation, would incite panic, lead to more injuries, and likely overload medical facilities with people suffering from phantom radiation sickness.

It was these psychological aspects of the threat that most

intrigued her. Terrorists didn't necessarily have to use exotic weapons of mass destruction to terrify us. Gasoline could do just as well. Terrorists didn't necessarily have to kill anyone. A contaminated water supply, rendering it undrinkable, but not deadly, would cause untold disruption to our society. It was this hypothesis that lead Dyan to formulate her theories. The terrorists were going to hit us, and hit us hard. But they would also hit us in ways we never thought they would, like they did on 9/11.

"We're focusing on the wrong threats." Dyan's voice broke the dead silence of her prison cell. "Nuclear bombs, especially those which our government originally lost and now can't find, are not what we should be scared of."

Seconds later, the silence was again broken by a loud knocking on the door.

"Yes?"

As the door opened, Blackman's intimidating figure filled the space. Prior to the tunnel bombings, less than four weeks ago, Dyan never met the man. In the intervening weeks, she often wondered if the serious, deadpan demeanor was the real Blackman, or had the recent terrorist attack temporarily blocked out a more personable human being. As he stood there, looking like the cat who just swallowed the canary, she got her answer.

"Grab your Domino file. There is a meeting in 1427A. We found a fourth cell."

16

"Cocamo Mo!"

Mozat, normally not easily startled, felt his body jerk as he opened his eyes and turned his head around in the direction of the main dock at the aft of the boat.

"Remember me? Dave Lawson. South Haven, Michigan. We're doing the Great Circle Route. We met in North Palm Beach. Sailfish Marina. Beginning of June. Actually June fourth. The day of the tunnel attacks." Lawson whispered the last sentence, as if the attack was some dark secret between him and Mo.

"Oh, yes." Although Mozat had immediately recognized the man, he only now let on that he had. "Nice to see you again." Mozat forced out the words. "I thought you were in a hurry to get north?"

"We were. Developed engine problems. Started a few days out of Sailfish, actually. We had the engine checked out in Savannah. Two different marinas in fact. Neither found anything wrong. A few days later, I had it checked out again. Bellhaven, North Carolina. They said everything was fine too. We made it all the way here before she finally quit. Somers

Cove Marina. That was two weeks ago. Unfortunately they don't repair diesels here, so they had to take the engine out and ship it a hundred miles north to a place outside of Annapolis to be fixed. In the meantime we've been sitting here just relaxin'. There are worse places than Crisfield, Virginia, let me tell you. If you like crabs, you've come to the right place. Oysters are great too.

"Do you have any plans for dinner yet?"

"No. We just got in an hour ago. I was taking a nap." Mozat slouched down in his chair again, hinting his nap wasn't over, though he was certain Lawson wouldn't get the message. He didn't.

"I tell you what. Anne and I will swing by here about sev-enish. We'll take you to a restaurant I know you and . . . Ziara, right? You and Ziara are going to love it. It's only about a ten-minute walk. Oh, and it's very casual."

"I am not sure if we can . . . " Before Mozat could finish, Lawson turned, walked back down the dock, and disappeared in the maze of boats.

17

HEPATITIS A OUTBREAK GROWS

ALBANY, NY, June 30 — The confirmed number of cases of hepatitis A stemming from the Thruway travel plaza just west of Albany, New York, has grown to 211. Because thousands of patrons, many of them from out of state, utilized the facility during the month of June, the New York State Department of Health estimates several thousand people could eventually contract the disease.

The volume of cases, although high, is not unusual. The most severe restaurant-related hepatitis A breakout in the U.S. occurred last year in Pennsylvania, in which over 600 people contracted the disease.

A nationwide hepatitis A advisory was issued on June 28 for people who may have eaten at the Pattersonville Travel Plaza, located twenty miles west of Albany, New York . . .

18

Dyan sat in her usual seat in conference room 1427A, directly across from Blackman. Actually it was only her second time in the high-tech room, the first being on June 5, the day after the tunnel bombings.

As she stared at the director, she felt like she was beginning to understand the man who less than a month ago was a total stranger to her. When she first met him, she wondered how the director of the FBI could afford to spend so much time on terrorism. Over the past few weeks she had come to understand that terrorism had dwarfed all the other issues that the Bureau is responsible for. When it came to hunting down terrorists, America's most wanted bank robbers, murderers, and extortionists could wait their turn.

The FBI, along with the rest of the federal bureaucracy, was under tremendous pressure to find the terrorists responsible for the tunnel bombings. Unlike the 9/11 perpetrators, whose suicide deaths somehow cheated the American public out of a more vengeful punishment, when it came to the tunnel bombers, you could smell blood. Unfortunately, neither the FBI nor any other law enforcement agency had a clue as to who they were.

The president was furious that the two deadliest terrorist attacks on American soil took place on his watch. While the first attack gave him a chance to display his previously hidden leadership skills, and deservedly resulted in high approval ratings, the second attack, though long anticipated by almost everyone, was now calling into question his administration's ability to deal effectively with terrorism.

With the election just four months away, the president was putting pressure on Blackman for some kind of a win in the terrorism arena. Exposing the three known terrorist cells would likely boost the administration's ratings. To date, Blackman was successful in convincing the president of the benefits of keeping silent, but in doing so he significantly damaged his relationship with him. The discovery of the fourth cell, at least temporarily, would vindicate his earlier recommendation.

"I'd like to first review what we know about the three previously identified cells." Although Blackman called the meeting less than thirty minutes ago, he briefed his staff on what he wanted to cover, and as usual, they were prepared. "Then we can cover what we know about this new cell."

Although Dyan listened intently to the presentation, she'd already memorized all of the information contained in the Domino file on the known terrorist cells. As is the case with many investigative breakthroughs, luck sometimes plays a role. That was certainly the case a little over a year ago when the first suspected cell was identified. The tip came from Scotland Yard. The British just arrested a half dozen suspected terrorists who were part of a cell that was manufacturing sarin gas in an apartment just outside of London. The apartment also contained several portable computers, cell phones, and a wealth of documents — address books, phone numbers, financial records — which linked the cell to several other individuals in Germany, Spain, Indonesia, and the U.S.

The U.S. suspect, Tarig Hazmi, had been in this country for

a year on a student visa, and was attending Boston University. He was renting a three-bedroom apartment near the campus, which seemed unusual for a single individual. Hazmi was put on twenty-four-hour surveillance. Under the auspices of the newly passed Patriot Act, warrants were issued for wiretaps and a full background check was completed. Throughout that summer, five more individuals from various Middle Eastern countries entered the U.S. on student visas, and moved into Hazmi's apartment.

In January of this year, Hazmi moved to Albany, New York, and transferred to Albany State University. He again rented a three-bedroom apartment, close to campus, and shortly thereafter, another stream of foreign students began arriving.

During spring break, Hazmi flew to Germany to attend what was believed to be a meeting of several al Qaeda operatives from around the world. Also in attendance was Ahmed al Sahari, an Afghan, who was enrolled at Chicago State University and living outside of Chicago. Within a month of their returning to the U.S., al Sahari moved into a larger apartment, which then became the location for what was believed to be the third terrorist cell.

On the outside, all three apartments took on the look and feel that their inhabitants wanted. That is, a group of foreign students attending college in the U.S. They attended all their classes, turned in their required assignments, and attained passing grades. Some of them even got part-time jobs. Within weeks they disappeared into the American mainstream.

There was very little communication detected among the three cells, although much more was suspected to be taking place. Communication modes were constantly changing. Prepaid phone cards and cell phones, used no more than a month then disposed of, made it difficult to track communications. There were never any face to face meetings. Until last week.

"Five days ago, on Friday, June 25, at 7:25 A.M., Tarig

Hazmi, believed to be the leader of the Albany, New York, cell, headed west on the New York State Thruway, toward Buffalo. At 9:55 A.M. he exited at the Warners Travel Plaza, which is five miles west of Syracuse. When he got out of the car, he put a dark green backpack on his back and entered the rest stop facility.

"Thirty minutes later, at 10:25 A.M., Hazmi exited the building. He was not wearing the backpack. Seconds later, a second man of Middle Eastern descent exited the building wearing the green backpack. Hazmi got into his car. The second man got into his car, which was parked three spaces away from Hazmi's.

"The agent continued to follow Hazmi, who exited the Thruway at the next exit, re-entered on the eastbound lane, and returned to his Albany apartment.

"The agent also copied down the license plate number of the second automobile. It is registered to a Turabi Zagreb, who lives in Buffalo, New York. Mr. Zagreb has been in this country for two years on a student visa and attends the State University of New York at Buffalo."

When Dyan heard that, a chill went through her body. She attended the same school just five years before.

"Mr. Zagreb appears to share an apartment with two, maybe three other men. We have positively identified one of the individuals. He too is a student at Buffalo, and here on a student visa."

"Is anyone else besides me seeing a pattern here?" Blackman barked.

"We've already started a search of the student visas issued in the past two years, matching them against like addresses. Unfortunately, many foreign students tend to share living quarters with people of their own background and culture. The initial search has turned up 8,000 hits. We're whittling that list down now."

"Just out of curiosity, did the search turn up the names of the individuals in the three cells we already know about?" Dyan asked.

There was a long, uneasy pause before one of the analysts spoke up. "No. They did not."

"Why not?" asked Blackman. "I thought foreigners on student visas were required to let Immigration know of their current address."

"They are, sir. But the computer only matches addresses if they are exactly the same. If you use the Arabic number '1' for apartment one, and someone else who lives at the same address uses the word, o-n-e, the address is correct, you'll get your mail, but the computer will not match the two addresses.

"In the case of the three cells, not one of the addresses matched due to these slight differences. There is no doubt that it was done purposely."

"One more question," Dyan spoke up again. "Do we know if there are any video cameras inside the building where the two gentlemen met, and have we pulled the tapes?"

This time the pause was longer than before.

"I don't know, but will find out."

Blackman's face went red.

19

HEPATITIS OUTBREAK SPREADS TO SECOND LOCATION

ALBANY, NY, July 1 — Health Officials have confirmed that more than two dozen employees at a second travel plaza on the New York State Thruway have tested positive for hepatitis A. The second location, the Schuyler Travel Plaza, is located five miles east of Utica, New York, on the westbound lane of the interstate.

Four days ago, three dozen employees at the Pattersonville Travel Plaza, sixty miles east on the same interstate, were confirmed to be infected with the virus. The number of confirmed cases of hepatitis A from that location has passed the 300 mark.

The CDC is still investigating to determine if there is any connection between the two outbreaks of the disease. In the meantime, the New York State Department of Health has ordered that all employees working at travel plazas along the interstate highway be tested.

20

"Dyan Galloway." Although she was expecting the phone call, its ring still startled her.

"Hey girl, ya still gettin' laid every night?"

"I sure am."

"You mean after four months he's not sick of you yet?"

"Not yet."

"Well, when he does, don't forget about my outstanding offer."

"Don't worry, I haven't forgotten. And believe me, my man hasn't either. How could he, the way you were hanging all over him and teasing him that night."

"Hey, if he's going to cheat on you, why not have him do it with someone you know? Plus, I read somewhere, if you let your husband do it with your best friend, it's really not cheating."

"Oh really."

"It's true."

"Uh-huh."

"And if you're really good to me, I might even let you watch. You might learn a thing or two about how to take care of your man."

"Ditto."

"If that's an invitation, I'll be up this weekend."

Dr. Lindsey Briant was Dyan's best friend since the third grade. They were college roommates, and she was the maid of honor at Dyan's wedding.

While Dyan went off to join the FBI after college, Lindsey pursued her Ph.D. in medicine. The brainy type, she chose test tubes over patients, and landed a position as a research scientist at the Centers for Disease Control in Atlanta.

"So, how's Washington?"

"How did you know I was in Washington?"

"Area code 202."

"Ah, right. It's good. I'm on a special assignment."

"So I guess you lied to me earlier."

"What do you mean?"

"You're not getting laid every night."

There was a short pause. "So, have you got an answer to my question?"

"I think so, but let me make sure I understand what you're asking. You have a worker at restaurant A with hepatitis A. A customer comes into the restaurant and is infected by the worker. The customer then visits restaurant B. Could the customer infect the workers at restaurant B?"

"That's the scenario."

"Under the right circumstances, yes, it could happen. But if what you are really asking me is, do I think that is what happened along the Thruway in upstate New York, I'd say no."

"Thruway? Who said anything about the Thruway?"

"What? You think I don't know about the outbreak of hepatitis A at the two travel plazas on the Thruway? Dyan, I work at the CDC, remember?"

"Gee . . . I forgot. So, why do you say that's not what happened there?"

"Because I think you are assuming that the customer who gets infected at restaurant A, drives down the Thruway, and an hour later stops at restaurant B, right?"

"Right."

"The problem is, when the customer first comes into contact with the hepatitis A virus, although he is infected, he's not contagious. There's about a two-week incubation period before he can pass the virus along to others. That's what makes finding the source of the virus so difficult. The virus can spread to many people before it's discovered.

"It appears the employees tested all contacted the disease about the same time, late May. In order for there to be a connection between the two rest stops, the contagious person would have had to have been the customer, and somehow he passed the virus to the employees at both restaurants, at about the same time."

"Is there any way for us to know if the virus at both restaurants came from the same person?"

"Let me see what I can do. I'll get back to you."

21

"Hi. This is Dyan Galloway. I was wondering if you found out if that Thruway travel plaza had any video cameras?"

"Yes I did, and yes they do. The state had them installed at all of the travel plazas when they renovated the facilities several years ago. State-of-the-art stuff at the time. Video though, not digital. They're sending the tapes overnight. We'll have them tomorrow."

"You wouldn't happen to know how far back their archives go, do you?"

"They can go back up to five weeks. After that they recycle the tapes."

"Okay. Thanks."

Dyan looked at her watch, then quickly dialed the phone.

"Jack Nelson."

"Hi."

"Excuse me. Who am I speaking to?"

"Funny."

"Is this the famous Dyan Galloway, the analyst who at one time worked in the Syracuse FBI Field Office? I haven't heard your voice in so long I didn't recognize it."

"I need you to do something for me."

"Anything you want, Ms. Galloway. Your wish is my command."

"I need you to send someone to two Thruway travel plazas to pick up their surveillance tapes from Memorial Day weekend."

22

"I still don't think you understand me. I was there for a whole week. I went through every square inch of his cabin, I talked to almost two dozen people who knew the man. I've gone through his files at home. His personnel files at the school he taught at. Everything.

"I can't find one thing to explain why he named me as the beneficiary of his estate."

Chapman leaned back in his chair, clasped his hands, carefully intertwining his pudgy fingers, and rested them on his round protruding belly. "I don't know what to tell you, Dr. Zola. You read his will for yourself. It's very simple. You've read his previous wills. On this one point he has been very consistent. I was his lawyer. I wrote the will as he instructed. I don't know why he wanted a scholarship set up, and I don't know why he left the rest of his estate to you. It was not my duty to ask why he did what he did. It was my duty to make sure his will reflected his wishes. Of that, I am confident it does."

Iullia did not need to say a word. She knew Chapman could read her thoughts by the frustrated look on her face.

"If you don't feel comfortable accepting the estate, there are several alternatives we can pursue. We could liquidate the entire estate and donate the money to charity. Of course we'd have to decide which one. Another possibility is, since we already know Mr. Williams wished to have a scholarship established, we could put the entire proceeds into the scholarship trust, to establish either more or greater annual scholarships. That would be more in line with his wishes.

"Whatever path we take, it should be your decision."

"What if I just refuse to be involved with this anymore?"

"Certainly, no one can force you to accept his estate. I would probably petition the court to allocate the entire estate to the scholarship fund. If I weren't successful, the state would get the funds.

"Look, you don't have to make a decision today. Take your time. Give it some thought. Get back to me in a couple of weeks."

"What would you do if you were me, Mr. Chapman?"

"Ethically, I can't answer that question. I am Mr. Williams's lawyer, not yours. Any advice I give you would probably be biased. I'm charged with trying to carry out the man's wishes. I'll do my best to do that."

"It just doesn't feel right to me. Not knowing why he did this. I'm sorry."

"The only other suggestion I have is for you to dig a little deeper to try to find the answer. You said you thought this lady friend of his," Chapman shuffled his scribbled notes, "Barbara Davis, might know more than she let on. Maybe you could go back and talk with her again.

"Another approach might be to hire an expert, a private investigator, to search Williams's background to see if there is anything that links him to you."

Iullia sat sideways on the old, two-person porch swing, her back against the metal chain that attached it to the ceiling above, and her feet resting on the pillow in the adjacent seat. It was a warm, sticky evening in the city. The sights, sounds, even the air, were much different than what she grew accustomed to during the past week at Williams's cabin. Although she didn't know why, somehow she felt she belonged there.

She looked down again at the piece of paper clenched in her fingers. Barely readable, in Chapman's scribbling, was the name and phone number of a private investigator. Iullia already decided she would call the man in the morning. She needed to find out who Williams really was.

As Iullia sat there, one image kept creeping into her mind. A box. Pandora's box.

23

As Dyan peeked into the doorway of her small office, she squinted her eyes from the bright sun, its silhouette still above the horizon, even at 8:45 P.M. It was one of the benefits of having an office on the west wall on one of the upper floors in the James A. Hanley Federal Building in Syracuse. The afternoon sun, when it did shine in the second cloudiest city next to Seattle, always seemed to lift Dyan's spirits, no matter what kind of a day she was having. Of course after being confined to her Washington, D.C., prison cell, any office with a window, even one overlooking an alley, would be a welcomed relief.

She put her briefcase on her desk, and stood in front of the window. The dark, energy-efficient glass shielded most of the sun's rays, but she could still feel the skin on her face go warm. There were only a few cars moving on the streets below and even fewer on Route 690, one of the main highways that criss-crossed the city. Although Syracuse had a population of 150,000, and a surrounding metropolitan area population of over 400,000, traffic was not an issue in central New York.

Dyan smiled as she gazed out over the city, which quickly transformed to the rolling green hills of the surrounding countryside to the south, and shimmering waters of Onondaga Lake to the north. She took in a deep breath, and exhaled slowly. She could feel her eyes tearing up. This was home. Syracuse and central New York were far enough away from all the anger and hatred in the rest of the world, so a person could actually feel safe, even in a world infected with al Qaeda.

"Welcome back."

Dyan's whole body jerked as she turned toward the loud voice coming through the doorway.

"Sorry. I didn't mean to scare you," Jack said, this time in a less enthusiastic tone.

"You didn't." Dyan wiped a tear from her eye. "Just glad to be back I guess." She turned her head to the side so Jack wouldn't see her wipe her eye a second time. "I see you got me the tapes." Dyan pointed to the video tapes, close to a hundred, piled on the table behind her desk. She didn't notice them when she walked in a moment ago, drawn instead to the sun-filled window.

"I got you a TV and VCR too." Jack pointed to the small TV mounted on the roll cart, squeezed into the corner, next to the table. Dyan had been oblivious to that too.

"Are you okay?"

"Yes. I'm fine."

Jack glanced down at his watch, then back up at Dyan. "I don't suppose you'd be interested in a quick dinner somewhere?"

"You haven't eaten yet?"

"No. I got busy working on something and lost track of the time I guess. How about you?"

"I had something at the airport in Washington. I'm really not that hungry. Thanks." She could see the disappointed look on his face. She then looked back at the pile of tapes on the table.

"I suppose you are anxious to start looking at those."

Dyan kept her eye on the tapes. "I don't know if anxious is

the right word." She then looked up at Jack. His white shirt glowed orange from the sun, accenting the dark brown skin of his face and arms. Staring at him, it wasn't hard for her to understand why she fell so hard for him the first time she laid eyes on him. Although, she was surprised at how quickly things went from a school girl crush to an office affair. A very hot affair at that.

"You're going to work through the weekend, aren't you?" Jack said as he stared at the tapes.

"Unfortunately, yes."

"It's Fourth of July weekend, you know."

"I know. I know."

"Your new husband is not going to be happy about this. Have you told him yet?"

"No, but I think he already figured it out. Luckily, he has some work he has to catch up on, and he's already lined up a few early mornings of golf with the guys."

"And at least you're not down in Washington, so you can . . ." Jack purposefully waited to see if Dyan, who was still staring at the tapes, would finish the sentence.

"Take care of my wifely duties."

"Well, I didn't want to put words in your mouth."

"Uh-huh."

"All I can say is, you must have one hell of a great husband."

"He's the best. And don't worry. I plan on taking care of my wifely duties. In fact, I have a couple of things planned that are gonna shock even him."

"How come I don't doubt that, even for a second?"

Dyan looked at her watch, then back at the pile of tapes. She had already put in a fourteen-hour day, her third in a row. The last two nights in her Washington hotel room were lonely, restless ones. She knew reviewing the tapes would be a tedious, boring task, with little chance of even finding what she thought might be on them. It was too much of a long shot.

76

She looked up at Jack who was staring straight at her. "Tell ya what. I'm not up for dinner, but I'll let you buy me a drink. Just one though."

"Name the place," Jack shot back, though Dyan was not surprised at the quickness of his answer.

"Can I get you another one?" Jack whispered, making sure a heavy dose of his warm breath played with the outside of Dyan's ear.

"Oh my god, it's almost midnight," Dyan shouted as she looked at her watch.

"What? Do you turn into a pumpkin or something at midnight?"

"No wonder I'm so tired."

"Remember when you could stay out till two o'clock every night?"

"See what married life will do to you?"

"So, do you want another one?" Jack reached over and picked up the empty Coors Light bottle that was on the bar in front of Dyan.

"I can't, Jack. I'm beat. I've already had three more than I said I was going to have. So much for one drink."

"I can't twist your arm?" He wobbled the bottle on the bar.

"Not even with one of your secret FBI moves. Besides, if I have another drink, I won't be able to perform my wifely duties tonight. And my husband won't like that."

"You're right about that. I'll walk you out."

Jack picked up the change from the bar, left a generous tip, then followed Dyan out the front door to the side parking lot. When she got to her car, she turned to Jack. "Thank you for the drinks and I'll see you . . . "

Before she could finish, Jack pushed his body against hers and covered her moving lips with his mouth. Dyan could feel herself melting under his probing tongue.

It was a full minute before they finally separated. Dyan opened her eyes and saw the passion on Jack's face. "You're making it very difficult for me to get home to my husband."

24

THE DEPARTMENT OF HOMELAND SECURITY ISSUES
WARNING FOR UPCOMING HOLIDAY WEEKEND

*WASHINGTON, D.C., July 2 — The Department of Homeland
Security reissued its warnings for Americans to stay vigilant over
the upcoming Fourth of July holiday weekend. Although the officials did not cite any specific terrorist plot, the warnings are based
on intelligence deemed credible, indicating an attack, similar to
the tunnel bombings a month ago, may be planned between now
and Labor Day.*

*That information dovetails with other intelligence chatter suggest-
ing that al Qaeda is pleased with the impact of the March 11 terrorist bombings in Spain and may want to affect elections in the
United States and other countries.*

*"There will be more people traveling, and more people gathered in
large groups, all of which appeal to terrorist activities," said one
federal official. "The fact that the tunnel bombings occurred on
June 4, exactly one month before the most celebrated American
holiday, may not be a coincidence."*

25

"Son of a bitch. There he is. Right on time."

Less than thirty minutes ago, Dyan's head was bobbing as she entered her sixth straight hour of reviewing video tapes. It wasn't until she caught a glimpse of him, although it wasn't hard to miss him in his long-sleeved flannel shirt and green backpack, that she suddenly got her second wind.

For most of the day, her mind kept drifting away from the boring video tapes to thoughts of what almost happened in the parking lot last night. She could not remember the last time she had sex in the back seat of a car, so Jack's offer was tempting, until they both suddenly realized neither of their cars had a back seat. They laughed so hard, that when they finally stopped, they agreed it was a bad omen, and decided it was better if they both went home. As tired as Dyan was, it didn't stop her from performing her wifely duties until well past three.

Knowing she would be stuck in the office all weekend, she decided to sleep in, and arrived at work just before eleven. By five o'clock, she was beginning to have her doubts about her plan to review the tapes. It was a long shot, but still it was based on one of the fundamental concepts in her report on low-tech, low-cost terrorist threats. Terrorists would exploit all opportunities available to them, including bio-terrorism. But her theory was that the biological threat did not have to be exotic, like anthrax, which was difficult to obtain, difficult to manufacture, and difficult to handle. It could be a simpler, more common virus, like hepatitis. The beauty of a disease like hepatitis was it was easily spreadable, it was weeks or even months before you realized you had it, and once you had it, there was no cure. You just suffered with the flu-like symptoms, sometimes for months. Although in most cases it was not life-threatening, infecting thousands or even millions of people would not only disrupt life as we know it, but it would send the more terrifying message of how vulnerable our society was to biological terrorism. Like the dirty bomb, the true terror would be more psychological than physical.

Being an upstate New York native, she followed the hepatitis outbreak, located just one hundred and thirty miles east of Syracuse near Albany, that was first reported in the news on Monday. She knew hepatitis was quite common in the U.S., infecting about 50,000 people annually, and in the beginning this case seemed like your typical restaurant outbreak. As the week progressed, although the number of cases increased rapidly, and appeared to be uncommonly high for an outbreak at a single restaurant, it was very similar to an outbreak a year before in Pennsylvania. At that restaurant, over six hundred people were eventually infected with the virus. Since the Thruway travel plaza had many more customers than the Pennsylvania restaurant, there was the potential for an even larger number of people getting the virus. However, it might be difficult to pinpoint the travel plaza as the source of many of the resulting cases, since many of those potentially infected were on route to destinations across the country.

By midweek the number of confirmed cases for the travel plaza grew to over two hundred, which was still far below the

Pennsylvania case. What finally piqued Dyan's curiosity was yesterday's news that a second travel plaza, just sixty miles west on the same interstate, had several employees who tested positive for hepatitis A. Her best friend confirmed that the first rest area could not have been the source for the second outbreak. It was more likely that a common carrier, traveling down the Thruway, was the source.

The scenario of someone driving down the interstate highway spreading a contagious disease, like hepatitis, was eerily similar to one of the terrorist plots described in Dyan's report. Although her report did not specify hepatitis, or the Thruway, it did mention a contagious disease, and the food supply chain. When you add to all of this the fact that suspected terrorists were observed driving up and down the Thruway, exchanging backpacks, the mere coincidence seemed too incredible.

Without sharing her hypothesis with anyone, except for her friend Lindsey who figured out what she was thinking, she went off to try to find the proverbial needle in the haystack. Since the first outbreaks of the disease coincided with the Memorial Day holiday weekend, she decided to start there. Even that seemed logical to her. What better time to begin spreading a contagious disease than the first busy traveling weekend of the summer. And what better place than a restaurant, or in this case six of them, located at an interstate roadway travel plaza.

Even though she thought she had the time and the place, she still wasn't sure what it was she was looking for. She hoped that by reviewing the video tapes, something would catch her eye. Something totally inconspicuous to everyone at the rest stop, but not to the video camera's eye.

After six hours of monotonous viewing, most on fast-forward, of thousands of people walking into the Pattersonville Travel Plaza, she finally saw him. Among hundreds of total strangers, almost no one there knew more than one or two people around them, he blended in perfectly. But under the watchful eye of the overhead video camera, where everyone became even more similar, he stuck out like a sore thumb.

The video tape said it was 12:11 P.M. on Saturday, May 29, 2004. Dyan still needed to verify the temperature that morning, but by the short-sleeved shirts and short pants worn by most of the people entering the building, and especially the youngest, she assumed it was a relatively warm day. So when she saw the man dressed in the heavy, long-sleeved flannel shirt, with all the buttons buttoned, stroll across the TV screen, her eyes popped wide open as she fumbled for the remote. It took a few seconds for her to find the pause button, since it was the first time she needed it in the past six hours. When she finally pushed it, the flannel-shirted man was nowhere to be seen. Rewinding, she again paused the video, this time with the man centered in the screen of the TV. She stared at him. He was young, maybe in his early twenties, with jet black hair, medium length, and a neatly trimmed mustache. At first it looked as though the man wore a pair of suspenders, but when Dyan pushed the slow-play button on the remote and the man moved to the left edge of the TV screen, she thought she started to hear her already throbbing heart when the green backpack appeared on the screen. She again pushed the pause button and looked closely at the screen. It was definitely a green backpack.

She fast-forwarded the tape, and at 12:18 P.M., the man appeared on the screen again leaving the building, carrying a cup with a plastic lid on it. This time, as the man walked away on the TV screen, the backpack was clearly visible.

Over the next twenty minutes, Dyan meticulously loaded the tapes from the three cameras inside the building and fast-forwarded to 12:11 P.M. The Backpack Man, as she nicknamed him, first went into the men's room, then a minute later visited every restaurant before returning to the first. He purchased a soda, which he then filled at a self-serve beverage station. Dyan saw nothing out of the ordinary, although the video camera, obviously mounted high in the interior of the building, made it difficult to review with any kind of detail what the man was really doing.

Next, she jumped to the video tapes from the Schuyler Travel Plaza, located sixty miles west on the Thruway, near Utica, New York. She calculated it would take about an hour to drive the sixty miles to the travel plaza, and fast-forwarded to 1:15 P.M. on the video tape. She rewound the tape to 1:10 P.M., then watched it up until 1:20 P.M. There was no sign of Backpack Man.

She stopped the video, leaned back in her chair, and stared out the window. The afternoon sun was just beginning to come into view at the top of the office window. She sat as still as she could watching the orange speck grow as it dropped down into view.

Slowly, a smile appeared on her face. Calmly she turned in her chair and reached for the remote. She fast-forwarded the tape five minutes to 1:25 P.M., then pushed the play button. Within a minute, the man dressed in the flannel shirt, carrying that green backpack, appeared on the screen. Dyan pressed the pause button.

"Son of a bitch. There he is. Right on time."

Dyan leaned back in her chair. Because she was a frequent traveler on the Thruway, she remembered there was another travel plaza, the Iroquois Travel Plaza, on the west bound lane, between the Pattersonville Travel Plaza and the Schuyler Travel Plaza. If you assumed the Backpack Man, for whatever reason, was stopping at every Thruway travel plaza, you would need to add five to ten minutes onto his arrival time at the Schuyler Travel Plaza. That would put him into Schuyler from 1:25 P.M. to 1:30 P.M. The video tape showed 1:26 P.M.

"Yes dear."

"Great. You're still there."

"Do you think I'd skip out without at least saying goodbye?"

"I need to have someone get another batch of tapes."

"Tonight?"

"If possible, yes."

"Where this time?"

"The Iroquois Travel Plaza, westbound lane."

26

"You have reached Dyan Galloway at the FBI Field Office in Syracuse. I can't come to the phone right now but if you leave your name and number I'll get back to you as soon as I can. If this is an emergency, and you need to speak to someone right away, please press zero and you'll be connected to the operator."

"Hey girl. It's me. Well, your hunch was right. The virus at the two Thruway travel plazas are the same strain. Haven't been able to link it yet with any strains that we've seen recently, but we're still lookin'. Good goin' girl. Although, I'm gettin' the credit for asking the question. Thanks. Got any more tips for me?

"It's about seven o'clock. Give me a call if you need to, although I'm outta here in a few minutes. Happy hour is calling. I'm going to be into work in the morning, so you'll have to go it alone with that hunk of yours this weekend. Don't hurt him.

"Oh, one more thing. It's probably totally unrelated, but there's been an outbreak of hepatitis A linked to a restaurant in California. Less than two dozen cases so far. Keep in mind we get about a thousand cases of hepatitis A in the U.S. weekly. So it's probably all just a coincidence. Anyway, call me if you want.

"Love ya. Bye."

27

Dyan was not a field agent. She was a desk-bound, pencil-pushing, computer geek, FBI analyst. She was never on a stakeout in her life. The only things she knew about them she learned from TV shows and movies. She knew she should look inconspicuous, but not be so obvious about it that she looked conspicuous. She knew there was a perfect gray area where you went unnoticed. She decided hers was to sit in her car, seat back reclined, although in a Miata it wasn't much of a recline, and pretend to catch a power nap. She counted at least three others doing the same thing in the crowded parking lot that afternoon. She doubted any of them had a pulse rate as fast as hers though.

She had arrived at her office earlier this morning, 6:45 A.M. Since her husband had an early morning golf date, it was useless for her to try to sleep through all his commotion anyway. How could a shower be so noisy? she thought.

As Jack promised, the Iroquois Travel Plaza video tapes were on her desk. After calculating an approximate arrival time, she popped in the Saturday, May 29, video tape, and fast-forwarded it to 12:55 A.M. Within five minutes of viewing the tape, Backpack Man appeared. The inside videos showed him going through the same ritual as at the other two travel plazas. A visit to the men's room, a tour of the eateries, then the purchase of a single drink, self-serve. She again saw nothing out of the ordinary. He exited the building seven minutes later.

"What the hell is he doing?" Dyan kept asking herself, and although she had no proof, kept coming up with the same answer. "Somehow he's spreading the hepatitis A virus around."

The words sent a chill down her back. Unfortunately, the whole thing made sense. Holiday weekend. Crowded interstate. Thousands of people using the travel plaza facilities. It was the perfect place and time to spread a contagious virus.

Still, she had no conclusive proof. She kept viewing the videos, over and over again, searching for some corroborating evidence, but found none. Then suddenly it dawned on her. Memorial Day weekend was three days long. The same people would not be traveling on the west bound lane of the interstate on each of the three days. There'd be a different group each day. In order to get the greatest exposure over the weekend, you'd want to make sure the virus was around the entire weekend.

"What are the chances . . . " Without finishing the statement, she searched through the video tapes for the one of Sunday, May 30, and fast-forwarded to 12:05 P.M. Her heart pounded as she watched the tape. She gasped when Backpack Man appeared on the screen.

It took her less than an hour to verify Backpack Man's daily visits over the Memorial Day holiday weekend. Each day's visit at each of the three travel plazas was timed within minutes of the next. But even after viewing the three days' worth of video tapes, she still had nothing to show what the man was doing.

Dyan leaned back in her chair and closed her eyes. It was then she noticed her head pounding. Too much TV, she thought. She glanced at her watch. 1:15 P.M. She had been at it for six hours. Add to that the eight hours from yesterday, and it was more TV than she normally watched in a month.

"What a way to spend a holiday weekend," she said as she stretched her arms up to the ceiling. Then she froze. With her eyes closed, she started calculating. She jerked her right arm down and looked at her watch again. "I can make it," she said as she ran out of her office.

Just as she calculated, it took her just forty-five minutes to drive down the eastbound lane of the Thruway, make an illegal U-turn just past the Chittenango Travel Plaza, proceed westbound, and exit at the travel plaza.

It was 2:00 P.M. She leaned her head back against the head rest. Within fifteen minutes she'd know if her hunch was right.

28

"Hey girl. It's me again. It's two o'clock, on Saturday afternoon. I just left you a message at your house. We need to talk. The shit's hitting the fan. Call me ASAP."

29

Dyan jerked forward so quickly her head almost hit the convertible top of her car. So much for her inconspicuous stakeout she thought. Anyone watching her would have thought she just saw a ghost. Fortunately, no one had, not even Backpack Man as he walked through the parking lot, less than five feet in front of Dyan's car. As he went past, his green backpack hung from his shoulders. She glanced at her watch. 2:10 P.M. "You can set your clock by this guy."

Dyan waited until he entered the building before she got out of her car. As she started to slam the car door with her left hand, she suddenly punched her right hand into the space between the closing door and the door frame. "NO!" The pain of the slamming door banging on her forearm shot through her entire body. She looked around. No one heard her scream. She pulled open the door and saw her keys laying on the black leather passenger seat. She leaned in, grabbed the keys, slammed the door shut, then walked briskly to the doorway of the building, all the while rubbing the now reddening welt on her right forearm.

Just as she walked through the second set of double glass doors, she saw Backpack Man walk out of the men's room doorway to her right. He turned right in front of her, then headed down the wide hall to the back of the building where the eateries were located. When he got to the end of the hall, he turned left and headed for the restaurant at the far end of the room. Dyan glanced to her right. At the far end was a restaurant with a self-service beverage station. She got in line, purchased a small drink, then headed for one of the booths directly across from the beverage station. Backpack Man was now in the same line she had been in just a minute before. He purchased a small drink, then took his cup up to the beverage station.

As he stood there, Dyan now saw what none of the videos was able to reveal. Backpack Man placed his left hand into his pants pocket, and from where Dyan was sitting, it looked as though he was squeezing something in his pocket, over and over again. As he glanced around the room, his right hand wandered over the entire area of the beverage station – the plastic tops to the cups, plastic spoons and forks, wooden coffee stirrers, napkin holder, and even the straw dispenser.

As quickly as he arrived, he turned and walked toward the doors of the building.

Dyan got up and walked over to the beverage station. She noticed the entire area was covered with tiny droplets of liquid. She picked up one of the wet plastic tops and put it in the empty cup she was holding. She took another top and sealed her cup. She then headed for the front door. As she got to the long wide hallway, Backpack Man was nowhere in sight. She ran toward the double glass doors and looked out. Still no Backpack Man. She ran toward her car. As she ran out between two parked cars, the blare of the horn to her right was just enough warning to make her come to a stop. She stood still as the car drove in front of her. "Sorry," she said as the car was directly in front of her. When she looked down into the open window, she immediately recognized Backpack Man's flannel shirt.

When the car passed by, Dyan glanced at the rear of it, then turned and walked toward her car. As soon as she unlocked her car, she opened the door and tossed the cup she was carrying onto the passenger seat. She then reached under the driver's side seat, and pulled out the small pad and pen she kept there.

She repeated out loud what she just wrote. "Light blue Dodge, Pennsylvania plate 9A6-471."

30

"What the hell is he getting off at Exit 36 for?"

Dyan's talking out loud habit was getting worse. At this point, she didn't care though. She was on a mission. Caught up in the excitement of the chase.

Dyan followed Backpack Man as he headed west on the Thruway. With no tailing experience either, she thought it would be best to keep as much distance between her and Backpack Man as possible. Most of the exits on the Thruway were at least ten miles apart. It wasn't like she could lose him. Anyway, she was certain she knew where his next stop was. The Warners Travel Plaza was just on the other side of Syracuse.

When she saw Backpack Man signal to get off at Syracuse Exit 36, which was at least ten miles before the Warners Travel Plaza, she panicked.

"He knows I'm following him."

She decided to continue down the Thruway. She wasn't a field agent. She didn't know what she was doing. She had enough evidence to convince the authorities of what she saw. Assuming the car wasn't stolen, she had Backpack Man's license plate number. It was time to turn over the chase to the experts.

Suddenly she pressed in the clutch pedal, slammed on the brakes, and turned the steering wheel hard to the right. The tiny sports car was inches from flying off the left shoulder of the exit ramp. A dust cloud appeared in the rear view mirror. She downshifted into third, and eased her way back onto the curved roadway.

"I couldn't have called more attention to myself if I tried."

Luckily, Backpack Man was already in line at one of the toll booths. She doubted he saw her.

On this busy holiday weekend, at least a dozen cars waited in line at each of the toll booths. Dyan eased into the line to the left of the one Backpack Man was in. Although he was three cars ahead of her in his line, she wasn't worried about losing him. The only roadway off Exit 36 was Interstate 81, which ran from the Canadian border to the north, to Tennessee to the south, and she had a clear view of both entrance ramps.

As luck would have it, Dyan's lane seemed to be moving exceptionally fast while his was going nowhere. Within seconds, her car was even with his. Backpack Man was now less than ten feet away from her. She didn't dare look out her passenger window.

"Damn. Why is this line moving so fast?"

Now Dyan found herself one car away from the toll booth. Backpack Man was two away. The car in front of her pulled ahead and within seconds drove away. Dyan did not pull the car ahead. Instead she fumbled with her purse. She glanced over her shoulder to see Backpack Man was still two cars back from the toll booth. Suddenly the blast of a horn, a semi tractor trailer's horn one car behind her, was all the nudging she needed to stop the stall tactic and drive up to the toll booth.

"Sorry, it's all I've got."

The man looked at her with one of those "dumb broad"

looks. Dyan forgot she entered the Thruway on Exit 34A, less than ten miles to the east. Although she traveled well over fifty miles on the roadway, her illegal U-turn, and back tracking to the Chittenago Travel Plaza, then to Exit 36, meant she only had a twenty-cent toll. She handed the tollbooth operator a fifty dollar bill.

She turned to her right side and saw that Backpack Man was still one car back in his lane.

"Could I have a receipt please?"

Finally, she pulled ahead. As she edged forward, she saw Backpack Man paying his toll in the next booth. But it was too late. She could never go slow enough to let him pass without being obvious about it. When she looked in the rearview mirror, he was now closing in directly behind her. She put her right directional on and headed for the entrance ramp for Route 81 South. Backpack Man followed. Instead of merging to the left onto the highway, she noticed he was staying on the ramp which in less than a quarter mile turned into the exit ramp for Seventh North Street. Dyan headed for the exit. Backpack Man followed. At the stoplight at the end of the exit Backpack Man still had his right signal light on so Dyan turned right. A hundred feet down the road, as Dyan continued straight, Backpack Man made a quick right turn into a parking lot. Dyan saw him make the turn but didn't panic. Instead she turned into the next parking lot. It was for the restaurant adjacent to the one Backpack Man pulled into.

There were a half-dozen restaurants within a half-mile of the Thruway, Route 81 Interchange. It took Backpack Man less than thirty minutes to hit them all. By 3:15 P.M. he was back on Route 81 heading south.

31

"Jack Nelson."

"Jack?"

"Dyan. I've been worried sick. Security said you left the building at one-twenty this afternoon. Why haven't you called in?"

"I left my cell in my charger on the desk. I ran out without it. This is the first opportunity I've had to call."

"It's seven-thirty. You've been gone for six hours. Where the hell are you?"

"Philadelphia."

"What?"

"I'm in Philadelphia."

"New York or Pennsylvania?"

"Philadelphia, Pennsylvania."

"What the hell are you doing in Philadelphia?"

"It's a long story."

"I bet it is."

"I can't get into it right now. I need for you to get ahold of Director Blackman for me."

"Gee. What a coincidence. He's been trying to get ahold of

you. For the past four hours I might add."

"What?"

"That's right. He's got half the agents in Syracuse looking for you. You've got a bunch of pissed-off co-workers wondering why they are working a holiday weekend looking for you."

"Did he say why he wanted me?"

"Sorry Dyan. The director doesn't let me in on everything like he does you. But . . . haven't you been listening to the news? This hepatitis outbreak has mushroomed. Millions might be infected. It's all up and down the eastern seaboard, from Boston to Miami, and as far east as Chicago. Even the West Coast has been hit. Southern California and the Seattle area. Although there hasn't been anything official out of Homeland Security, rumors are flying about a terrorism plot. The hospitals are being overrun. People are panicking. Blackman wants you in Washington tomorrow for a 10:00 A.M. meeting."

"Tomorrow?"

"Yes, Sunday. Tomorrow."

"Do you have a number where I can reach Blackman?"

"Yes I do. Hold on a second. So, I take it since you are in Philadelphia you'll just continue on down to Washington so you can make the meeting tomorrow."

"Let me think."

"While you're thinking, here's the number. Got a paper and pencil?"

32

"You are not a field agent, Ms. Galloway. What you did today was stupid. You could have gotten yourself killed. Worse yet, you could have exposed a year's worth of trying to uncover and track what is probably the largest terrorist network to ever infiltrate our country.

"You are damn lucky I don't make decisions when I'm in a bad mood like this, because if I did, I'd probably have you thrown in jail for jeopardizing our national security.

"Now get out of my office."

Dyan witnessed Blackman in many different moods, from melancholy to excited, and everything in between. She saw him hold his cool during some difficult times. The person now sitting across the desk from her was none of those.

She just spent the past hour briefing Blackman on the investigative work she did to uncover the hepatitis contamination. Except for two minor clarification questions, points she hadn't yet covered, but was about to, he said nothing else. She thought she would get some reaction when she told him about Backpack Man's contamination of several grocery stores in the Binghamton area, along Route 81, which to her meant a much greater part of the food supply chain was now at risk. Instead, he just sat there taking notes. Even news that she thought she uncovered another terrorist cell in Philadelphia, Backpack Man's final destination point, elicited no reaction from him. When she finished talking, he continued writing for several minutes, then looked up and started his ranting.

Dyan risked her life. She thought she went above and beyond the call of duty. She didn't have time to get the field jocks involved. Ten minutes later and she would have missed Backpack Man. She wouldn't have known what he was doing. She wouldn't have known how widespread he was doing it. And she wouldn't have found his cell. She thought she was a hero.

Dyan got up from her chair, turned and headed for the door out of Blackman's office.

"Dyan." For the first time in their hour-long meeting, the tone of Blackman's voice was civil, even smooth. Dyan stopped and turned.

"I believe this is al Qaeda's big effort to try to break our will. To destroy the U.S. Their next 9/11 attack. Their Armageddon." There was a long pause, but when Blackman spoke up again, his voice was still calm. "If this backpack person spotted you, even suspected you were following him, it would have been all over. The existing cells would be disbanded by now without a trace. They'd be reorganizing into something new. We'd be starting from ground zero again.

"You've been right about their tactics. But I still believe they are up to something big. Even bigger than 9/11. Finding those cells is our only hope to stop them."

"I'm sorry. I thought I was doing the right thing."

"I know you did." There was another long period of silence. "It's already midnight. You've got a lot to do to prepare for tomorrow's meeting."

Dyan turned and walked toward the door.

"One more thing Dyan." Dyan stopped and turned toward him again. "In the end, results are what count, especially when fighting terrorism. And today, you got results. Between you and I . . . great job."

33

"Hey girl." Although the words were there, the usual excitement wasn't.

"Dyan, where the hell have you been? I've been trying to reach you all day."

"I know, I know. I'm sorry. It's been a long day. Maybe I'll be able to tell you about it someday."

"Are you okay?"

"Yes. I'm fine. Can you tell me what the hell is going on?"

"Oh boy. Let's see . . . where do I start."

After Dyan left Blackman's office, she went back to her office. She resigned herself to the fact that she was going to be pulling an all-nighter. She found a small TV, brought it to her office and tuned in CNN. The scenes reminded her of the films she watched in high school about the civil rights riots in the 1960s. Only now people were storming hospitals and clinics.

Because of the emotionalism, she couldn't really tell from the TV reporters how accurately they were reporting on the extent of the hepatitis outbreak. If what they were saying was true, the situation was turning pretty bleak. And it had done so in less than a day. She decided to go to the best source she knew. Unfortunately Lindsey's report was not any better.

With hospitals now guarded by state National Guardsmen, it was difficult to get an accurate estimate of how many people were infected with the virus. A statistical analysis performed by CDC projected over a million people could by now already be infected. A vast majority of those individuals would still not be showing any symptoms. The more sobering projection was the total number infected could eventually reach ten million. That statistic assumed a majority of the at-risk public, those individuals who may have contracted the virus within the past fourteen days, received an injection of immune globulin, an antibody treatment that would greatly lessen the chances of acquiring the disease. However, there were several problems with that assumption. A massive testing program would be needed to determine who was at risk. Testing would take days to set up, and each day that went by rendered the injection more useless. Even if the testing program was in place, there wasn't enough antibody to treat all those in need. In other words, the estimate of ten million could go much higher.

The sources of the virus seemed to surround several major roadways of the Interstate Highway System. Route 90, east to west, from Boston to Chicago seemed to be the northern most corridor, with three major highways extending from there to the south: Route 95 from Boston to Miami, Route 81 from Syracuse to Knoxville, and Route 65 from Chicago to Louisville. Two areas on the West Coast had also been identified: San Diego and Seattle, although the Los Angeles and San Francisco areas might be involved too.

Dyan told Lindsey what she knew about how Backpack Man was spreading the virus. She suspected the backpack held a container of infectious feces suspended in water. A plastic tube attached to the container ran under the man's loose clothing to a hand operated pump, similar to the one on a common household spray bottle, located in his left pants pocket. Another tube was connected to the end of the pump and ran under his shirt sleeve, to the palm of his right hand where the solution was sprayed. Backpack Man could stand at a salad bar, and with a few squeezes of his left hand, concealed in his pants pocket, spread the virus without being detected.

"Did you actually see him spray an area?"

"Yes. I was less than ten feet away from him when he sprayed a self-serve beverage station. After he left I went up to the counter. It was covered with a fine mist. I grabbed a sample. One of the plastic cup lids. In fact it's still in my car."

"I'm going to have someone drop by tomorrow and get that from you."

"No problem."

"How many places did you follow the guy to?"

"Thirteen places. I have a feeling he was running out of the virus though."

"Why do you say that?"

"As we traveled down Route 81 at first he stopped at every exit with a fast food restaurant. Then he skipped a bunch of exits. Didn't get off again until he got to Binghamton. The grocery stores he hit there were his last stops."

"What did you say?"

"Binghamton was his last stop."

"No. What did you say about grocery stores?"

"He went to three grocery stores in Binghamton. They were his last stops."

"Oh my god."

"What?"

"The analysis we performed to predict the extent of the outbreak limited the sources of the virus to restaurants. If they've contaminated the food supplies in grocery stores, that would significantly increase the number of people infected."

"By how much?"

"I don't know . . . I gotta go."

34

HEPATITIS A VIRUS INTENTIONALLY SPREAD: MILLIONS AT RISK

WASHINGTON, D.C., July 4 – The Department of Homeland Security issued a statement today indicating that one or more individuals may have intentionally spread the hepatitis A virus across hundreds of restaurants in the U.S. However, officials declined to speculate that this was an act of terrorism. Meanwhile, the number of confirmed cases of the disease has surpassed 100,000. A source at the CDC who wished to remain anonymous, indicated up to ten million people could eventually be stricken with the virus.

Hospitals have been inundated with patients who suspect they have the virus. Hundreds were arrested at a hospital in Albany, New York, when patients, told there was no cure for the disease, stormed the facility demanding treatment. The outbreak prompted the governor of New York to activate the National Guard and deploy them at several of the larger hospitals in the state.

Although there is no cure for hepatitis A, an antibody injection is available to lessen the chance of getting the disease. However, it must be administered within fourteen days of exposure to the virus. The injection is rendered useless to anyone already exhibiting the flu-like symptoms of the disease.

The CDC stressed that hepatitis A, although highly contagious, is normally not a life-threatening disease. One official was quoted as saying, "It's more like a three-week flu."

35

"Wait a minute. Let me see if I have this straight. You know who the person is who spread the hepatitis A virus around. You know how he did it. You have him on video tape, caught in the act of actually doing it. You have an eye-witness, an FBI agent no less, who saw him do it. You have a sample of the actual virus.

"The bastard is responsible for possibly millions of people getting sick. God willing, not many, but some are going to die. The National Guard is controlling the crowds around hospitals. It's probably going to result in billions of dollars in damages. Hundreds of restaurants are shut down. Some will never reopen.

"Why don't we already have him in custody?"

David Cross was one of the personal assistants to the president. He was assigned by the president to basically keep an eye on things at the FBI. Cross did not like Blackman, which was okay with Blackman, because he didn't like Cross.

"The one piece of information you left out David," Cross preferred the name Dave to David, so Blackman always called him David, "was this man belongs to an al Qaeda terrorist cell, the fifth we have confirmed of a dozen or more in this country."

"A dozen or more you BELIEVE to be in this country." Cross was a details man. A lawyer by training. He was famous for correcting errors of speech, and he particularly liked doing so to Blackman.

"You're right David. We believe there are a dozen or more. Unfortunately, each day our belief gets more real. A year ago we knew of none. A week ago we knew of only three. As of yesterday, we have identified five.

"It's also clear to us that more than one person, and probably more than one cell, was responsible for spreading the hepatitis A virus across such a wide geographical area."

"What happens if this guy jumps in his car tomorrow morning and starts spreading the virus around again? Are we just going to sit back and let him do it?"

"We don't believe he will do that."

"What makes you so sure of that?"

Blackman pointed to Dyan to answer. "The cat's out of the bag so to speak. People will be on the lookout for anything suspicious. That is, if there are any people actually going to restaurants anymore. The ones that are still open, I mean. Why risk getting caught when you won't be spreading the disease to very many people?"

"Terrorism under your watch is getting out of control. The president wants action, not words. When can we start to make some arrests in both this and the tunnel bombings?" demanded Cross.

"I can't answer that question," Blackman was quick to answer.

"That's unacceptable to the president."

"I am not about to jeopardize a year-long operation . . . "

"I'm only asking when we can expect to see the results of this operation."

"We are seeing results. Two more cells identified in the past week."

"I mean, when are we going public? When will arrests be made?"

"I don't know the answer to that."

"It's already been a year."

"And look at the progress we've made."

"And look what the terrorists have done. They've killed over a thousand people. Now they've infected millions. All while you were supposedly keeping an eye on them."

"And that's precisely my point, David. We were keeping an eye on these cells. Yet terrorist acts continue. Which further supports our theory that there are more cells in this country. Many more. Cells we haven't found yet."

"And all I'm asking is, when do you think we are going to find the rest of these damned cells?"

"I don't know the answer to that."

"So in the meantime we just let the terrorists have free reign on the American public?"

Blackman sat frozen, staring at Cross.

"Wait a minute." Cross's voice went noticeably lower in tone. "Are you saying if you knew one of these cells was about to commit an act of terror, that you would let them do it, just so your year-long operation could continue?"

"Depending upon what they were planning to do . . . "

"Stop right there Director. This is totally unacceptable. This president has already endured more than his fair share of terrorist attacks on American soil. I believe he made it clear when the two of you met that you are to use every means at your disposal to stop these attacks. Did he not?"

"Yes he did David, but let me finish."

Cross sat still, staring at Blackman.

"Al Qaeda has a tremendous amount of patience. More than we Americans have, unfortunately. It took them over two years to plan and execute 9/11. They have obviously been spending years establishing these cells in our country. We were lucky to stumble upon the first one. There were some who wanted to haul them in, just like we did with the scores of other suspicious people we rounded up since 9/11. But we held off. Yes. We took a risk. We waited and watched. And although al Qaeda is very smart, although they know how to remain very stealth, to assimilate into our society, we also know they are human beings. They will eventually make mistakes. Get cocky. Get careless. That's how we found the rest of the cells. That and a little luck.

"We believe there are anywhere from eighty to one hundred skilled al Qaeda terrorists in this country at this very minute. It's taken them years to get here. And it now appears their reign of terror has started. But it's not going to stop here. There is more to come. Some, like myself, believe much more.

"So, depending upon what they were planning to do, we need to weigh the risk of letting them do it against the benefit of being able to continue to spy on their every move without them knowing it.

"This strategy is no different than what we've used in the past to defeat an enemy. We broke the German and Japanese secret codes during World War II, yet we kept it a secret. We knew our enemies' every move. There were attacks we knew about well ahead of time. Attacks we didn't stop. Attacks that resulted in our soldiers getting killed. Those painful, but small-er sacrifices were made to achieve a greater goal.

"As of right now," Blackman glanced at his watch, "12:55 P.M. on July 4, 2004, we have possibly identified thirty-one al Qaeda terrorists living in this country. They are our only hope of identifying the rest."

Even though there were over two dozen people in the room, there was dead silence. All eyes were on Blackman. His eyes hadn't moved from Cross.

"No one is doubting your tactics Director. But I believe, the president believes, that it isn't just a coincidence that these attacks have started now. It's obvious al Qaeda is out to destroy our society. Our way of life. And one way to start doing that is to undermine our governmental system.

"What do you think would happen if our government were forced to postpone the election this fall? Some believe it would be the first step toward the downfall of our government as we know it today. Those are some of the risks you need to consider as you continue to let these terrorists run free, Mr. Blackman.

"This administration will not tolerate another major terrorist attack on our soil. I hope the president's previous direction to you on this point has been clear."

Seconds later, the silence in the room was broken when a young man, obviously nervous about entering the room, slipped through the doorway, eyed his way around the table, then walked over to and handed Blackman a folded five-by-seven-inch piece of paper. As Blackman read the note, half of the men seated around the table simultaneously reached for their pagers. Blackman looked up.

"A massive power blackout occurred a few minutes ago in New England. There is no indication yet as to what caused it, but it appears to be very similar to the one that occurred last August."

As soon as he was done reading the note, Blackman looked over at Dyan.

36

"What else is going to happen?"

"Why, what's wrong?"

"Do you know where the circuit breaker box is? The stove just went dead."

"It's over here, but it's probably not the circuit breaker. It's something you'll have to get used to if you move up here. We lose power all the time in the Adirondacks. It's one of the things you put up with to keep things wilderness-looking."

After meeting with the private investigator on Friday, Iullia decided to spend the Fourth of July weekend at Williams's cabin. It would give her a chance to once more search for any connections between her and him. More importantly, she hoped to meet up again with Barbara, who she was sure knew something more about Williams's past.

When she arrived on Friday evening, as she emerged from the pine tree cave and spotted the cabin, a sense of calm came over her. It was like the feeling you get when arriving back home after a long vacation. A sense of calm, of being safe, of belonging. Although it was only her second time at the cabin, she felt as if she belonged there more than in her own home.

Early yesterday morning she set out on the back trail in search of Barbara's cabin. Barbara had been right. The well-worn path led right to her back door. Unbeknownst to Iullia, Barbara just minutes before set out on a day hike on the Indian Pass trail near Lake Placid. Later that evening, Iullia decided again to hike the back trail, only to run into Barbara. Their initial uneasiness with one another quickly faded when Barbara invited her on an early morning hike for the following day.

"I guess you were right. It's not the circuit breakers. It just seems funny that we would lose power on such a beautiful afternoon."

"Honey, anything's possible in the Adirondacks."

They both walked back to the front porch chairs with the coffee Iullia had managed to warm before the power outage.

"You know," Barbara spoke up, then took a sip from her mug. "You know a lot about me, but I know almost nothing about you."

"There's really not much to know."

"Married?"

"Nope."

"Ever?"

"Nope."

"Then no kids obviously?"

"Obviously."

"Seeing anyone?"

"I date occasionally. Actually, less than occasionally. Mostly to charity functions where you are required to show up with a partner. Not too romantic obviously."

"I know you're a professor at Syracuse University. What do you teach?"

"Russian Studies, mostly modern Russian History."

"Do you speak Russian?"

"Da. Fluently."

"Well there you go. That's another thing you have in common with Richard." As soon as she said it, Barbara realized her mistake.

"I didn't know he spoke Russian."

37

HEPATITIS OUTBREAK CLAIMS FIRST FATALITY

SARATOGA SPRINGS, NY, July 5 – A patient infected with hepatitis A died last night at Saratoga Hospital, the first fatality in upstate New York stemming from the largest known outbreak of the sickness in U.S. history.

The patient was identified as Jessica McNeill, age 5, daughter of Mrs. Debra McNeill, 9157 Canton Street, Saratoga Springs, according to the Saratoga County Coroner's office. Her death has shocked this affluent upstate community, because authorities have been saying that hepatitis A is usually not fatal and normally runs its course in a few weeks.

A spokesman for the CDC indicated that the fatality rate for hepatitis A is one to three deaths per 1,000 cases, though it can rise to ten times that much, or 20 cases per 1,000, for the elderly, and even higher for those with chronic liver problems.

Yesterday, the Department of Homeland Security issued a state-

ment indicating that the current outbreak of hepatitis A may have been intentional. However, officials declined to speculate if it was a deliberate act of terrorism. To date no organization has claimed responsibility.

38

"Was this or was this not an al Qaeda-coordinated terrorist attack?" Blackman finally realized he let the meeting go far too long. After listening to almost two hours of a point-counter-point debate between the two factions in the room, he had enough.

For Blackman, the most important question he wanted answered was did the blackout involve terrorism. A month ago the question would have never crossed his mind. That was before he read Dyan's report.

Immediately following word of the blackout, he sent a small investigative team to upstate New York. Their mission was to cut through the politics that dominate events such as this, and bring back a quick and dirty assessment of what might have caused it. Ironically, a year earlier, a very similar blackout occurred, affecting over 50 million people in eight states and Ontario, Canada. More than a dozen electric utilities were involved. Their six-month investigation determined that a number of human and operator control errors that "shouldn't have happened," happened. Blame got distributed, which then meant no one was held at fault. With hundreds of millions of dollars in potential compensatory claims from the twenty-four hour outage, it was the safest answer for all. Blackman didn't care about the politics. He wanted the truth.

Little or no damage occurred to the electrical distribution system during last year's blackout. Restoration involved switching circuits back on, and restarting power plants. The entire process took less than twenty-four hours. This was certainly not the case with the current blackout. Several major transmission lines carrying power from Canada, Niagara Falls, and the Nine Mile Point nuclear complex were simultaneously knocked out. These lines carried over half the power consumed in New York and New England. With these lines knocked out, the rest of the system could not handle the load, and it too went down. The resulting blackout was as big as last year's, and after forty-eight hours the system was still not fully restored.

"The bolts were removed from the plates connecting the legs of the transmission towers to its base. Six to ten towers in a row in each line. Then at exactly twelve noon on the fourth, someone used a rope to pull over one of the towers in each line. They all toppled like dominos. It was all well-coordinated. They also knew which lines to hit to cause the most widespread blackout."

Blackman looked across the table at Dyan who was doodling on the yellow pad in front of her. Her report summarized the vulnerability of the electric grid and how simple it would be to cause a major outage anywhere in the country. For years terrorists in other countries blew up transmission towers to knock out the power. During the first war with Iraq in 1992, and especially during the second in 2003, transmission lines as well as major electric generating stations were some of the first facilities taken out by our bombs. During the Cold War we knew our major electric power complexes, especially nuclear stations like the Nine Mile Point complex near Oswego, New York, on the southeastern shore of Lake Ontario, were targeted by

Russian intercontinental balistic missiles. Knock out a country's electric infrastructure, and you turn it back to the stone age.

It was obvious the terrorists figured this out too. But as summarized in Dyan's report, without a supply of explosives, the terrorists would need to resort to other methods if they were to topple the transmission systems. Unfortunately they didn't need high explosives to do it, just a wrench. Even the largest of transmission towers were at some point bolted to massive concrete bases buried deep in the ground. But to avoid problems with corrosion, the bolts were always above ground, and accessible. A terrorist could either keep removing bolts until the structure toppled over, or take out just enough to leave the structure standing, then either let the next strong wind blow it over, or come back later and pull it over with a rope.

"You mean to tell me no one saw these guys unbolting these things?" David Cross asked when he saw how a total of thirty-one towers were taken down.

Blackman guessed how it was done, but motioned to Dyan to answer the question.

"The electric utility industry has been going through a massive restructuring ever since it was deregulated about ten years ago. A number of utilities have either merged or been taken over by other companies. When this happens, the newly formed company is under tremendous pressure to cut costs. One way to do that is to cut back on some of the long-standing preventative maintenance practices. For example, the transmission line right-of-way, or the one-hundred-foot-wide corridor that the line runs through along the country side, is originally cleared of trees and brush when the line is first built. Long-standing utility practices called for continued clearing of this right-of-way when the underbrush got to about three- to five-feet tall, or once every four to five years. In order to save money, new practices have been adopted to clear the transmission right-of-ways every seven to ten years. This results in a ten- to twelve-foot growth of bushes and trees. This is still low enough such that the transmission lines do not normally contact the underbrush, which would ground the line, shorting it out."

"What do you mean 'normally'?"

"A few years ago in California, a line operating at one hundred percent capacity in hot weather sagged, and made contact with an overgrown tree in the right-of-way."

"Thank you."

"Even though the lines may not contact the taller underbrush, that same undergrowth now provides perfect cover for anyone wanting to vandalize the towers, especially at its most vulnerable point, where it contacts the ground. The company that owns most of the toppled towers, the Northeast Transmission Company, recently bought the utility that originally built and operated the lines. They implemented the cheaper, but less effective brush-clearing program.

"Whoever removed the bolts probably did it in broad daylight, totally unnoticed."

"How the hell did they know which ones to hit?"

"One of the biggest relay sub-stations in the northeast is located in the center of New York State near Utica. The Marcy sub-station is the major intersection point for transmission lines transversing west to east from Niagara Falls, and north to south from the Nine Mile Point nuclear complex on Lake Ontario and Canada. These lines then proceed downstate to the New York City metro area. It doesn't take a rocket scientist to know knocking out a few of these lines would probably bring down much of the system."

"Still sounds like an inside job to me."

"Which leads us to one of the theories as to who may have done this," Ryan Reynolds interjected.

Blackman had sent a team of four FBI investigators to New York headed up by Reynolds. Three of the investigators were seasoned veterans. The fourth was Dyan. It was clear as soon as the team started their investigation that the three veterans had formed their opinion of who was responsible for taking down the transmission towers.

The Northeast Transmission Company takeover had not been fully embraced by the highly unionized workforce. With the union contract due to expire at the end of the month, negotiations were at a standstill. The company was looking for concessions from the union to justify its buyout to Wall Street. The union, led by the hard-core linemen, was not budging. There was an increase in petty vandalism — like wooden utility poles cut down with chain saws and insulators shot out with high-powered rifles — that rumor had was instigated by union radicals. But there was also a hint of more extreme tactics if an acceptable agreement could not be reached.

The three veterans on the team were convinced this was a coordinated act of vandalism by a small group of hard-core company linemen.

"They had the knowledge of which lines to hit, where the most remote spots were where they would go undetected, and the know-how to take apart the transmission towers. Couple that with motive . . . "

"Which is?"

"Show the company how vulnerable it would be if they ever went out on strike."

"That's crazy." Dyan, the lone dissenter on the team, couldn't hold back any longer.

"Crazy or not, the company seems to be coming to the same conclusion," Reynolds replied.

"Of course they are. That's what's in their best interest. Defeat the union, lower their costs, and raise their profits."

"The union made their own bed."

"What kind of public support do you think the union would have if it were caught pulling off a stunt like this? Millions of people were without power. It's probably caused hundreds of millions of dollars in lost productivity, lost consumer sales, and other damages. If and when these people get caught, they'd be put in jail forever. Shooting out an insulator is one thing. Knocking out power to millions is in a whole other league.

"Just because bombs aren't involved, don't think it can't be terrorists."

"I think you're stretching things here, Dyan. Your wanting it to be terrorists doesn't make it terrorists." Reynolds's voice was getting louder.

"I don't want it. I believe that's the most reasonable answer."

"They aren't sophisticated enough to pull this off, and even if they were they wouldn't use wrenches."

"Like they weren't sophisticated enough to pull off 9/11 or the tunnel bombings."

"Look here you . . . "

"All right, all right, that's enough." Blackman's words silenced the room. His stare kept it that way. "Did any of you go back over the surveillance records of the three original cells, especially the Albany and Boston cells, to see if any of them could be traced to the geographical areas where the towers were toppled." No one responded. "I suggest you pull that string."

"Are we saying this is not a terrorist attack?" David Cross desperately wanted to report to the president that the FBI's preliminary conclusion was this was not a terrorist act.

"I don't know the answer to that."

39

TOPPLING OF TRANSMISSION TOWERS DELIBERATE BUT NOT TERRORISM

SYRACUSE, NY, July 8 – Investigators have concluded that the massive blackout across New York and New England on July 4, though deliberate, was likely not the result of terrorists. Although the Joint Terrorism Task Force and the FBI have not yet completed their investigations, sources reveal they have found no links to terrorist groups.

Michael Dayton, a Homeland Security Department spokesman, said in Syracuse today that the government is unaware of any credible evidence linking the blackout to al Qaeda or any other terrorist group.

The timing of the blackout, which took place exactly one month after the deadly tunnel bombings of June 4, has fueled speculation that it was carried out by al Qaeda. Immediately following the tunnel bombings on June 4 al Qaeda came forward claiming responsibility. However, following one month of intense investigations by a number of law enforcement agencies, no link has been found to the terrorist organization.

Authorities continue their investigation into what is now being described as an act of vandalism that mushroomed out of control. Meanwhile the Northeast Transmission Company, owner of most of the downed towers, has offered a reward of $100,000 leading to the arrest and conviction of those involved.

40

"Dyan Galloway."

"Hey, girl."

"Do you look as bad as you sound?"

"Nope. Worse. In fact, I look like shit."

"That's good, because that's how I look too."

"I bet I've gotten just about as much sleep as you have in the past week."

"How come in college we could survive on even less sleep?"

"And still look pretty damn hot, right?"

"Right."

"Must have been the drugs."

"We didn't do drugs."

"I meant alcohol."

"Excuse me, Doctor. Only you would define a can of Coors Light as a drug."

"A can?"

"A six-pack?"

"Keep going."

"So you're saying if I was half in the bag right now, I'd look and feel great?"

"No, but you'd think you did."

"Oh good. So . . . I take it this isn't a 'hi, how-ya-doin' ' call?"

"No, not really. Just thought I'd give you an update as to where we were with our analysis."

"That hasn't been you they've been quoting in the newspaper is it? The 'unnamed source at the CDC.' "

"No. But if there really is such a source, and they find out who it is, look out. Their ass is grass."

"Okay, go. I'm all ears."

"First, the viral strain is the same across the entire country. Second, it looks like the virus appeared at the same time all across the country."

"Memorial Day weekend?"

"That's right."

"East and West Coast?"

"East, west, north, and south. Third, we've been able to identify the source of the strain, at least geographically."

"Let me take a wild guess. Afghanistan."

"You're close. We can't get it down to a specific country, only a region of the world. It's definitely from the Middle East. Afghanistan, Iraq, Iran, Saudi Arabia. Take your pick."

"Do you guys have any ideas as to how they got it into this country?"

"We had quite a few brainstorming sessions on that one. We listed a hundred scenarios. Most of them only a Ph.D. would think of. Manufacture feces to look like candy bars. Refill water bottles with contaminated water, then reseal the plastic tops. It wasn't until after hours of these meetings that a summer intern, not more than twenty-one, who was assigned to take notes, blurted out what became the most likely scenario. It was so obvious, we couldn't believe no one thought of it before."

"Well are you gonna tell me?"

"The human body."

"What?"

"They carried it in their bodies."

"You mean like the drug runner who uses a mule?"

"A what?"

"A mule. He fills a condom with cocaine, ties and swallows it, crosses the border, then craps the rubber out the next day?"

"You are in one sick line of work girl. I suppose they could use a mule, but in this case there's no need to be that sophisticated about it. All you need to do is ingest the virus."

"But then you've got the disease."

"Exactly. You purposely come in contact with the virus. Travel to the U.S. with the virus tagging along. Two to four weeks later, when the symptoms confirm you have hepatitis, you start manufacturing it."

"How?"

"Dyan, do I have to spell everything out for you? By eating. The human body becomes the factory for producing the virus. If you need to increase output, all you need are more willing humans to become contaminated and voila — more factories."

"But then they've got the disease."

"Dyan, this is hepatitis A. Most people in third world countries get the disease before they are three years old. The probability of death is two to three per thousand cases. Most people are sick for a month or two at most. If they can find people who are willing to commit suicide for their cause, they can certainly find a volunteer or two to suffer with the flu for a month. Their biggest problem was probably finding someone who hadn't already had the disease so they weren't immune."

"Lindsey, how confident is the CDC of this scenario?"

"It fits all the evidence we have to a tee. In fact, a report is being circulated for final review. It's due at Homeland Security by the end of the day tomorrow. I have no idea when it will go public."

"Any new estimates on the number of people that will contract the disease?"

"As of today, we have two million confirmed cases. Assuming the virus is no longer being intentionally spread, and the public has implemented the hygiene measures we've published, we're now estimating over the next month, twenty to thirty million more people will get the virus."

"My god."

"It gets worse."

"How could it get any worse? That's ten percent of the population of the U.S. all sick at once. Granted it's like the flu, but some of them are going to require medical attention. There's going to be an economic impact from all the lost productivity. It's a disaster."

"Dyan, you still there?"

"Yes. Just thinkin'."

"Your report?"

"Yes."

"There was nothing you could have done to prevent this. First of all, no one would have listened to you. And if they had, no one would have spent a dime to change the way we distribute food in all of the restaurants and grocery stores. Get real. We've known about this risk for a long time, and still we did nothing about it."

"I know, but . . . ."

"But nothing."

"You said it gets worse. Lindsey, you still there?"

"Yes." Lindsey cleared her throat. "People are going to die."

"But you said it was a low probability."

"Do you remember the probabilities?"

"Two to three deaths per thousand cases."

"Right. It doesn't sound so bad when you're talking about a thousand cases. But as with any small probability, when you start multiplying it by big numbers of cases, well . . . with twenty to thirty million infected people, we're projecting 40,000 to 90,000 deaths.

"Dyan, you still there?"

41

Mozat dialed the number slowly and carefully. It was the second time he did so in the last two minutes. This time he would not have to hang up after the thirteenth ring. He looked at his watch. Just as the second hand swept past the number twelve, he pushed the send button on the cell phone. "Calling" appeared on the small luminescent screen. He counted the rings. When they stopped after the tenth, he again looked at his watch, waiting for the second hand to travel around the full circumference of the watch face, or sixty seconds.

"Hello."

"How are you?"

"I am doing well. And you?"

"Very well."

"How has your trip been?"

"Everything has been going well. We are right on schedule. Exactly where we should be."

"Glad to hear that."

"I see that you have been very successful with your project."

"Yes. It went much better than expected. It lasted much longer than we thought it would. We reached many more customers than we originally planned."

"The chairman of the board will be glad to hear that. Will you be submitting a report to him soon?"

"Yes. Very soon."

"I look forward to seeing the final report."

"It should not be long before you do. I am sure the chairman is anxious to make the announcement to the world."

Mozat pushed the red button on the front of the cell phone and held it for several seconds until the words "power off" appeared on the small screen. Even though it was the first time he used the new phone, he walked to the edge of the rocky shore, bent down, and placed it into the cool, seaweed-strewn salt water. A minute later, he stood up, phone in hand, and slowly strolled back in the direction of the marina. By midday they would be back in the Intracoastal Waterway, far from shore. There the phone would find its final resting place.

42

"We took a statistically valid sample of video tapes from over four hundred restaurants along the four major interstate highways where the outbreaks occurred."

Where the hell is Blackman, Dyan thought. She would have bet money that he'd be at this meeting. One of the analysts working on this part of the investigation already hinted to her that she was going to be pleased with the results. "Another homer for the rookie," as he put it. Although getting a pat on the back was always nice, especially in front of your boss, it was not the reason why she wanted Blackman there. Lindsey's voice kept echoing through her mind.

"Once we identified the suspect along a particular route, it was easy to track him down at the locations prior to and after the one he was spotted in. From there we were able to map out his entire route."

As Dyan sat there, she thought about the same analysis she performed five short days before. She couldn't believe how much happened in just five days. What was a minor hepatitis outbreak had now spread nationwide. Millions had the disease. Millions more would get it. People were fighting over a vaccine

131

that either didn't exist, or if it did, wouldn't help them anyway. The stock market already dropped a thousand points anticipating the impact that millions of sick people would have on the economy. Restaurant chains, devoid of customers, were petitioning the federal government for financial assistance. Dyan wondered what was going to happen when people started dying.

"Fuckin' bastards."

"I'm sorry, Dyan. Did you have a question?"

"No." Her habit was getting worse.

"As I was saying, we've been able to map out the route of each of the Backpack Man suspects." Everyone in the room seemed to cast their eyes toward Dyan. "We have determined a total of eight men were involved in spreading the virus."

"Only eight? That seems like too few to have done this much damage."

"That's all we have been able to identify, eight. They each covered five to six hundred miles a day. Some establishments were hit every day, most every other day. This appears to have gone on for the entire month of June. It appears they started Memorial Day weekend and stopped throughout the early morning hours on Sunday, July fourth."

"Any thoughts as to why they stopped throughout the morning on the fourth?" As usual, Reynolds had his list of questions ready.

"The only thing we could think of was July fourth was the one month anniversary of the tunnel bombings. They only made enough of the virus to last them through that date."

"Seems odd that they all ran out during an hour or two period that morning. You'd think they would have at least a full day's supply. By then they certainly knew how much they used each day. Are you sure there wasn't something else? Some other reason why they stopped at that time?"

"It was the headlines." Dyan spoke up.

"Headlines?" Reynolds looked at her with one of his condescending stares.

"The newspaper headlines. Not all, but most of the places they hit sold newspapers. They'd be on display as soon as you entered the building. Sunday morning's paper was the first to cover the story that the hepatitis virus was being intentionally spread. It was probably their agreed-upon signal to stop doing what they were doing. There was an increased risk of getting caught. It's how they communicated to their people in the field.

"Have we been able to identify any of the eight? Tie them to any of the known cells?"

"We haven't tied any of them to the Boston, Albany, Buffalo, or Chicago cells. So far we've tied two, the one you followed that day Dyan, and one other, to the Philadelphia cell. But that's it."

"So that confirms there are more cells out there."

"Definitely."

Dyan sat quietly thinking. Twenty-two terrorists had killed 3,000 people on 9/11. It appeared less than a dozen terrorists killed 1,300 on June 4. Now eight people were going to be responsible for tens of thousands of deaths. The odds were getting worse. Much worse.

"We found another cell," the agent yelled into the conference room before the door was even half open. The guy looked like he hadn't slept in a week, which was because he hadn't. But the expression on his face was like a kid who'd just found his presents from Santa, the day before Christmas. He sat down and took a deep breath before talking again.

"A cell phone in the Chicago cell, one we thought was disposed of several months ago, was activated yesterday evening. A long distance call was placed to a cell phone with a San José, California, area code. Here's a recording of the call." The man placed a micro-cassette recorder on the table in front of him, and turned it on.

"Hello."

"Satam?"

"I miss you."

"What are you doing calling me?"

"I told you. I miss you."

"Satam, you could get into trouble."

"I need to see you."

"You know that is impossible."

"Nothing is impossible. Isn't that what we are told?"

"Satam, you must hang up now before the others find out."

"But."

"The woman on the other end of the line hung up. This morning, another call was placed to the same number. We were able to trace down the location of the phone. The apartment in San José is rented out to a Jamel al Quasi. He is in this country on a student visa. He attends San José State. There appears to be three, maybe four other people living in the apartment. Two of them are females. We got a good shot of them leaving the apartment about an hour ago. We're checking their photos against the two Backpack Man suspects that worked the West Coast."

"Great job. We need to get word to Blackman."

"Where is he?" Dyan asked.

"I'd say he's just walking into the Oval Office."

43

Iullia's hands shook as she inserted the key into the ignition on the steering column of her car. The new car smell, heated by the midday sun, was more pungent than usual. Still, it was the first time in the month that she owned the new car that she did not notice the odor. She put both hands on the steering wheel to try to stop them from shaking. It worked for her hands, but not the rest of her body.

"Who the hell are you, Richard Williams?"

An hour ago Iullia walked into a meeting with the private investigator she hired, thinking she was about to hear the answer to that question. Instead, she was leaving with more questions.

Benjamin King could have easily passed for Randal Chapman's twin brother. Even their voices were similar. When she met him one week ago, she blinked twice to make sure it was the private investigator and not the lawyer standing in front of her.

King assured her from the beginning that his was a reputable agency. He would do a thorough investigation, but not spend one dollar more than was needed to find the answer she was looking for. When he called her earlier today to ask if she could stop by his office, her first thought was, "that didn't take long."

"Dr. Zola, come in. Sit down. Can I get you some coffee?" Iullia held up her Dandee Donuts coffee cup. "I trust you survived last weekend's blackout?"

Iullia had to admit, King was one of the most polite men she had met in a long time. If only he were twenty years younger, she thought. "As a matter of fact, I was at Mr. Williams's cabin. You could almost survive in that place without electricity, so I fared just fine." As she watched King sit back in his chair, she was again reminded of Chapman.

"I'm not one to beat around the bush Dr. Zola, so I'll get right to the point. I've invested a little over thirty hours trying to find a life for Mr. Williams prior to 1963, and I've gotten nowhere. Like you said last Friday, it's as if he was born in 1963, which we know is not the case. But all the evidence I found surely points to that conclusion.

"His Social Security number is in the same sequence as those issued in 1963. He has no record of paying into Social Security before then. I could find no bank records, no court documents, and no tax returns prior to 1963. He was not in the military. His fingerprints are not on file anywhere. There is no record of him ever being arrested. Not even a parking ticket. His driver's license was first issued in New York state in 1963, the same year he first registered a motor vehicle in the state. There is no record of him having a license in any other state.

"In his life prior to 1963, he must have acquired some money, though. He paid cash for his cabin when he purchased it in March of 1964."

"Cash? But . . . "

"Keep in mind, we're talking 1964. Although the place is probably worth a couple hundred thousand today, in 1964 he paid $10,000. Though that was a tidy sum back then. The average American made about $5,000 a year, including school teachers. So he had to have saved quite a few years to have accumulated that kind of cash — if he was a school teacher before 1964."

"You sound like you have your doubts?" Iullia immediately picked up on the tone change in King's voice. He would not make a good liar, she thought.

"I'll be honest with you. It is very rare that I cannot find out the background on an individual. Even something. A birth certificate. Long-lost relative. Something. This one has got me stumped."

"You said rare. Have you ever come across anything like this before?"

King leaned forward in his chair, reached for his large ceramic coffee mug, and took a long sip. "Only once." He took another sip of the coffee, placed the mug back down on the desk in front of him, and leaned back in his chair. "It was about ten years ago. I retired from the police department five years earlier, so I'd only been in business for a short time. Most of my cases involved a spouse wanting to know what their better half was doing when they were away from home. One day this very attractive woman walks into my office. Expecting the usual story, I was surprised to learn she was a widow. Her late husband left her very financially secure. I mean millions.

"She met a man, only months before, and he asked her to marry him. Although she was in love with the man, there was something about him that bothered her. His past. He didn't seem to have one. Their discussions were always void of anything beyond five years back. She asked me to check him out.

"Dr. Zola, have you ever heard of the Federal Witness Protection Program?"

"Isn't that where a witness testifies, say against the Mafia, and because of the danger he is now in, the government sets him up in a new life somewhere?"

"That's a pretty good definition. Anyway, I'm researching

this guy's past and five years into it, I run into a brick wall. It's as if he never existed. On a hunch, I call a friend of mine, he's a U.S. marshal. They administer the program for the Justice Department. He got pretty antsy over the questions I was asking, so I backed off.

"Two days later, my client's fiancé gets arrested for the murder of her husband. The guy was in the Federal Witness Protection Program. He had been a paid hit man. Murdered over a dozen people in his past life. In exchange for his testimony, he served three years in a country club federal prison, then was given a new identity, and bank account, which he depleted quickly. Hence the plan to marry a rich widow, which he had a hand in creating.

"If you follow the rules of the program, it's very successful. That is, a person's past is erased. They are virtually nonexistent. You have a new name, new social security card, new everything. And changing your identity means you can't take your resumé with you, and you can never again contact outside family, friends, or associates. You are given money. After the witness gets established, contact with the government is required only once a year."

"Is there any way you could contact your marshal friend and . . . "

"Unfortunately he's retired. Moved to North Carolina. I was able to get ahold of him though. His wife passed away a month ago, so he was pretty depressed. We talked for over an hour. I think he was thankful for the conversation. Anyway, I know more about the Federal Witness Protection Program than I'll ever need. Unfortunately, nothing was of any value to your case, except maybe one thing."

"What?"

"Well, it may have nothing to do with anything, but ironically the program started in late 1963, early 1964."

44

"Who the hell told you that?"

"It's a credible source."

"I don't give a goddamn how credible it is. I haven't heard anyone talk about those kinds of numbers. Nobody's said anything about this being more than a fuckin' pain-in-the-ass nuisance. A three-week flu. Hell, wash your hands and you won't even spread the goddamn thing around."

As soon as Dyan walked into Blackman's office, she knew it was a mistake to wait until so late in the evening to meet with him. She could have waited until the morning. When she laid eyes on him, she wished she had. She knew the information she was about to share was going to further ruin the disposition of the man standing behind the desk.

"Who is this credible source?"

"She works at the CDC. I've known her for a long time. I called her a week ago when I first started pulling the string on the hepatitis case. She gave me some good input. She's a Ph.D."

"I don't care if she's Einstein reincarnated. Where the hell is she getting these numbers from? How come nobody else knows about them?"

"She said there's a confidential report going through a final review at the CDC. It will probably be sent to Homeland Security tomorrow."

"Goddamn it. I was just in a meeting with the president. No one said anything about this. How can no one else know about it? They talked about twenty million getting infected. Inadequate supplies of the vaccine. The financial assistance that's going to be needed. How they've been dealing with the panic. Then they shit all over me. Why the hell haven't we been able to find one fuckin' clue as to who was doing this? Why haven't we come up with anything on the tunnel bombings? Bastards. They have no idea what we are up against."

Blackman's speech was interrupted by two knocks on the door. Before he could respond, the door opened.

"We've confirmed the suspects in the San José cell were the Backpack Men who spread the hepatitis A up and down the West Coast."

Blackman stared directly into the man's eyes. "Good job. Thanks." As quickly as the man entered, he turned and left, closing the door without a sound.

Blackman sat down in his chair and glanced up at Dyan. "They wanted me to round up the cells we've identified. I'm sure Cross is behind the idea. The administration is going down in flames. The tunnel bombings. The hepatitis outbreak. No vaccines. No suspects. They want some fresh meat. Something to show the voting public they're making progress. Thank god we've got some love-struck terrorists. If I hadn't walked in with the news about the San José cell, right now we'd be rounding up the other cells. Cross looked like an idiot in front of the president. I'm not sure how convincing I was when I told them I just got the word on the latest cell. Cross certainly didn't believe me. He thought I was purposefully holding back the information so I could spring it at the meeting. Anyway, I was able to convince them to wait. We'll never find the other cells if we jump now. They are all scared to death knowing there are more cells out there that we don't know about. But for some reason I think it would make them feel safer to gather up the ones we have. Bird in the hand syndrome."

"You're doing the right thing."

"You better hope so. If this whole thing blows up in our faces . . . if we should lose these six cells, god, I don't even want to think about it." For the first time since she walked into his office just minutes ago, Blackman seemed like Blackman. Cool, calm, and collected.

"Sit down. Let's call Cross." Blackman pushed the speed dial button on his phone.

"Cross."

"David, Bill."

"I'm reading the report on the San José cell now."

"I have Dyan Galloway here with me. I'm going to put you on the speaker phone. Can you hear me?"

"Yes I can. Good evening Dyan."

"Good evening Mr. Cross."

"Please call me Dave."

Blackman pushed the mute button and looked at Dyan. "No, call him David, just to piss him off." He took his hand off the button.

"David, there is something you should know about that is not in the report you are reading. It just came up a few minutes ago, and I'll get you a revised report. We just confirmed that the San José cell was the one responsible for spreading the hepatitis A virus on the West Coast.

"Are you still there David?"

"Yes. I'm just thinking. Does this change any of your thoughts and recommendations from our meeting earlier today?"

"Not in the least." Blackman did not hesitate with his answer. "We still need to find the rest of the cells. We know there have got to be others."

"But we now know conclusively that al Qaeda is responsible for spreading the virus. We know who the people are that did it."

"Not all of them. So far we're not confident all the identified cells had a hand in this."

"Yes, but we do know some of them did."

"David, I need to ask you something, and let me be blunt. Don't fuck with me on this."

"Bill, you know I'd . . . "

"At the meeting today, there was no mention of what the eventual death toll would be from the hepatitis outbreak. I was wondering if the president has seen anything on this?"

"I don't know what you mean. All the reports I've seen have put the risk of death as being very low."

"That's true. Well, let me have Dyan explain it to you."

"The risk of death is very low. Two to three per one thousand cases. But when you have twenty to thirty million infected people, you end up with the potential of almost 100,000 deaths."

"Dyan, who is coming up with these numbers?"

"David, I understand there is a draft report circulating in the CDC that is coming up with these estimates. Are you telling me that you or no one in the administration is aware of this report?"

"Well I can tell you that I am not aware of it, and I doubt seriously that anyone in the administration is aware if it. News like that could destroy our . . . let me see what I can find out and I'll get back to you."

"Thank you David. I would appreciate it if you could get back to me tonight."

"I think he already hung up."

This time the door to Blackman's office started opening before the knocking.

"Sorry to interrupt you, but CNN is carrying a live report from the al-Jazeera news network. Earlier today they received a video from al Qaeda claiming responsibility for the hepatitis outbreak."

Blackman picked up the remote control from the corner of his desk and switched on the large flat-screen TV that was mounted on the wall above the corner conference room table. The voice of a man speaking in Arabic filled the silence in the room. A few seconds later the crackling screen came to life. Two men, clad in white robes, were seated on the floor. Though rarely seen, they were probably the two most recognizable human beings on the face of the earth. On the left was Ayman al Zawahiri, bin Laden's top lieutenant. On the right was Osama bin Laden himself.

"I guess this puts to rest any fantasies we had that he was dead."

Dyan could feel her heart pounding as she stared into the man's eyes. She saw how people could be mesmerized by him. Though she didn't understand the words he was speaking, they somehow felt soothing to her. Almost calming.

45

"Jack Nelson."

"You're putting in a long one today."

"If we had a full complement of agents back here in Syracuse, I wouldn't be putting in double-duty now would I?"

"I'm really not doing much down here, just waiting for my husband to call like he promised."

"Maybe your husband did try to call you and you weren't there. You never are you know."

"You're right. I did just get out of a meeting."

There was a long pause. They were both too tired to argue, even jokingly.

"Did you see the news?"

"About the video tape?"

"Yes."

"We're waiting for an exact translation now."

"What's the reaction down in Washington?"

"I haven't really talked with anyone, but I'm guessing all hell is going to break out tomorrow."

"This isn't good, is it?"

"You know me. I know nothing when it comes to politics.

But even from my low-level perspective, I can already see the back-stabbing and finger-pointing starting. Heads are going to roll."

"Heads? Dyan, you've obviously been cooped up too much in your closet down there . . . "

"What are you talking about? I was just up in Syracuse on Monday and Tuesday."

"And how many hours were you around? You were off looking at toppled over transmission towers the whole time you were here. Get your head out of your rear end. The country you are trying to save is falling down around you. Haven't you been paying attention to what's happening?"

"Yes . . . yes I have."

"That sounds real convincing. Heads are gonna roll? Haven't you seen the president's ratings? Nader's got a shot at coming in second, that is if the president even survives until the election. The public rallied around him a month ago following the tunnel bombings, just like they did after 9/11. But this hepatitis outbreak. Millions infected, no vaccine, rumors we knew it was coming. People are pissed off. Hell, they're rioting in front of hospitals. And now we find out bin Laden is still alive and he masterminded the outbreak. Yeah, I'd say heads will roll."

"Jack."

"Yeah."

"It's gonna get worse."

"Well it better not get too much worse because from where I sit, people are at their breaking point."

"A lot worse."

"You be careful."

"Me? What about you? You're the one out in the field."

"How are you feeling?"

"Exhausted. Lonely. Sick of Washington."

"No. I mean . . . "

"Do I have hepatitis? I doubt it. Why? Do you think you do?"

"I feel exhausted, but . . . "

"Look at the hours we've been putting in. We should feel exhausted."

"You're probably right. It's all in my head. I should probably go home and get a good night's sleep."

"That's a great idea. Since my husband is obviously not going to call me, I think I'll go to my lonely hotel room and dream about him."

"Maybe I'll go home and dream about you."

46

BIN LADEN ALIVE — AL QAEDA SPREAD THE VIRUS —
100,000 COULD DIE

July 9 — Osama bin Laden is alive and well. So is al Qaeda.
Yesterday they released a video tape to Qatar's al-Jazeera news
network in which the organization claimed credit for the massive
hepatitis A outbreak in the United States. Bin Laden is quoted as
saying, "Millions of U.S. citizens will suffer and die from the dis-
ease we promised would be spread across the land."

A spokesman from the Department of Homeland Security again
stressed that the virus is normally not life-threatening, except in
rare cases. However, CNN has learned that government scientists
at the Centers for Disease Control in Atlanta have calculated that
up to 100,000 people could die from the current outbreak.

Hospitals, health clinics, and doctor's offices have been swamped
with callers demanding to know the truth of the effects of the virus.
Several individuals stormed a hospital in . . .

47

"Where the fuck else would they have gotten the tapes from if not you?"

"David . . . "

"Don't David me. You were the only law enforcement agency reviewing those tapes. Am I right?"

"As far as I know, yes."

"Then they had to come from you."

"David . . . "

"If I find that someone in the Bureau leaked those tapes, the president will be looking for your resignation."

The two men were now in a stare down.

"Are you through?"

Cross did not answer. He did not blink either.

"We confiscated the tapes from about four hundred restaurants across the country. It wouldn't take a good investigative reporter long to figure out what we were doing. There are hundreds, probably thousands of other restaurants with video taping systems. They would easily be able to find what we found."

Even though Blackman blinked long ago, he swore Cross still hadn't.

"That may sound like a reasonable explanation to you, but not to me. There is going to be an independent probe into this and we are going to get to the bottom of it." Cross turned, marched toward the door, opened it, stepped out, then slammed the door so hard you could feel the building vibrate.

"Fucking asshole," Blackman mumbled under his breath.

He saw the 60 Minutes report the evening before. He wondered why it took so long for someone to pull and view the video tapes from one of thousands of private surveillance cameras across the United States. Of course their report indicated hundreds of potential terrorist suspects, from double-dippers to people sneezing onto a salad bar. And if you looked hard and long enough, one of the would-be suspects was bound to resemble a Middle Eastern terrorist.

Fortunately, none of the suspects pictured on last nights show was a Backpack Man. Blackman concluded that the terrorist cells still felt as stealth as they did before the show aired. But he wasn't certain how much longer he could keep them that way.

48

"They arrived at the San Francisco International Airport at 5:30 A.M. PST. There were six of them in the Bonneville. They spent the next two hours watching the traffic coming into the parking garage. As each minivan was picked out, they'd follow its occupants into the terminal, making sure they all went through security."

"To make sure no one was coming back to their vehicle for a while."

"That's right. They picked out over two dozen targets. At 8:00 A.M. PST they started breaking into the vehicles, one at a time. They ended up breaking into nine of them before they found five to their liking. When we later went through the ones they left behind, we didn't find a parking garage ticket in them. Probably why they decided not to pick those. The five minivans and the Bonneville left the parking garage a few minutes apart and they arrived back at their San José apartment at 10:40 A.M. PST."

"Then what?"

"For the past two hours they've been making trips to local gas stations, filling up two-gallon gas cans. They are emptying the two-gallon cans into larger containers in the minivans. We estimate there are about twenty to thirty gallons of gas in the back of every vehicle. All five minivans and the Bonneville are now parked in the apartment complex parking lot."

"What are the suspects doing?"

"Sleeping. Or resting anyway. There doesn't appear to be any movement. The drapes are drawn on the windows. It's dark inside."

"We need to know what actions you want us to take should they start moving again."

Blackman's answer was instantaneous, almost rehearsed. "Tell me what you think they plan to do and I'll tell you what actions to take."

Blackman prepared for this day for over a year, ever since the first cell was identified. He always knew there was more than one cell in the United States. Al Qaeda's plans were bigger than that. He also knew that if they were patient, the others would appear. So far he had been correct. The discovery of a total of six cells, with forty-one terrorists, all under twenty-four hour FBI surveillance, kept those in the administration anxious for a quick win at bay. But Blackman knew that today would eventually come. This was the day he might have to trade a terrorist attack for the continued illusion of secrecy.

He rehearsed a thousand different scenarios in his mind, but it always came down to one question. How much death and destruction would he trade to keep the cells in place? Approaching it coldly, which he felt was the only sane way to deal with terrorists, one life or even ten, though unfortunate, would be too little of a sacrifice to breach the secret. Even one hundred innocent lives, sacrificed to potentially save many thousands, still would not be enough. But there is where he drew the line. Anything over a hundred and he would expose the secret.

Destruction of property was another matter. Blackman felt

buildings and other physical assets could be replaced. They were much more expendable than the loss of a life. Even a national treasure to some extent might have to be sacrificed.

"Whatever they have planned is probably going to occur in the next twelve to eighteen hours, before anyone returns and finds their vehicle missing. We don't expect an attack like June fourth. Most of the tunnels out west are through the mountains. Deaths would likely be minimal.

"They might try to close off the Golden Gate Bridge. Explode the vans at each end of the bridge. It might shut it down. People would panic. But there isn't enough explosive power to collapse it. Therefore, there probably wouldn't be a lot of casualties.

"We also thought about them returning to the airport parking garage, dumping the gasoline, then blowing up the garage. Again, a lot of damage, probably not a lot of deaths. And if that is their target, there's an easier way for them to pull it off. Poke holes in five or ten gas tanks in the cars already parked in the garage. Why go through the trouble of carrying the gas in yourself?

"There are dozens of other scenarios involving large office complexes in the Silicon Valley, housing developments, subways. None of them too exciting and unless they are carried off in broad daylight, the riskiest time for them to do it, loss of life would be minimal."

"Anything else?"

"Dyan will cover the last scenario."

"I believe whatever they have planned will take place later this evening before anyone misses the minivans they stole. My guess is they will head east. I'm not sure of their exact destination, but it will be a heavily forested area where they will spread out, drop their cargoes of gasoline, and start what will be one of the largest forest fires in California history. The summer in California has been much dryer than normal. They have already experienced a few fires. The conditions are perfect. The terrorists don't need a lot of gasoline to exact a tremendous amount of damage."

"I wouldn't think there would be many lives lost."

"No there won't. They're doing it for effect. Burning America, so to speak. It's more psychological. Shows how vulnerable we really are as a society."

"So which scenario do we think is most probable?" Everyone expected the question from Blackman. Dyan was the only one to speak up.

"I believe bin Laden himself has told us what he plans to do." Eyes not on Dyan a second ago, were now. "If you go back and analyze the statement al Zawahiri made on June tenth, when al Qaeda took credit for the tunnel bombings, he also said, and I quote, 'we will spread disease throughout the land of the infidels,' close quotes. Obviously we know now what he meant. The hepatitis outbreak.

"In bin Laden's July eighth video, where they claim responsibility for the hepatitis outbreak, he said, and again I quote, 'the flames from hell will grow upon your land,' close quote. The literal translation from Arabic to English isn't exact, but I think you get the point. He's warning us he's going to use fire . . . "

"He could also be warning us he's going to use a nuclear weapon. Nuclear weapons have been referred to as the devil's fire," Reynolds interrupted.

"Anything's possible, but these guys have several minivans filled with containers of gasoline, not atomic bombs. I believe he's again telling us what he's going to do."

Though Blackman sat perfectly still, his mind was racing. To him, none of the scenarios warranted exposing the cells. The loss of life would be minimal. Collateral damage acceptable. This was especially true if the minivans headed east, as Dyan was predicting.

Suddenly the nightmare that awakened him so many times

during the past month filled his brain. He is sitting in an eerily similar meeting, listening to the experts as they review the deadly scenarios, all projecting little loss of life. He gives the order. Do not intercede. Let the terrorists carry out their deed. He always awakens just after he notices it's early afternoon on June 4. Blackman knows that is the biggest risk with the decision he is about to make.

If he makes the wrong decision, there may be no time to stop what unfolds before them. If there had been a meeting on June 4, if he had given the orders to follow but not intercede, no one would have been able to react in time to stop the death and destruction that followed.

49

"When is all this going to stop?"

"Not for at least another three or four weeks. That's if the public has done what we've asked and stopped the spread of the virus."

"Have you gone grocery shopping lately?"

"No. When have I had time to go shopping?"

"I went a few days ago. There is no fresh produce, no fruit, and no fresh baked goods on any of the shelves. They're bare."

"Probably because everybody stopped buying the stuff."

"The only things people were buying were canned goods, sealed packages, or things you have to cook the hell out of, like macaroni."

"Hopefully it'll help eliminate the virus and things can get back to normal around here."

"What's your shift?"

"Eighteen on, six off. Been doing it since the fourth . . . nine days in a row. Got tomorrow off though. Twenty-four straight hours in bed, alone. How about you?"

"I've been on twelves. Eighth day in a row. I've got Thursday off. I suppose we should be getting back to the E.R."

The nurse slowly pulled herself up from the couch, and walked over to the window. "Jesus, there must be two hundred people waiting in line." She glanced at her watch. "It's already four-thirty. That last guy in line won't get into the E.R. before mid-night."

The doctor got up from the couch, walked over and stood next to the nurse. "It's still hard to believe there are National Guardsmen surrounding the building."

"With rifles over their shoulders, no less."

They both turned, walked out of the break room, then down the hall to the E.R.

"Have you seen what the latest death toll is?"

"No. I've been too tired to watch the news."

"It's up to a little over two thousand. A lot less than what they thought it would be by this time."

"We still have weeks to go before we're out of this thing. It's going to get a lot worse before it gets better."

"Do you know how many deaths we've had?" It was proba-bly because she was so tired that she didn't realize what she said until she was done saying it.

"No."

The two of them didn't speak another word as they walked down the hall to the E.R. They both stepped in front of the dou-ble stainless steel doors that separated them from the commo-tion on the other side, took a deep breath, and pushed on the doors.

Minutes later, the doctor slipped through the opening in the curtains. "Hello. I'm Dr. Cantor." As the patient stared back at him, Cantor wondered if he knew he was being treated by the doctor who had the distinction of being the first to lose a patient to the current hepatitis outbreak.

50

UTILITY REPORT CONCLUDES VANDALISM CAUSE OF BLACKOUT

SYRACUSE, NY, July 12 — At a news conference earlier today Edward F. Coles, president of the Northeast Transmission Company, indicated the results of its internal investigation had concluded vandalism as the cause of the July 4 blackout that affected 50 million people in New York and surrounding states. "It was vandalism, pure and simple, and we are confident those responsible will be caught," said Coles. The company has offered a $100,000 reward leading to the arrest and conviction of those responsible.

When asked if he thought the current difficulties with their union workforce may have contributed to the blackout, Coles responded, "For their sake I hope not." The difficult negotiations surrounding the union contract that expires at the end of the month have lead some to speculate that union radicals may have caused the massive blackout. Relations between the company and the union have been strained following the takeover of the local utility by the Northeast Transmission Company.

157

In an unrelated matter, the Syracuse Utility announced today that it had signed an agreement with the Balfour Energy Group for the sale of its Nine Mile Point Nuclear Generating Station. Unconfirmed sources indicated the final price was considerably above Wall Street's projections. The announcement was viewed favorably by Wall Street. Northeast Transmission's stock was up almost thirty percent by mid-afternoon. The stock had seen a ten percent decline following the July 4 blackout.

51

At 5:00 P.M., exactly the time they planned, the same time they rehearsed two weeks before, the six — five men and one woman — exited the apartment building. Instinctively they all looked up at the boiling sun as it beat down on their still air-conditioned bodies. Dressed in similar hiking apparel — khaki shorts, loose-fitting button-down shirts, white socks, and leather ankle-high boots — they looked like anything but terrorists. The five men got into the minivans. The woman got into the Bonneville. They each turned left as they exited the apartment complex parking lot, about a minute apart, and quickly disappeared into the five o'clock traffic.

The six FBI bloodhounds, as they called themselves, exited the various parking areas surrounding the apartment complex and drove on different streets in the same general direction as the vehicles they were following. Although the bloodhounds were never in visual contact with the tailed vehicles — in fact they were at times miles from their prey — the homing devices installed on the car and minivans earlier in the afternoon kept track of their exact locations, plus or minus one foot. This made for a precise yet leisurely pursuit.

Within an hour, it was clear that the six vehicles were tracing a path east to the parched mountains of central California, just as Dyan predicted. When Blackman heard, he fought back the slight smile that wanted to form on his lips, then took in and exhaled a deep breath.

Four hours later, as darkness blanketed the desolate dirt roads, the vehicles, parked miles apart, waited in the cool, quiet mountain air.

At 11:00 P.M., exactly the time they planned, the same time they rehearsed two weeks before, the couple exited what was for the past six hours a very quiet apartment. With eight sharing the three-bedroom, two-bath living space, the peace was a welcome change.

Within forty-five minutes they arrived at Dirty Al's, a popular summer hangout in Palo Alto. Even though it was a Monday night, as expected they found the place as crowded as it was two weeks before, but not so much so that there was a waiting line. This made their repeated trips back and forth to their car go both quickly and unnoticed.

In less than fifteen minutes they completed all of their pre-rehearsed tasks. The slow-leaking, gasoline-filled, rubber water bottles were in place, the two emergency exits were pad-locked closed, and the detonators were armed. There was only one thing left to do.

52

"Is there any chance those assholes could have done it?" Blackman asked basically the same question three times over the past fifteen minutes.

The success of last night's operation, if you could call letting al Qaeda start one of the largest forest fires in California history a success, was overshadowed by the news that over two hundred people were killed in a nightclub located just twenty miles from the San José cell. The nightclub fire started at midnight, the exact same time the forest fires were first ignited. Though still not confirmed, gasoline may have also played a role.

"The San José apartment has only been under surveillance since last Thursday, July eighth. That's less than six days. We were ninety percent certain that six people lived there. There could have been more, there could have even been less. When they left for the airport yesterday, it was the first time we actually saw all six of them at the same time. Are there more than six? We still don't know."

"Is there any chance . . . "

"Yes, sorry to interrupt. Yes, there is some chance there could be others living in this apartment who carried out the

Palo Alto operation. We just don't know for sure."

"Excuse me sir." No one heard the conference room door open or close, although it must have since the young agent, who was not there seconds ago, suddenly was. "Al-Jazeera is broadcasting a new bin Laden video."

"Why do I get the feeling I'm going to get the answer to my question?" Blackman said under his breath, as he turned his chair in the direction of the large video screen at the far end of the conference room.

Suddenly there they were, al Zawahiri and bin Laden, dressed in the same white robes, and seated in the same room as the video released just four days before. It was like watching a sequel to a bad movie. A bad horror movie.

"Does anybody know what the hell they are saying?" Blackman wasn't sure if anyone in the room could interpret the words streaming from bin Laden's lips.

A few seconds later, as if he purposefully delayed his response so as not to overstep his bounds with any of the more senior people in the room, the young agent standing next to the door spoke up. "As Allah has commanded, the destruction of the lands of the infidels continues. Our army of one thousand soldiers will cut off the head of the snake and bring hell on earth as Satan's own fires cast death shadows upon the stone."

The voice on the video was garbled for a few seconds.

"I cannot make out exactly what he is saying . . . I think he said al Qaeda caused last week's blackout." For what seemed like an eternity, bin Laden's voice was the only one echoing through the room. Several people turned and looked at the young agent. He finally spoke up again. "The only thing I could make out was something about hundreds of sinners being consumed by the devil last night."

53

"I would like each of you to report-out on the issues we identified from the three al Qaeda videos."

Blackman assigned a team of the FBI's top analysts to review word for word the three video tapes that al-Jazeera broadcast over the past month, the latest less than twenty-four hours ago. Like the one broadcast five days before, authenticity was not an issue. It was bin Laden. It was his top lieutenant al Zawahiri. They both were alive. They both had no fear of being together. The tapes were recorded within days, if not hours before they were broadcast. What was at issue was how much of the information was true. There certainly was evidence to support some of the claims. Blackman was also hoping there was evidence to refute others.

"Let's start with the blackout. Can al Qaeda's claim be substantiated?"

"There is no evidence to tie the blackout to any of the six known cells. In fact, there are no suspects in the case. Circumstantial evidence does point to al Qaeda. It fits the low-cost, low-tech approach used by them over the past two months. The most important evidence is their claim that they were responsible. We have found no instance over the past ten years where a claim by them to have committed an act of terror was not eventually corroborated."

"What about the company's claim that this was not terrorism but vandalism?"

"They will tell you off the record that they suspect union radicals are responsible. We have told them that we do not agree. The union had nothing to gain by causing such a massive blackout. One tower would have gotten their message across. They did not need to topple thirty-one.

"Frankly, the company has a vested interest in concluding this was not an act of terror. First, in order to cut costs, they recently eliminated acts of terror from their insurance coverage. Saying this was an act of vandalism results in several million dollars of reimbursements. Second, they are in the process of selling their electric generating stations. Part of the selling price is tied to how well their stock is doing. Admitting al Qaeda targeted them would more than likely tank their stock.

"Everything points to this being a terrorist act. Al Qaeda has admitted to it. We agree. As a side note, since neither the Albany nor Buffalo cells appeared to be involved in this attack, it probably means there is another cell located in upstate New York."

"Let's look at the forest fire out in California next."

"We have direct evidence that the fire was set by the San José cell."

"What about the Palo Alto club fire?"

"The fire was definitely a deliberate act of arson. It fits the profile of a low-cost, low-tech act. Al Qaeda has claimed responsibility for a very similar nightclub fire in Singapore earlier this year. They admit to being responsible for this one, though we do not have a direct link to any cell, including the San José one.

"From all of this, we conclude . . . "

"There's one other piece of circumstantial evidence I think we should consider with these two fires." By now Dyan was expert at interrupting Reynolds, especially when he failed to include her thoughts in these presentations. "In the past it has taken days for al Qaeda to issue a statement claiming responsibility for a particular act of terrorism. 9/11. The tunnel bombings. The blackout. But for the California fires, a video tape surfaced within hours of the attacks. I don't believe it would be possible for them to do that unless they had prior knowledge of exactly what was going to happen, and more importantly exactly when it was going to happen."

"Is there some strategic reason for them to admit to the attack so soon afterwards?"

"Shock value. Don't let people speculate about all the ways these terrible events could happen. Let them know up front, while the horror of it is still fresh, that al Qaeda did it."

"Any more questions? Based on the circumstantial evidence, we conclude al Qaeda was probably responsible for the Palo Alto fire."

"Let's go to the hepatitis outbreak."

"We have video evidence of two of the cells spreading the virus. We have an FBI eyewitness to the act. No doubt it was al Qaeda."

"One question. Based on what was just said about al Qaeda wanting to take credit for things soon after they performed them, why did they wait so long to admit to the hepatitis outbreak?"

"The hepatitis virus takes weeks to incubate in the human body before it becomes contagious. Then it's contagious for weeks after that. In this case, the longer they could keep what they were doing a secret, the more people they would infect. They let this one go on for as long as they could, not going public with admitting responsibility until the outbreak was uncovered."

"Thank you, Dyan."

"Next, the tunnel bombings."

"We still have no direct evidence linking them to al Qaeda. But it fits all of the circumstantial evidence we spoke about for the Palo Alto fire. In addition, it was a well-coordinated, well-executed attack. Tell-tale attributes of al Qaeda. Circumstantial evidence points to them."

"Is that all of the known terrorist acts?"

"Yes."

"All right. Let's move on to the prophecies if you will."

"I'll handle the June tenth video. There were two items. The video promised more strikes would take place in the U.S. That has occurred. It talked about spreading disease throughout the land, hence the hepatitis outbreak. That was all we found."

"The July eighth video had one prophecy. It indicated millions would suffer and die from a disease that they had previously promised in their June tenth video would be spread across the land. Again the disease is the hepatitis A virus. We know millions of people are going to get the disease. The CDC estimates between twenty and thirty million. However I think there is a problem in the literal translation of this statement to English when you try to apply 'millions' to the number of people who will die. The CDC's estimate is less than 100,000. But that calculation depends entirely on what assumptions you make about the future course of the disease. We asked the CDC how many people would need to get the disease in order to see a million deaths. Their projection was that the entire U.S. population would need to contract the disease, and then some.

"Therefore it is difficult to say what bin Laden was trying to say with this statement. I'm not sure if he really meant to say millions of deaths, too."

"Unfortunately, if you were to ask the American public who do you believe more, the government or bin Laden, bin Laden would come out on top." David Cross had not said a word since he entered the room at the start of the meeting. Blackman thought about debating Cross on the trustworthiness of the government, but knew this was not the time or place.

"Was that it for the July eighth video?"

"Yes."

"Moving on to the July thirteenth video."

"There are two statements in the July thirteenth video that we need to focus on. First is bin Laden's claim that there are 'one thousand' of his soldiers living in the United States. If he had said there were 'thousands' of soldiers, I might agree with the statement. 'Soldier' is sometimes translated to mean a defender of god, or in this case a Muslim. I am sure there are thousands of Muslims in the United States, and many Christians for that matter, who at least have some sympathy for bin Laden and his cause. Hence the statement would be the truth. Unfortunately, that is not what he said. He used the exact number 'one thousand.' By using the exact number, it appears he is saying he has one thousand al Qaeda-controlled terrorists in the United States, or under their current organizational structure, about one hundred cells. As you know, we have only identified six cells with a total of forty-one suspects.

"As ominous as that may be, his second prophecy is even more disturbing. He says his soldiers 'will bring hell on earth as Satan's own fires cast death shadows upon the stone.'

"There is a museum in Japan called the Materials Hall that has a display named the 'Human Shadow Stone.' The stone came from the steps of the Hiroshima branch of the Sumitomo Bank, which on August 6, 1945, was located about a thousand feet from ground zero, the spot where the atomic bomb was dropped. At 8:15 that morning, somebody was sitting on those steps. When the bomb detonated, a nine thousand degree inferno melted the surface of the stone and turned it white. However, a black mark was left on that part of the stone shadowed by the persons body. That black mark, which resembles Rodin's

'Thinker,' is called the 'Death Shadow.'

"'Satan's fire,' or 'the devil's fire,' was a phrase supposedly spoken by one of the Manhattan Project scientists as he watched the first atomic bomb blast twenty days before in Alamogordo, New Mexico.

"The phrase 'hell on earth' was a description given by the first U.S. servicemen to enter Hiroshima several days after the bomb was dropped."

If thinking brains made noises, the conference room would have been deafening. Luckily they didn't, and it wasn't. In fact there was silence. A dead silence.

54

SEC TO INVESTIGATE THE NORTHEAST TRANSMISSION COMPANY

SYRACUSE, NY, July 15 — The Security and Exchange Commission announced today that it will conduct a formal probe into the allegations that executives at the Northeast Transmission Company falsified documents related to the investigation of the July 4 blackout. On Monday the utility claimed that vandalism was the cause of the outage that knocked out power to 50 million customers over the holiday weekend. The next day, a taped message from al Qaeda leader Osama bin Laden claimed his organization had masterminded the blackout.

The public as well as several government officials were quick to criticize the utility following the al Qaeda confession. One official, who wished to remain anonymous, stated, "The public has a right to know if there are terrorists in their backyards. Why would the utility want to cover that up? As far as I am concerned, they've lost the public's trust and confidence. I know I'll never trust them again."

Northeast Transmission Company President Edward F. Coles stated at a news conference earlier today that, "Their findings were based on the evidence they had at the time and were consistent with those of several other law enforcement agencies." However, when asked, he could not name any of those agencies.

Northeast Transmission's stock price has fluctuated wildly over the past two weeks. Buoyed by news earlier this week of a buyer for their Nine Mile Point Nuclear Station, the stock rose over thirty percent. Following the announced SEC probe, the share price was off forty percent.

55

"How deep is it?"

"Saeed . . . do not torture yourself like this."

"How deep is it?" This time Saeed's voice was noticeably louder.

Aman reached down between his feet and lifted the neatly folded towel. The aqua-blue glow of the depth finder illuminated the white bottom of the inflatable boat. He quickly recovered the instrument, extinguishing the light. "Eighty feet." He lied. It was really one hundred and one feet. He knew Saeed would, for some strange reason, feel more at ease knowing they were in less than one hundred feet of water.

A year ago, neither man could swim. There was never a need for it in the desert lands of Saudi Arabia. A six-month membership at the YMCA solved that, although they almost quit after their first lesson. The two twenty-four-year-old men could not take the stares from the dozen ten-year-olds in the class. Luckily the teenage instructor was quick to pick up on their embarrassment and recommend they transfer to the adult swim class.

Even though they both swam miles of laps in the pool, Saeed

was still uncomfortable with venturing into water deeper that ten feet. It didn't matter that he was in a boat. It didn't matter that he wore a full-body wet suit, with enough buoyancy to keep him afloat. It didn't matter if it was a windless, waveless, balmy summer night. A shiver still shot through him at the sound of the words "eighty feet."

Saeed turned and looked at Aman. "You're lying."

"What difference does it make how deep it is? Eighty feet or eight hundred feet. You are in a boat. Stop worrying and pay attention to what you are doing. How much farther do we need to go?"

Saeed faced back toward the bow of the boat and pushed the large red button on the GPS unit mounted between his legs. The light from the small, four-inch LCD screen was still bright enough to cause him to squint. "We are still one half-mile away."

Aman stared at the giant buildings along the dark shoreline in front of him. The thousands of lights, pointed in every direction except out into the lake, made it appear as if they were much closer than a half mile.

Nine Mile Point was a stable geologic rock formation on the southeast shore of Lake Ontario. It was home to one of the largest electrical generating complexes in the world. Three nuclear plants, Nine Mile Point Units 1 and 2, and the James A. Fitzpatrick Nuclear Plant, produced enough electricity to meet the needs of about three million households.

Nuclear plants were near the top of everyone's terrorist target lists. These concrete monoliths represented the supposedly god-like smugness that came to represent America. For the average American, these facilities were a deep dark mystery. Nuclear was synonymous with Hiroshima, the arms race, the Cold War, Three Mile Island, Chernobyl, and more recently, dirty bombs and weapons of mass destruction. In other words, nuclear meant bomb. As in nuclear bomb. That in itself made it an ideal terrorist target. What better way to terrorize the public than to bring down one of these giants?

However, what most people didn't realize was that the inherent complexities of containing a controlled nuclear reaction within the confines of a building also made destroying the facility from the outside almost impossible. Three- to ten-foot-thick steel reinforced concrete walls, eight-inch-thick stainless steel reactor vessels, and duplicate — and in some cases triplicate — backup safety systems meant you almost needed a nuclear bomb to blow up a nuclear plant. Even a plane, like those used on the World Trade Center, would likely not result in the release of radiation if crashed into these giants.

Al Qaeda knew this. But they also knew that even a strike against one of these facilities, no matter how ineffective, would accomplish their overall objective, to spread terror and fear across the American landscape.

Their plan was cunningly simple. Rather than hitting the plant with one massive bomb, which they did not have anyway, they chose to strategically strike at a number of points around the plant. Their hope was to cause so much confusion that the plant operators might cause even more damage, like they did at Three Mile Island and Chernobyl.

As with all of al Qaeda's missions, the meticulous planning and rehearsing was usually more rigorous than the actual attack itself. The end result of crashing planes into buildings was straightforward compared to the planning needed to steal the airplanes to begin with. Rehearsing the actual event, like flying weeks before on the same flight you plan to eventually commandeer, not only enhances the probability of a flawless execution, but also prepares the terrorists mentally for carrying out the real attack.

After Aman's and Saeed's venture tonight, they would be ready to execute their attack.

Saeed leaned forward again and illuminated the GPS screen.

"We should be over it right now."

Aman stopped the silent electric motor that propelled the ten-foot inflatable boat over the past two hours. Both men listened for any sign that their journey had ended in the right location.

"Do you hear or feel anything?"

"No . . . but we must be very close to it."

Nuclear generating stations, and especially Unit 1 of the Nine Mile Point complex which did not have a cooling tower, required massive amounts of water to cool the steam that was produced in the nuclear reactor. That water, thousands of gallons per minute, flowed into the plant via a twelve-foot-diameter pipe that extended a thousand feet into Lake Ontario. Aman and Saeed hoped they stopped their boat directly over the large intake structure they knew was in the lake directly in front of the plant, right where the GPS unit said it was located.

"Lower the weight."

Saeed picked up the six-pound lead ball and lowered it over the side of the boat until the full length of the twenty-eight-foot rope, which was tied to the seat of the boat, was in the water. Aman switched on the electric motor and started the boat going in random circles. Suddenly they both felt it. The lead ball struck something. Since they were in thirty feet of water, it had to be the intake structure which extended several feet off the bottom of the lake. They waited. They hoped they would feel the water move as it was sucked into the intake structure far below.

"I do not feel anything."

"This must be the location." Aman looked up at Saeed. "Mark the GPS."

Saeed picked up the GPS unit and pushed the waypoint button. The unit beeped and the message "waypoint 6" appeared on the screen. With waypoint six now permanently programmed into the locating device, the next time they ventured

174

out into the lake, they would be able to plot a course directly for the intake structure.

"Pull up the weight. We can head back now."

Saeed could not pull the weight up fast enough.

56

Iullia glanced at her watch. "Five more minutes." It was the third time she said it. After each five minute interval passed, instead of leaving, she talked herself into investing another five. After forty-five minutes, how much longer could it be? After all the receptionist originally said, "Have a seat and he will be with you in a few minutes." She knew if she left now and returned tomorrow, she'd probably just start the waiting process all over again.

With nowhere else to turn, Iullia decided to take her problem to the authorities. Law enforcement to be exact. But with no crime to report, local officials were no help. The U.S. Marshal's Office, or at least the clerk she spoke with, made it clear that anything regarding the Witness Protection Program was highly confidential. So as a last resort she turned to the FBI.

As soon as she walked into the office, she confirmed her suspicion from earlier in the morning. This was not the right time to be visiting the Syracuse Field Office of the FBI. With the terrorist threat at level orange, terrorist acts like blackouts and hepatitis outbreaks happening right in central New York, and al Qaeda promising more, she had the feeling there would be little empathy for her problem. Hell, most people wouldn't even call it a problem to begin with. A smirk came across her face.

"Dr. Zola."

Iullia did not notice the woman who was now standing three feet in front of her.

"Our agent will see you now."

Iullia followed the young woman back through the labyrinth of cubicles to a doorway which she suspected was one of the corner offices on the floor.

"Dr. Zola?" Jack asked as he extended his right hand to her. "My name is Jack Nelson. Please come in. Sit down. What can I help you with today?"

Iullia had to admit, even though the agent must have had more pressing issues to deal with, he was thoroughly attentive to her. The only time he took his eyes off hers was when he jotted notes on the yellow pad on the table in front of him. By the time Iullia finished reviewing the sequence of events that started just one month ago, she noticed the agent flip over another page of his pad and write the number four on the upper right hand corner of it.

"I'm sure you can understand the reluctance of the marshal's office to want to talk to you about this issue."

"Oh believe me, I do. I was just hoping that since Mr. Williams had passed away, and if he was connected with the program, they might be able to share something with me."

"I am not sure what the protocol is there. My gut tells me though that they still would not share anything with you."

Jack could feel Iullia's eyes as they stared at him from across the table. The look, one of hopelessness, confusion, distraught, and even fear, was one that he saw far too often in the past month. It reminded him of the days and weeks following 9/11 when fear dominated everyone's minds. That same fear was back.

"I am not sure what I can do with this."

"I know you are very busy with everything else that is going on."

"No, that's not it. I'm just not sure I am going to be able to find you an adequate answer." Again, he felt her eyes on his. "I am going to be in Washington next week. I have a few contacts who might be able to help me do a little digging. I might not be able to answer all of your questions, but if we are lucky I might be able to tell you definitely that Williams was not in the program. At least you could eliminate that scenario."

"I would appreciate any help you could give me."

"I'll call you when I get back, probably towards the end of the week."

As Iullia waited for the elevator, she glanced up and down the hall. There seemed to be a constant flurry of people. She thought again about how much the world had changed in the past thirty days and how those events dwarfed her own problems. She took in a deep breath, letting it out slowly. In that instant she made up her mind. If Jack Nelson came up empty-handed, she would call it quits. She would stop searching for an answer to the question why. She would accept that Williams had taken the answer with him. She would agree with everyone else that she really did not have a problem.

Another smirk came across her face.

57

BEEP, BEEP, BEEP, BEEP . . .

He reached over and depressed the red reset button. The beeping noise stopped.

"Goddamn it. I thought you said they fixed that detector."

"They did. Last week. Didn't I forward you the e-mail? Wait a minute, I did. Remember? I looked it up. It only took them two months to get to it."

BEEP, BEEP, BEEP, BEEP . . .

"Does that sound like it's been fuckin' fixed to you?"

Within a month of 9/11, U.S. intelligence was receiving information from a number of reliable sources that another al Qaeda attack was imminent in which they would use a weapon of mass destruction. For years the U.S. was aware that al Qaeda was trying to obtain WMDs, including nuclear weapons. In late October, the CIA received reports from a Russian source indicating al Qaeda may have obtained a suitcase nuclear device from somewhere in the Soviet Union, and planned to detonate it in New York City.

Although the reliability of the intelligence was suspect,

the consequences of the threat, should it be true, were too horrific to ignore.

Stopping a nuclear 9/11 became the administration's number one priority. By the end of 2001, the government put into place a number of steps to provide some assurance of protection against a nuclear attack. One of those measures was to deploy a number of advanced radiation sensors, called gamma ray detectors and neutron flux detectors, designed to detect nuclear weapons grade material.

Ultimately the sensors, as well as those used for detecting biological releases, would be everywhere, but initially they were placed around key ports, border crossings, and major highways.

The shroud of safety these sensors provided was broken when the devices, rushed into service, proved so unreliable that spurious operations became the norm. Like the little boy who cried wolf, soon the alarms were completely ignored by those monitoring them. In some cases they were disconnected altogether. Malfunctioning sensors took months to get repaired and many times failed again within days.

The sensors operated by the New York Port Authority in and around New York Harbor were no different than the rest. The first time the alarm went off was on December 20, coincidentally the hundredth day since September 11. The Port Authority operator on duty that day actually suffered a heart attack when the alarm sounded.

It would be the first of hundreds of false-positive alarms over the ensuing years.

BEEP, BEEP, BEEP, BEEP . . .

"Goddamn it!"

"Which alarm is it, anyway?"

"B-21, George Washington Bridge."

"That's way up river. It's obviously a false-positive. If it were real, how did whatever it was that was making the alarm

go off get by all the other sensors? Disconnect the goddamn
thing and send in another repair order."

58

Dyan did not know where she was, nor did she care. She was out there somewhere, in the nothingness that existed between sleeping and being awake. As a kid, she visited the place often. Almost every morning, until the noise of the alarm clock took that joy away.

Now, in the rare times she was able to go there, her thoughts, at least the ones she remembered, were of him. Each time the setting was different. A deserted beach, hotel room — sometimes expensive, sometimes cheap, sometimes very cheap — her own bedroom, it didn't matter. He was always there too.

It had been that way since she first met him a year ago. As soon as he entered her mind she would feel her body go hot. She knew she was now his, to do with as he pleased. He never spoke a word, yet she always knew his wants and desires. She made sure she was the one to fulfill them. His arching body and loud unrecognizable screams told her that she did.

Her mind tried to drift out of the place, but she fought back. She had pleased him . . . was it last night? Yes, last night. He had been there. The carnal scenes flashed before her. Her pleasing him. Him pleasing her. Both pleasing each other. The moans. The screams. The musty sweat. The warm body fluids. The room was filled with all of them, then just the two of them, as they drifted off to sleep.

It had been like that the first time they were together in that way, and every time since. Even the anticipation of them meeting seemed to build up like static electricity. There were times when she could not stand it, counting down the hours, minutes, and seconds until they would touch again. And when they did, the sparks would fly and the tingling would get even worse.

After they were married, it got even hotter. Although it had only been months, it seemed whenever they were together, they could not keep their hands off one another. That was especially so behind closed doors. She knew what parts of her body most excited him and he knew what parts of his most excited her. Neither hesitated to use them on the other.

But the past month and a half had been difficult on their young marriage. She went from being with him two to three times a day to only five nights in the past six weeks. She understood the world had changed. She understood things might never be the same again. But she said the same thing after 9/11, and at least for her, life seemed to eventually get better. Much better. After all, she was now married to the man of her dreams. He took her to places no man had ever taken her to before.

She was there again. Had he really been there last night? Had he taken her to those places again? Or had she been dreaming about him, like she had so often over the past six weeks? It couldn't have been a dream, she thought. If only she could move. If only she could touch the places on her body that she knew he would have made sore. If only . . . she knew it was useless to even think it. She had come to understand long ago when you were in that place, your mind could only control itself. The rest of your body was lifeless.

He must have been there last night. Her thoughts were too erotic. She sensed her body felt too used. Much more than the feelings she got when she was alone, without him. She was too satisfied. He had to have been there.

Suddenly, as if a hypnotist snapped his fingers, she was no longer there. She drifted too far to the other side. Experience told her she could not go back, at least not now. Slowly the rest of her body began to awaken. Then she felt it. First it was only a presence. Then the hand cupping her right breast. Warm legs against the back of hers. Something warmer against her backside. Long hot breaths across the back of her neck. Am I still dreaming? she wondered.

Last night's memories flooded her brain. He had been there. The thought made her squirm. She felt the soreness. Tingles shot through her body as she felt his now hot hand gently squeeze. With both their bodies frozen in place, his hardness thickened against her.

"Good morning."

Dyan froze. It wasn't a dream. Jack had been there last night.

59

SHOTS FIRED AT WHITE HOUSE, PRESIDENT SAFE

WASHINGTON, D.C., July 18 — A demonstrator pulled a rifle from a baby stroller he was pushing and fired six shots at the White House yesterday afternoon. Within seconds he was shot and killed by a U.S. Marine sharpshooter standing less than one hundred feet within the treed grounds of the White House.

The assailant has been identified as John Davenport, 68, from Chambersburg, Pennsylvania. Neighbors say Davenport was despondent over the death of his wife, who passed away six days ago from the hepatitis A virus. He blamed the president for the out-break and lack of adequate supplies of vaccine.

At the time of the shooting, the president was in the Oval Office. At no time was he in any danger. He was immediately taken by Secret Service agents to a secure location in the building.

Davenport was with a crowd of over 50,000 demonstrators angry over the government's handling of the hepatitis terrorist attack.

"Thousands of needless deaths are occurring because the government has misled the public over the severity of the disease," said one of the organizers of the demonstration.

The latest tally puts the death toll from the hepatitis A outbreak over 10,000. Some health officials believe the final toll could approach ten times that much.

60

"The president wants all the known cells brought in."

"But why?"

"He is in a free fall. Christ, the whole government is in a free fall. People are in a panic mode. There are rumors flying that the country has been infiltrated by thousands of al Qaeda operatives. They have each been assigned a high-level government official and at some appointed time, September eleventh, Election Day, the day before Election Day, who knows, there is going to be a mass assassination. You can bitch all you want about your government officials, but think what it would be like if suddenly they were all gone.

"Anyway, the president is looking for a quick win. Something to boost the government's credibility with the masses."

Blackman had just left the White House. He knew what the topic of discussion was going to be before he walked into the hastily called meeting. It was the same topic he had been called in for during the previous two White House visits. Only this time he knew that he was going to lose the argument.

To anyone on the outside it appeared as though America was losing the war with al Qaeda. Thousands were dying, people were panicked, the economy was in a nose dive, and Osama bin Laden was not only alive, he appeared to be executing a well-thought-out offensive to destroy our society, with promises of worse things to come. If you weren't scared, you had no idea what was going on.

"What about the other cells? Those still hidden? The thousand soldiers bin Laden says are out there? The known cells are our only hope of finding the others."

"I think he's lying." It took less than a second for everyone in the room to turn their heads toward Dyan.

"I'm listening," Blackman finally responded.

"I think bin Laden is lying about the thousand soldiers. Look, we all know over the years that al Qaeda has trained tens of thousands of fighters. Most of them were used in the mountains of Afghanistan to defeat the Russians. Now many of them are in Iraq. Except for the one-man suicide bombers, count up the number of true terrorists al Qaeda has used to carry out its deeds around the world. It's no more than a few hundred. And most of those, if they could even get into this country, wouldn't last very long before they were discovered.

"You've got to have a certain mindset, a certain set of unique skills to transplant yourself into another society. Think about it. How many of us would survive if we were asked to live a covert life in say, Japan? Most of us wouldn't last a week. Look at the guy in the Chicago cell. Love has been his downfall.

"We haven't found more cells because there aren't many more to be found. Certainly not a hundred.

"And quite frankly they don't need a thousand soldiers to destroy us. They can do it with much less than a hundred. Twenty-two for 9/11, less than a dozen for the tunnel bombings, even less for the hepatitis outbreak. We have thousands of unguarded targets for them to pick from. There is no way for us to even begin to try to protect ourselves from them. The odds are overwhelmingly in their favor. They don't have to be sophisticated about it. They don't even have to hit many targets. If they plant the seed that no place is safe, that our government is helpless to protect us, they've won. It only takes a handful of them to do that.

"He's lying."

"I hope to god you are right."

"It doesn't matter if she is right or not," Blackman interjected. "We are going after them tonight."

61

"The director is waiting for you Ms. Galloway."

Dyan wasn't even out of the elevator and the blond bitch was already barking her orders. Don't you ever sleep? Dyan thought to herself as she walked by the receptionist's desk. No matter what hour of the day she ventured into Blackman's office, she was always greeted by Ms. Rock's dominating voice. Dyan smiled as she walked past. The only thing she got in return was a slow but deliberate elevator stare from the woman. I hope she doesn't think . . . Dyan kept her eyes focused on the doorway in front of her.

"Congratulations. It looks like you got them all."

Blackman looked up at Dyan. "You mean all we know about."

Yesterday's roundup of the six known terrorist cells in Boston, Albany, Buffalo, Philadelphia, Chicago, and San José netted a total of forty-three suspected al Qaeda terrorists. The operation went off without a hitch. For the past twenty-four hours the FBI searched every square inch of the six apartments for links to other cells. So far they found nothing.

"How was your meeting at the White House?"

"The president is happy. Cross is happy. The initial public reaction is, on balance, favorable. I think people are shocked when they first hear the news. That there were terrorists living among us. Especially people who live in those same cities. Everyone wants to know how they got into this country. But then there appears to be a sigh of relief that they've all been apprehended. But it hasn't taken people long to start asking the $64,000 question. How many more are there out there? I know its got people spooked."

"You probably didn't see it, but it was the key question being raised by every one of the national news programs earlier this evening."

"I don't think anyone has a good answer for it yet. I was hoping we'd find something to lead us to some of the other cells."

"My guess is any other cells out there have broken up and disappeared by now anyway. At least we've disrupted them for a change.

"You wanted to see me?"

"Yes. There is something you should be aware of. One of the major news networks has contacted the Bureau and the White House. They are working on a story about the California fires and they supposedly have an informant who is telling them that we knew about the attacks and let them happen anyway."

"But we did. That was our modus operandi all along."

"No, Dyan. I'm not talking about the forest fires. I'm talking about the nightclub fire."

"But we didn't know about that."

"I know that and you know that, but you also know the news media has a way of adding two and two and coming up with five. Anyway, this investigative reporter is apparently doing a lot of snooping into the California fires and the hepatitis attacks. Just make sure the task force notes and materials are all up to . . . "

"I've been on top of it since the first day I started," Dyan interrupted.

"I know you have. Make sure the rest of the task force is aware of the issue. That's all. Thanks."

As the elevator doors closed, Dyan didn't even notice if the blond bitch was sitting at her desk. Her mind was racing over what Blackman just told her. She sensed he did not share everything he knew about the media's investigation. Although Dyan did not know it, as usual her intuition was right.

62

"Hello."

"Dr. Zola?"

"Yes."

"Jack Nelson from the FBI."

"Yes, Mr. Nelson. I wasn't expecting to hear back from you so soon. I thought you said you were going to be in Washington this week."

"I am in Washington, but I was able to find out some information on the issue we talked about. Rather than wait until I got back to Syracuse, I thought that I would call you, if that's okay with you."

"Yes. It's fine."

"First of all, I was not able to find out anything specific about Mr. Williams. But I think we can pretty much conclude that he was not in the Witness Protection program starting in 1963."

"If you didn't find anything specific, how can you be so certain?"

"The program did in fact start up in late 1963, but at that time it was in its infancy. All of the program participants, and there weren't many, were men in high-security federal prisons. The program did not start placing people back out into society until late 1965, early 1966, and then it was only a handful of people. So I think we can pretty much rule out any involvement of him in that program. I'm sorry I couldn't be more help to you."

"Thank you, Mr. Nelson. You've been very helpful."

"I'm not so sure if I have."

"No, you have. I guess I've just got to accept that this man had his reasons for doing what he did and wants to remain anonymous."

63

"I can't tell you what, I can't tell you where, I can't tell you when. But what I can tell you is it is going to be more spectacular than anything they've done to date. We have indications from everywhere. There's been an unprecedented spike in the number and severity of threats. The system is blinking red, from what we can see, even more so than it did in the summer before 9/11.

"There is no doubt that it is in direct response to the roundup of the six terrorist cells earlier in the week. Al Qaeda was dealt a huge blow. Their reputation has been tarnished. It is possible they think we are on the heels of other sleeper cells, so before they are caught, they want them to accelerate carrying out their intended missions." The analyst making the presentation to the task force looked as frightened as the words were he was saying sounded.

Dyan looked around the room at the faces of the other task force members. She was sure her face mirrored theirs. She knew everyone was asking themselves the same questions. How many more cells do they have? What do they have planned? Can we figure it out and stop them?

Although it was almost two days since the six terrorist cells were rounded up, the FBI found nothing to link them to any other cells operating in the country. If al Qaeda had more cells here, they had nothing to fear about us finding them.

"You're saying with all this intelligence coming in, there is nothing specific we can prepare ourselves for? Area of the country that might get hit? What they might have planned?" As usual, Reynolds asked the first questions.

"Most of the information is too vague. It's chatter. Al Qaeda is going to attack, and it's going to be big. That's it."

"What about the last bin Laden video? His threat to use a nuclear weapon? Is there anything to substantiate that threat?" Reynolds's voice was now louder, and the rate at which the words flowed from his mouth quickened.

"We found nothing in the six apartments to support that any of them had anything to do with a nuclear device. We even did a thorough gamma scan of the apartments and a whole body count on each of the forty-three suspects. A whole body count is where you scan each person to see if they have come into contact with or ingested any radioactive materials in the recent past. All of them had normal background readings. It appears none of them has come into contact with either dirty bomb material or highly enriched bomb material."

"So if their threat is real, it supports the theory that there are more cells out there."

"That is probably a good assumption."

"If their threat is real, if they had a bomb in this country for some period of time, why risk having it found? Why not detonate it ASAP?"

"My guess is they were so confident of their operations, they were planning to detonate it on a specific date. September eleventh. Election Day."

"And now they aren't so confident that they can keep it hidden that long."

"Exactly."

"I hate to be a naysayer on this," Dyan said. "I think you can all recall that we had the same concern following 9/11. Al Qaeda was going to follow-up with another attack, this time a nuclear weapon. Hell, we even had intelligence that New York City was the target. But cooler minds eventually prevailed. If al Qaeda had a bomb, why didn't they use it as soon as they were able to? Again, as was said, why risk having it discovered? Back then the suspected source for a suitcase-sized nuke was Russia. Since then, their security, although not perfect, has tightened considerably. If we assume al Qaeda has only recently obtained a bomb, where did they get it from?"

"There are a number of rogue nations . . . "

"And if we ever found out any of these nations supplied a nuclear weapon to al Qaeda that al Qaeda used on us, what do you think would happen to them? Hell, post 9/11 the administration was considering preemptive strikes against the 'axis of evil' countries because we thought they were developing the capacity to produce a bomb. Any country that would knowingly supply a bomb to al Qaeda would be gone, just like Afghanistan was invaded after we found out al Qaeda called it home. Again I ask, where is the source for such a bomb?"

"Unless it was somehow seized years ago, we don't have a source."

"Then why are we wasting our time on this scenario?"

"Because bin Laden threatened it, and he usually carries out what he says," Reynolds interjected.

"In this case, I believe he either doesn't have the capability to carry it out, or he means something else other than a nuclear weapon. What that might be I don't know."

"Do you realize what the consequences are if you are wrong?"

"Yes."

"Well so do I. The consequences are too great to ignore this threat. I want all our resources focused on the nuclear weapon scenario. Is that clear?"

"I think you are making a big mistake."

"Look, Dyan. I will admit that you have been right in predicting al Qaeda's attacks in the past few months. But the playing field has changed, especially in the past few days. We know al Qaeda has wanted to follow-up 9/11 with something spectacular."

"What do you think the hepatitis outbreak is?"

Reynolds was speechless.

Dyan knew she had him, so she pressed on. "I know it was not a very sexy attack, but you have to admit it was devastatingly effective. Five times as many dead as 9/11, and the number is still climbing."

"And do you think that's the end of their attacks?"

"No, but . . . "

"That's right. It's not. They have more planned. And the collective judgment of this task force is, it is something that will make an even bigger statement from al Qaeda."

"All I am asking is, if it is a nuclear weapon, where did they get it from?"

"Instead of wasting this task force's time, why don't you help us find out the answer to that question? It's time you became a team player Dyan, instead of trying to grab all the glory for yourself.

"This meeting is over. You have your orders. Let's get to work."

64

"Ryan, you got a minute?"

"Sure, Sam. What is it?"

"A few hours ago we intercepted a cell phone call on one of our Afghanistan-Pakistan border monitoring sites. It wasn't a strong signal so we didn't get it all. It was a totally one-sided conversation. There is a high probability it was Ayman al Zawahiri doing the talking. There is also a high probability that bin Laden was on the other end."

"Wait a minute. If it was them aren't they getting a little sloppy? Using a cell phone? They have to know we are monitoring."

"They are either sloppy, cocky, or they wanted us to hear them. Unfortunately, I don't know which."

"What did he say?"

"Again, we didn't get it all. It was a short call and we only got about half the words. It translates to, 'black rain will fall by the weekend.' "

"What the hell does that mean?"

"We believe it is another reference to Hiroshima."

"Hiroshima?"

"Immediately following the Hiroshima explosion, many of the survivors remember a sudden downpour of rain over parts of the city, or what was left of it. The raindrops were black, probably contaminated from the blast debris. This downpour has been nicknamed 'the Black Rain.'"

65

As soon as Dyan walked into Blackman's office, she knew this was not going to be a friendly chitchat of a meeting. Not with Reynolds sitting at the far end of the hexagonal table with his head slightly tilted to one side and that cocky smile on his face. She felt her heart sag in her chest as Blackman walked out from behind his desk and without a word motioned her to the table. It didn't take her long to figure out she was about to get her ass reamed out. Why couldn't she use a little more tact to get her message across to people, she thought. She knew at times she appeared overbearing and stubborn. She was told that in the past, even by those closest to her, like Lindsey and her husband. Why hadn't she listened?

"Dyan, when we met . . . "

"I apologize for my behavior at the task force meeting this morning."

Reynolds stared at Dyan with raised eyebrows. He couldn't believe she interrupted Blackman.

"But I just do not believe we should be wasting time chasing a phantom bomb while al Qaeda launches their next terrorist attack."

201

Blackman, who was looking at Dyan, turned toward Reynolds.

"We have a difference of opinion as to where we should be applying the task force's resources." Reynolds's calm voice immediately told Dyan this was not the reason why she was seated at the table. A very uneasy silence filled the room.

"As I was saying, Dyan, the issue we spoke about two days ago — late Tuesday night actually — the investigative reporter who's uncovered some information about the California terrorist attacks, they've informed us that they are going to come out with the story, probably over the weekend."

"Have we had a chance to review their work?"

"Yes. David Cross and I were briefed by them earlier today."

"Did they have the facts straight?"

"Yes, their facts are accurate. There is nothing to suggest we knew about the nightclub fire. We will take a hit for the forest fires, but they are fair about balancing that against finding more cells."

There was another uneasy silence. Dyan glanced at Blackman, then Reynolds, then Blackman again.

"They have also completed an investigation into the hepatitis outbreaks. Apparently they pulled and reviewed video tapes from thousands of restaurants in an attempt to try to observe the terrorists in the act. In fact they were able to identify several of the terrorists, once they knew what to look for."

"Backpack Man?"

"Yes."

"It sounds to me as if they have done a thorough job."

"Dyan, one of the tapes they have shows the terrorist you first saw at the Thruway travel plaza in Chittenango on Saturday, July third."

"I thought we collected those tapes."

"We did. What we did not know was they record duplicate copies from all of their video cameras.

"The video shows you watching Backpack Man, they even use that term, spreading the hepatitis virus at the beverage bar, then following him out of the building."

"Yes, I've seen the video."

"What you may not have seen was minutes later a family with four-year-old twin girls went to the same beverage bar. Last week one of the twins died from hepatitis A. A lot of questions are being asked regarding when we knew about the outbreak and what we did to stop the disease from spreading."

"That exact instant was the first time we had confirmation of what Backpack Man was even doing."

"Dyan, you need to understand, we are being held accountable for our actions just as much as we will eventually hold al Qaeda accountable for theirs. Just as the 9/11 Commission looked at the circumstances and facts surrounding the September eleventh attack, there are going to be similar investigations into how we handled these attacks. Unfortunately, the Monday morning quarterbacks are going to get their shot at us first."

"But we have nothing to hide."

"That's your perception."

"We did not know what al Qaeda was doing."

"You started compiling a report months ago outlining new tactics you thought terrorists would use against us. As it turns out your report was frighteningly accurate. There are some who might question why we did not act on the report sooner. And if we had, could we have prevented some of these attacks. Couple that with our desire to find the other cells, even at the expense of more attacks, and you can see how the conspiracy theorists are already salivating."

"I still do not see how we would have done anything differently."

"Damn it Dyan, take off your rose-colored glasses. By this weekend 20,000 people are going to be dead because of terrorists who spread one of the most common viruses on earth into our food chain. It's the worst attack ever to take place on our soil, and it's not over. Thousands more are going to die. The average citizen wants to know why. The average citizen is beginning to wonder if its government can protect them from these terrorists. Some are even beginning to think we let these attacks happen on purpose."

"Just because I sat there and watched . . . "

"Emotions are replacing facts, Dyan. Thousands are dying, including little four-year-old girls. The public is going to want to know we did all that we could to protect them.

"I've asked Internal Affairs to do an independent investigation into how we have handled the attacks over the past two months."

Dyan, who was still sitting with her head down, looked up at Blackman.

"I am sure things are going to work out, but in the meantime it is going to get ugly around here. I think it would be best for you if you went on a paid administrative leave."

"But wouldn't that be . . . "

"No, it wouldn't be admitting anything. I just think it would be best if you let Internal Affairs do their work without any interference."

"But . . . "

Blackman held up his finger. "Ryan. Would you please excuse us."

Reynolds, who had not said one word since Dyan entered the room, got up and left. Blackman waited until the door to his office closed before he spoke up again.

"Dyan, you need to trust me on this one. The administration is in a death spiral. The election is less than four months away. There are people who will stop at nothing, destroy anybody's career, to achieve their own goals. They are looking for a scapegoat. To be honest . . . it will probably be me. For the sake of your own career, agree with me on this one."

66

. . . seven, eight, nine, ten. As expected, the ringing stopped. Mozat looked at his watch and waited.

"Hello."

"It is me."

"I have been waiting for your call."

"I have been very busy."

"We have been asked to move up our plans."

"I suspected that we would be asked to. Do we have a new date?"

"How soon can you be ready?"

"I will call you back in one day with a date."

67

*NATIONWIDE TERRORIST THREAT RAISED TO SEVERE –
CODE RED*

*WASHINGTON, D.C., July 23 – The federal government raised the
terrorist threat level today to "severe," or Code Red, citing a new
stream of intelligence suggesting al Qaeda operatives in the United
States are preparing to mount a large-scale terrorist attack. This is
the first time the Code Red rating has been issued on a nationwide
basis since the system went into effect over three years ago.*

*The attacks over the past seven weeks have caught counterterror-
ism experts off guard in both their simplicity and devastation.
However, more recent intelligence seems to indicate we are in the
midst of al Qaeda efforts to attack the United States on a scale similar to 9/11. One administration official was quoted as saying, "We
should be prepared for weapons never before used by terrorists."
When asked if he meant weapons of mass destruction, the official
declined to comment.*

68

The sounds of millions of raindrops falling onto the front lawn flooded through the open living room windows. Iullia, sitting in her large antique wooden rocking chair, was lulled into a dreamlike state by the rain. Of course the wine helped too. What should she do, what should she do, what should she do . . . the thought had been racing through her mind for the past two days, ever since her phone call with Jack Nelson.

Even with her eyes closed and her mind miles away, she sensed the silent white flash, then waited. The crackling thunder still made her jump. Her eyes opened, bringing her back into the living room. Within seconds, they dropped shut and she again drifted away.

What should she do? The cabin flashed in her mind. A calm feeling came over her as she mentally walked around and through it. It was a gift. Take it. You don't always have to know why things happen, she thought. Why did her mother die giving birth to her? Why did her father die in a car accident a year later? Why did she become a college professor? Why was she not a mother? She lived with these unanswered questions. What difference would one more make? He wanted her to have it.

There was a reason. There was an answer. Only it was not for her to know. Could she live with that? What should she do . . .

Another flash of light brought her back. This time she opened her eyes and waited for the sound of the rain to disappear under the rumbling thunder. Instead, there was another flash. Iullia jumped. It was much less than a second, but there it was, in the open window, the shadow of the woman she saw exactly one month before.

"Barbara?" She yelled the name out without thinking about it, only to have the sound of her voice drowned out by a roar of thunder. She stood up. "Barbara? Is that you?"

A flash of lightning answered Iullia's question.

"Yes, Iullia, it's me."

Iullia rushed to the front door. As she opened it, thunder crashed all around.

"What are you doing here?"

"I made a promise to him that I would give this to you." She handed Iullia a black book wrapped in rain-soaked plastic. "Iullia, Richard Williams was . . . " The crackle of thunder seemed to play forever.

"What did you say?"

"Richard Williams was your father."

69

Windy stood in front of the control panel and let out a long drawn-out yawn. He slowly gazed around the control room. No one, including the station shift supervisor, saw him. Although he was exhausted, he was good at hiding it. He glanced at the digital clock on the wall in front of him. 12:15 A.M. He was only fifteen minutes into his twelve-hour shift.

Weekend shifts were always hard, but the midnight-to-noon Sunday morning shift was especially so. With family activities filling up time on Saturday afternoons, many of the late-night shift workers usually arrived with having little or no sleep over the past twenty-four hours. Luckily, management had long ago figured this out and made sure no "real work" was scheduled for that time period. What that did, though, was make the already boring life of a nuclear plant control room operator even more so.

A normally operating nuclear power plant required almost no human intervention. With the consequences of an error being so great, the engineers designed the plants to respond on their own to problems that might occur, thereby taking the human element out of the equation. Human interactions, like the ones that occurred at Three Mile Island and Chernobyl, usually made things worse.

"What the hell was that?"

Everyone seated was now standing and staring at the control panel.

"It felt like an earthquake."

The Nine Mile Point Unit 1 nuclear plant, along with the two other nuclear plants next door, was built on one of the most stable geological rock formations in the northeast. Formed during the last ice age, the bedrock was so stable, over the plant's 35-year life no one felt even a vibration from the many minor tremors that occurred in the eastern United States.

Suddenly the main control panel started lighting up like a Christmas tree and the sound of the annunciator alarm filled the normally library-quiet control room.

"We have an indication of a fire in the screen house," Windy shouted, just as he was trained to do.

"I copy that," the station shift supervisor, who was now standing in the rear of the control room where he could observe the activities taking place in front of him, yelled back. "You have an indication of a fire in the screen house. Send an operator down there and report back immediately."

"Sending an operator to the screen house."

"Jesus!" The building shook again. "This has to be an earthquake."

"We now have an indication of a fire in the turbine building."

"Copy. An indication of a second fire in the turbine building."

"We have a loss of off-site power. Main buss breakers have opened. We have a turbine trip. We have a reactor scram."

"I copy. Loss of off-site power, turbine trip, reactor scram. Tell me those assholes knocked down the power lines again. Let me know when you have verified all control rods have inserted."

"I copy. Verifying control rod insertion . . . all control rods verified at position zero-zero. Fully inserted."

"Copy. All control rods fully inserted. Verify Light House Hill hydro station is up and running."

"Verifying Light House Hill operation . . . breakers for 104 line to Light House Hill are closed, but we have no power coming in. Repeat, no power coming in from Light House Hill."

"I copy. No power from Light House Hill. What is the status of the backup diesel generators?"

"Diesel generator 101 is operating. Diesel generator 103 is not operating. It's tagged out for emergency maintenance."

"I copy. No off-site power from Light House Hill. Diesel generator 101 is operating. 103 is out for maintenance. Find out how soon we can get 103 back in service."

"Copy. Checking on the status of diesel generator 103."

The station shift supervisor flipped through the pages of the emergency procedures to the section marked "Loss of Off-Site Power." During normal loss of off-site power events, the station has three back-up sources of emergency power. There were two redundant diesel generators on-site and the Light House Hill hydro electric station located about twenty miles from the station. With two of the three back-up emergency sources not available, the supervisor was searching through the procedures for the section on how to shut down the reactor with a total loss of power. From his training, he knew the procedure was there. He also knew it was a procedure never before tried on an operating plant.

"What's the status of checking out those fires?"

"The operator is still on his way to the screen house, but he just reported that he smells gasoline fumes in the turbine building."

"Gasoline?"

Suddenly, the annunciator alarm blasted out again. Windy looked at the computer screen in front of him, then turned to the shift supervisor. "We have a warning of a high-bearing temperature on diesel generator 101."

"Fuck."

70

"Come in, Ryan." Blackman put his pen down on his desk, stood up, and walked over to the hexagonal table. "As I said on the phone, I have a meeting with the president in an hour, so what do you have for me?"

"Right now things are stable at the plant. Off-site power has been restored. They are in what is called cold shutdown. That is where the reactor water temperature is less than two hundred and twelve degrees or the boiling point. There was no damage to the reactor core. No radiation was released. There was some damage to the turbine building and some other buildings, nothing major. The reactor building was not touched. Except for the explosions and loss of off-site power, the plant was shut down normally by the plant operators. They still have a site area emergency declared, but plan to downgrade that in an hour or so."

"Do we know what caused the loss of off-site power?"

"Same scenario as the July fourth blackout. Except this time they knew what towers to hit to knock out all the power to the plant, including a small emergency source of back-up hydro electric power. They did their homework."

"What about the explosions?"

"It looks like they used gasoline."

There was a long silence as both men stared at each other, knowing exactly what the other was thinking.

"They still do not know how the gasoline got into the building. They are theorizing somehow it got mixed in with the outside cooling water. Once inside the building, the gasoline, which is lighter than water, floated to the surface and vaporized, creating a highly explosive mixture. A spark from an electric motor probably set off the explosion."

"How the hell did they get so close to the plant?"

"It appears they came in by boat. Early this morning a fishing boat out on Lake Ontario came across two men in a ten-foot inflatable powered by an electric trolling motor about six miles out from shore, five miles east of the Nine Mile Point complex. The men said they were fishing, but they were dressed in wet suits and didn't have any fishing gear. The fishermen notified the Coast Guard and the two men were arrested.

"A car was found parked near the lake on a dirt road about five miles west of the plant. We believe the two men launched their boat there, made the trip over water to the plant, dumped the gasoline, and started back. However, shortly after midnight a west wind kicked up on the lake, which made it more difficult for them to get back to where their car was parked. Their batteries eventually died out and they were at the mercy of the wind and waves.

"The car was registered to an Amed Moqued. He had a Syracuse address and an apartment near Syracuse University. Earlier this morning we arrested Mr. Moqued and three other individuals who were in the apartment. One of the other individuals had a Dodge Durango registered to him. We searched it and found a number of large wrenches, a chain fall, and steel cable."

"Equipment needed to topple the towers?"

"We believe so. We are in the process now of matching the paint stains on the wrenches to the bolts removed from the towers. We've also taken mud samples from the car and the suspects' shoes to compare against the ground around the towers in question."

"Could this be cell number seven?"

"All six individuals are from Saudi Arabia. They are in this country on student visas. They have all been here for over a year. I would say it is cell number seven. It's all written up in here." Reynolds handed Blackman a red folder.

"Nice work, Ryan."

"Thank you, sir."

"One more thing. Have we gone public with this information? I mean, does the news media know this was a terrorist attack on a nuclear plant?"

"At first the company was playing down that aspect of the emergency."

"Is this the same company that was involved with the July fourth blackout?"

"Yes. The Northeast Transmission Company."

"What the hell is wrong with them?"

"Apparently there is a sale pending on the nuclear station. A multi-billion dollar deal."

"This is terrorism. We are at war for god sakes!"

"I understand they have since come out with a news release indicating it was a terrorist attack. Of course it was after the news media figured it out for themselves. Rumor has it the sale is now off, which is probably going to tank their stock come tomorrow morning."

"Do you think this was the nuclear attack bin Laden has been referring to?"

"We don't know. From what I understand, although the terrorists knew what they were doing, it was unlikely what they did would have ever resulted in a release of radiation from the plant. There would have had to have been a number of human errors to get that far."

"Maybe that is what they were counting on."

"That's apparently what happened at Three Mile Island and Chernobyl."

"Let's hope this is their nuclear threat. At least this should dominate the news for the next few days."

As Reynolds waited for the elevator he thought about what Blackman said about this story dominating the news. "I guess the little bitch will have to sweat it out a few more days. Fuckin' Dyan." Ryan smiled to himself.

71

"Jack Nelson."

"Mr. Nelson, sorry to bother you. This is the guard at the parking garage entrance. There is a woman out here who insists that she see you."

"It's six fifty-five in the morning."

"Yes sir. I tried to tell her that we don't open the building to the public until eight thirty, but . . . "

"What's her name?"

"Iullia Zola."

72

She could remember the dream. It took her to that place. Far away from real life. She could remember it ending and slipping back. She could remember seeing the alarm clock go from 8:10 to 8:11. But she could not remember her eyes opening, though somehow she knew it was hours before.

She rolled over. The bed was empty. She remembered. It was Monday morning. "Damn good thing somebody has a job around here."

Dyan was able to catch the Thursday afternoon flight out of Washington. She wasn't in the mood to spend another night there alone. She stopped into her Syracuse office hoping to surprise Jack, which she did. Then she surprised him again with her news. She needed to talk to someone about it and Jack was the perfect person. She left the building that night not knowing when she would return, if ever.

She slept away most of Friday and Saturday. She knew she'd need to sleep for a week straight to catch up on all that she lost over the past two months. But she also knew that was not why she was sleeping now. She remembered reading once that one way the human mind deals with depression is to shut down.

Sleep was the best way to accomplish that.

But Sunday was different. From the time she woke up, her eyes were glued to CNN watching the events unfold at the Nine Mile Point nuclear station located less than fifty miles from her bedroom. Several times throughout the day she wanted to pick up the phone and call Ryan Reynolds just to say, "I told you so." Or better yet, "I fuckin' told you so!" But she didn't. Instead she fantasized about him, or Blackman, calling her, telling her she was right again, and begging her to come back. But the phone never rang. Bastards. At least she knew that they knew that she had been right. And so did everyone else.

She jumped at the sound of the ringing phone, quickly reached for the receiver, then froze. This is probably the call, she thought. Let the answering machine get it. Maybe they'll think she's out golfing.

"Dyan, it's me. Pick up if you're there . . . Dyan."

Although it wasn't who she hoped it would be, it was a good second choice.

"Are you calling to check up on me? Don't worry, Jack. I haven't done anything stupid. I'm still alive."

"Dyan, you need to get down here right away."

"Excuse me. Have you forgotten that I've been banned from playing cops and robbers?"

"Dyan . . . "

"No can do, buddy. I wouldn't want your pretty black ass to get into trouble."

"Dyan." Jack's voice was noticeably louder. "Shut the fuck up and listen to me. You need to get down here right away. There is someone I need you to interview. I am dead serious. Do you understand me?"

"But what about the leave of . . . "

"Fuck the leave of absence. I'm ordering you to get in here. I'll expect you by 9:00 A.M." The phone went dead.

As Dyan stepped out of the shower, which took her all of

three minutes, something on the TV in the far corner of the bedroom caught her eye. Bin Laden was on CNN again. She walked to the night stand next to the bed, picked up the remote, and pushed the volume increase button. She looked up at the TV screen. Her heart started pounding seconds after she finished reading the words scrawling across the bottom of the screen. She didn't believe what she had read until the commentator's voice repeated the same words. "Osama bin Laden has been captured alive by U.S. forces."

73

"You're late. Come on." Jack turned and headed for his office with Dyan in quick pursuit.

"I'm late? Haven't you heard? They caught bin Laden alive."

"I heard. Right now this is more important for you to listen to."

"What the hell could be more important than . . . "

"Dr. Zola, this is the person I was telling you about, special agent Galloway." Dyan shook Iullia's hand and wondered what would happen if Blackman or Reynolds knew Jack just put her back into service.

"Dr. Zola, I'd like you to start from the beginning, from the day you received the letter in the mail from the lawyer."

For the first fifteen minutes Dyan kept glancing at Jack wondering why she was sitting there listening to this woman across the table from her. Jack was always looking at his yellow legal pad of hand-written notes, adding more words in the margins as the woman told her story. The only time he looked up was when he coached the woman, "When we met before, you also said . . . " which would start her off on a more detailed explanation of a just-covered point.

Several minutes later Iullia's words started to take on a new meaning for Dyan. This time when she looked at Jack, as if he somehow knew, his eyes were staring back at her. But it wasn't his eyes as much as the whisper of a smile across his lips that silently told her there was more to come. A minute later Dyan was the one asking the questions.

"If only half of what she said is true, it's still almost too unbelievable to believe."

"Now do you understand why I wanted you to get in here?"

Dyan's mind was racing, like a computer crunching millions of pieces of data at once, she looked zombie-like. Her body was stiff, her head was raised, and her eyes were focused on something miles away. Jack knew enough to leave her alone until she came to on her own.

Finally, Dyan turned and looked up at Jack. "There is no way anyone is going to believe this, in fact I still don't believe it, without hard proof. Right now all we have is the journal of a dead man. For all we know, this could all be a big hoax on his part."

"I agree."

"I am going to want to read the journal for myself."

"Iullia said she'd have a translation of it in a few days."

"We should have made a copy of it."

"It was in Russian. What would you have done with it?"

"I don't know, but when she comes back, let's get a copy."

"Fine."

"We should have the bodies exhumed."

"I was thinking the same thing. I'll take care of that."

"DNA analysis will either confirm or refute the claim that Williams is her father. If he's not, the rest is probably a hoax."

"And if he is?"

"Then we'll have to find out if the other things he claims are true."

"We're talking about something that happened over forty years ago."

"I know."

"If this is true . . . if this is true, it changes history."

"If this is true, it's one of the best kept secrets of our generation."

74

"I know I don't say this enough, but I'd like to thank you for the time and effort you have all put in, especially over the past two months. This has been a very trying time for our country. Tens of thousands have died, and before it is over tens of thousands more will die. But without your efforts, there is no doubt in my mind these numbers would be much greater. And more importantly, the enemy would still be among us.

"I didn't want to take up too much of the task force's time. I know you have a lot of issues to discuss. But if there are any questions, I would be glad to try to answer them." Blackman looked around the conference room table.

"Do you know what the plan is yet for bin Laden?"

"Good question. No we don't. I met with the president this morning on that issue. As you know we have only had him in custody for a little more than seventy-two hours. I can tell you he is in the United States, but for security reasons, I can not disclose the exact location. The administration is still trying to determine the next steps."

"Did anyone anticipate the effect his capture was going to have on the American public?"

"I do not think anyone expected this kind of reaction. If they had we probably would have sent a million-man army searching for him long ago.

"I think one of the reasons people are looking at this so positively is because of all the death and destruction this man has masterminded against us, especially in the past two months. His capture is a huge win, and I believe some people think the worst of the terrorism might therefore be over. But we cannot let our vigilance down. This war is still not over.

"If there are no more questions, I will let you get back to work." Blackman stood up from the table along with Reynolds. "Thank you for your leadership," Blackman said as he shook Reynolds's hand, "and again, thank you for all of your efforts." Blackman then left the room.

"He was in a great mood."

"Who isn't these days?" Reynolds chimed in. "We've captured al Qaeda's leader, the stock market posted its biggest two-day gain ever, the president's ratings are up twenty points. But as the director said, the war isn't over. So with that segue, let's get started. First agenda item. How are we coming assessing al Qaeda's threat to use a nuclear weapon?"

"We still have no leads on a source for such a weapon, and nothing to indicate any of the captured cells, including the seventh cell uncovered in Syracuse last weekend, are dealing with nuclear material."

"How do you factor in last weekend's nuclear plant attack?"

No one was anxious to answer Reynolds's question.

"One could interpret bin Laden's words to mean their plan was to try to cause a radioactive release from a nuclear plant versus exploding a nuclear weapon. Last week's attack is consistent with the tactics used by them since the tunnel bombings."

"I assume you mean Dyan's low-tech, low-cost theory?"

Everyone in the room was surprised to hear the sound of

Dyan's name coming from Reynolds's lips.

"Yes, that's correct."

"I am still not convinced al Qaeda doesn't have something else planned. So I think we still need to keep working this issue.

"Let's move on to the second item . . . " Reynolds stopped mid-sentence when he noticed the agent's hand out of the corner of his eye. He reached for the note, unfolded it, and read it. His face went white.

"Al Qaeda has just released another video. Ayman al Zawahiri is threatening to explode a nuclear warhead in New York City unless bin Laden is released within forty-eight hours."

75

Jack walked into Dyan's office and silently closed the door.

"Just let me finish this one page." Dyan was holding one of a dozen books piled on the desk in front of her. Half of them, obviously the ones she read so far, contained scores of yellow post-it notes sticking out from between the pages.

"This stuff is fascinating." She looked up at Jack. "What?"

"Williams's DNA matches Iullia's. He was her father."

"Then who is buried in the grave in Virginia?"

"No one."

"What?"

"The casket was empty."

"Son of a bitch."

"Soooo . . . what now?"

"Let me think. What was Williams's previous name?"

"Aleksandr Popov."

76

It was well over a hundred degrees outside. And sticky. The relief felt upon first entering an air-conditioned office building quickly disappeared when your body figured out that the interior temperature was in the eighties. But that was not the reason Ryan Reynolds's face was red.

"Is this unanimous?" His eyes circled around the conference room table at the nodding heads.

"We cannot find a credible source for such a weapon, especially a more recent source. And if they did have such a weapon for some time, we believe they would have already used it rather than risk having it discovered."

Why do these words sound so familiar? Reynolds thought to himself. The bitch isn't even here and she still has an influence over the group. Fucking Dyan Galloway.

"What about al Qaeda's threat? The fact that they have carried out everything they have promised?"

"We believe that threat had to do with the attack on the Nine Mile Point nuclear station."

"And yesterday's threat?"

"We believe he is bluffing."

"Bluffing?"

"Yes. Look at all of the attacks al Qaeda has launched in the past two months. They have been well-planned and well-executed. But none of them was very . . . "

"Sophisticated," Reynolds interrupted, "right?"

There was no response.

Even though the room temperature had not changed, Reynolds's face looked cooler.

"I can't dispute your findings, even though something tells me . . . I guess the facts are the facts and that is what I will report to the director. Thank you."

"Fucking bitch." Reynolds waited for the elevator door to close before he blurted out the curse. He knew the woman for less than six months, yet despised her from the beginning. She had been a threat. He was the fair-haired boy. Blackman's favorite. She tried to change that. So she had to go. His leak to the media did the trick. Yet even with her gone, he knew his report to Blackman would remind him of her. "Fucking bitch." He mumbled the words again just before the elevator doors opened.

"Mr. Blackman is expecting you. You can go right in."

"Thank you, Ms. Rock." Speaking of bitches, Ryan thought to himself, there's one he wouldn't mind trying out sometime.

As he walked toward Blackman's office, a warped thought entered his mind. What if the task force was wrong? What if Dyan was wrong? What if al Qaeda wasn't bluffing? He slowed his pace as he thought about how he could twist his report to make sure he'd look like the hero either way.

77

"Are you done?"

By the tone of Blackman's voice Dyan wasn't sure if he heard a thing that she said during the past fifteen minutes.

"Yes."

"First, let me repeat what I said at the beginning of this call. You are on administrative leave. That means you are not allowed to be in your office, you are not allowed to utilize any of the Bureau's resources, you are not allowed to interview people on behalf of the Bureau, and you are not allowed to masquerade as an FBI agent.

"Second, this theory of yours is ridiculous. You are saying that the highest levels of this government, as well as two other governments that we were for all intents and purposes at war with, agreed to a cover-up that has been kept secret for forty years. And the only proof you have for this theory is a dead man's diary.

"Third, in case you haven't heard, al Qaeda has threatened to detonate a nuclear bomb in New York City in twenty-four hours, which means that, contrary to your previous theory, the one you were preaching less than a week ago, al Qaeda already has a nuclear weapon.

"Fourth, and this will be my last point, unless you are out of your office in ten minutes, I will have you arrested and jailed for trespassing on federal property. Do I make myself clear?"

"Yes sir."

"Thank you. And if we ever speak again, it will only be because I called you."

The line went dead.

Jack spoke up as soon as he saw Dyan coming through the doorway to his office. "What did he say?"

"I need to get more proof."

"That's it?"

"He said a few other things that aren't important. Here." Dyan handed Jack a large inter-office envelope. "See what you can do to get this stuff for me." Dyan turned and started to leave.

"Where are you going?"

"To get more proof . . . and to find a place to hide."

78

NO EVIDENCE OF BOMB: THOUSANDS LEAVE CITY ANYWAY

NEW YORK CITY, July 30 – Although the government has stated it has no credible evidence to support al Qaeda's threat to detonate a nuclear bomb in New York City, thousands have still opted to leave. One resident cited al Qaeda's track record over the past two months of carrying out what they threaten as reason enough to get out.

With al Qaeda's 48-hour deadline for the release of Osama bin Laden due to expire at noon today, and the government adhering to its policy of not giving in to terrorist demands, the majority who remain were quick to criticize those who have left. The economic impact has already been felt as hotels, normally filled to capacity, have seen up to ninety percent of their reservations canceled. One merchant was quoted as saying, "These guys are bluffing and I'm going to call them on it."

79

"Oh my god, oh my god, oh my god. There he is again."

Jack. He was the first person she thought of. She had to call Jack. He has to see this. Instinctively she reached to her left for the phone, but it wasn't there. She twisted to her right, spotted the ill-placed phone, reached for it, then abruptly pulled her hand back when it rang.

With Dyan banned from her own office, she found refuge in another one, two floors below where the IRS worked. It was recently emptied by a retiree. Yesterday it was a barren work space; desk, chair, table, phone, and PC. Now littered with books and papers, it became the perfect hiding place for Dyan to work from.

"Hello." It was not her usual "Dyan Galloway" greeting. Even her voice was deeper.

"Dyan Galloway please."

The slow southern drawl coming through the phone told Dyan it was safe to acknowledge it was her. "Speaking."

"Hello, Ms. Galloway. This is Sumpter Jackson from Vector Electronics. I am returning your call from this morning."

"Yes, Mr. Jackson. Thank you for getting back to me so quickly."

"I understand you have some questions about our FXM-22 gamma ray and neutron flux monitors."

"Yes. I understand that you are the company that supplied the monitors to the Department of Homeland Security in late 2001, early 2002."

"That is correct."

"The monitors were installed in and around ports, border crossings, major highways, and other transportation routes."

"That is also correct."

"And I understand that there have been a number of problems with these monitors failing."

"Let me assure you, Ms. Galloway, that all of the problems that we first experienced in the field have been rectified. To be honest, yes, there were several problems with the system. This is not unusual with the introduction of any new piece of electronic instrumentation, especially one as complicated as this. We have replaced every monitor with the updated design, and I am happy to report that over the past six months, we have had no failures."

"I was reviewing a recent GSA report on these monitors and it indicated that recently three of the monitors along the . . . "

"Ms. Galloway," Jackson interrupted, "I personally visited all three of those sites, and I assure you there was nothing wrong with any of those monitors. They were in perfect working order. They absolutely did not fail."

"Thank you for the information, Mr. Jackson. You've been very helpful."

"My pleasure, Ms. Galloway."

"I do have one last question."

"Yes, Ms. Galloway."

"If the monitors were working correctly, what do you suppose made the people who were operating them report that they had failed?"

"Pavlov's Dog Syndrome."

"Excuse me?"

"I call it Pavlov's Dog Syndrome. It is when people automatically respond without thinking about what they are doing. When we first installed the monitors, we had so many failures, people operating them came to assume that an alarm meant a failed monitor. Now, whenever they hear the alarm, they automatically assume it is a failed monitor and shut it down."

"If these three monitors were not failed, then what caused them to go off?"

There was a long silence.

"That I do not know."

Unfortunately, Dyan now thought she did.

80

Blackman sat and stared at the silent TV monitor hanging on the far wall of his office. If something were going to happen in New York City at noon today, he didn't need to hear it. He was confident however, like everyone else, that nothing was going to happen. Of course his confidence was somewhat bolstered by the fact that he was sitting in his office in Washington, D.C.

Although yesterday's news report indicated fewer than 100,000 inhabitants fled, during the past two hours an exodus of people jammed the major highways out of the city. At 11:00 A.M., Times Square was bustling with people. Now, at 11:55 A.M., the place was deserted, as if staying inside somehow protected you against . . .

"Nothing is going to happen," Blackman said aloud. Still, he wondered how many people across the world were now glued to their TVs, like he was. CNN superimposed a digital clock in the lower right hand portion of the screen showing the time in hours, minutes, and seconds. It was as if they were telling al Qaeda, if you are going to do it, make sure you do it on time.

11:57:24. Less than three minutes.

He looked down and noticed his hands were gripping the

edge of his desk. His fingertips were turning white. He loosened his hands and lifted them. The desk was wet with his warm sweat.

He looked up at the screen. 11:58:04. Less than two minutes.

For some reason an old movie title flashed into his mind. "The Day The Earth Stood Still." He remembered the title, but couldn't remember what it was about. It didn't matter. The title alone was fitting.

11:58:35.

"This is stupid." If it was, why could he now feel his heart beating?

11:59:00. "Less than a minute." He took a deep breath.

Suddenly the screen went dark. A second later a new image appeared. Scrolling along the bottom of the screen were the words, "Live report from al-Jazeera news network." Ayman al Zawahiri filled the screen.

"No, no, no," were the only words Blackman could speak as he fumbled for his remote.

81

"Does it look like the same boat to you?"

Jack backed away and looked at the three pictures displayed on the monitor.

"Boy, it's hard to tell. Wait a minute . . . look. Right there." Jack pointed to what appeared to be a flag mounted on the antenna on each of the boats in all three screens. "It's a flag . . . no wait . . . it's a red, white, and blue wind sock."

Jack turned and looked at Dyan, who was sitting on the desk directly behind him.

"Where did you say these were taken again?"

"This one was taken on July first in Norfolk, Virginia. This one was taken on July seventh near Baltimore. And this one was taken on July sixteenth near the George Washington Bridge in New York City. All three shots are taken from video cameras mounted near where each of the gamma ray and neutron flux monitors went off on those days."

Jack looked down at his watch. It was 11:59 A.M.

237

82

"God damn it!"

In fumbling for the remote, Blackman had accidentally switched two channels up. He pressed the channel button with the arrow pointing down, twice. Al Zawahiri popped back up on the screen. 11:59:14. This time he carefully pressed the volume button with the up arrow on it. Though heavily accented, he began to pick up the interpreter's words.

" . . . is unfortunate that your government has not complied with our demands to release our spiritual leader. Your president has the blood of millions of our people on his hands, yet even that is not enough. He wants your blood also.

"Your president knows we have Satan's fire, yet we do not believe you are willing to spill your blood for him. Therefore we will expose the secret he keeps from you. We will show you what he knows. Then you too will know his evil ways."

Blackman looked at the clock. 12:00:00. He held his breath.

83

Blackman jumped when he first heard the noise, then refocused on the screen. Al Zawahiri was gone. Times Square was back on. It was 12:00:10. New York City was still there.

The second time he heard the noise, he was able to figure out what it was. "Come in."

"Sorry to bother you, sir. We just received word that someone placed an anonymous call to the NYPD several minutes ago. They claimed to represent al Qaeda and indicated that a nuclear device was in the Empire State Building. A Delta Force team and NEST team are en route with an ETA of 12:05."

"Thank you. And get me Reynolds . . . please."

"Yes sir."

84

One dozen Delta Force soldiers emptied from the two vehicles in seconds. They were completely dressed in black, which only made them stick out like sore thumbs on this bright, cloudless, summer day. As if previously choreographed, eight of them raced to the buildings entrance, clearing a pathway for those that would follow.

The remaining four soldiers gathered around the black GMC Yukon. The glass was tinted so dark it was impossible to see inside. Suddenly the doors opened and four middle-aged men, dressed in pure white coveralls, complete with booties, stepped out. Written across the back of the coveralls in large bold black letters was the word "NEST." They went to the rear of the vehicle and opened the hatch. Each of them grabbed a large white duffel-like bag and placed the dangling straps on their shoulders. The four black-clothed soldiers then escorted the four white-clothed men into the building.

Following 9/11, the government feared the next al Qaeda attack would involve a nuclear weapon. In addition to hurriedly deploying monitoring devices around the country, it also created various response teams that could be deployed should a nuclear bomb be detected. Delta Force teams were trained to deal with the special precautions needed to take control of a renegade nuclear weapon. The NEST teams, or Nuclear Emergency Search Teams, were comprised of scientists and technicians trained to keep a nuclear device, once found, from detonating.

"I'm getting a reading." As soon as they walked off the elevator on the eighty-eighth floor, the ultra-sensitive neutron flux monitor began reacting. The NEST team froze.

"Are you certain?"

"Positive."

The four knew they were the only ones standing there who understood the significance of the detector reading. A mass of highly enriched uranium was within fifty feet of where they were standing.

85

"Its been identified as a Russian-made tactical nuclear weapon with an estimated yield of two kilotons."

Blackman was dumbfounded with the relaxed ease at which Reynolds was briefing him on the NEST team's findings. He also wondered why they were discussing the technical attributes of the recovered nuclear weapon, and not the horrific death and destruction that was originally intended.

"The firing mechanism has been disabled. The warhead will be moved during the night to the nuclear weapons storage facility at Oak Ridge, Tennessee, where it will be dismantled."

Al Qaeda had the opportunity to finish what they started on 9/11, yet they decided not to. Why? Blackman thought. Why go to all the trouble and obvious expense to procure such a weapon, smuggle it into the country, prepare to detonate it, then change your mind and turn it over to your enemy? Why?

"We've sent the weapon's technical information to the Russians, including the serial number. We expect a reply from them within the hour."

The news media, tipped off by the same anonymous caller as the police, arrived on the scene only minutes after the Delta

Force team. Although it was less than four hours since the device had been discovered, the Department of Homeland Security already held two press conferences, their main objective being to control public fear. Based on the reaction of the people in and around the Empire State Building, and even the rest of the city, no one appeared to be fleeing the scene. Either the press conferences resulted in the desired calming effect, or people felt it was useless to run from a nearby nuclear bomb.

"The NEST team's preliminary investigation indicated the device, although dated, is real, and if it had been activated would have in fact detonated."

With the release of the two kiloton yield figure, about a tenth of the size of the bomb dropped on Hiroshima, every news organization in the world was projecting the death and destruction that would have resulted assuming the bomb detonated at noon. Although difficult to determine since only two cities have ever had nuclear bombs exploded over them, most concluded there would have been about a square mile pile of demolished buildings with as many as a million dead.

"The bomb itself is a tactical weapon, small and compact. It appears it was designed more as a defensive battlefield armament rather than an offensive one. It is very similar to the tank and cannon projectiles we have in our arsenal. The NEST team indicated the weapon was quite old. They believe it was built in . . . "

"The early sixties," Blackman interrupted.

"How did you know that?"

The ensuing silence was broken by three knocks on Blackman's office door.

"Come in."

"Excuse me. I thought you might want to see this." The woman handed Reynolds the note, then left, closing the door behind her.

"The Russians have confirmed that the serial number was one of theirs. It was one of forty tactical warheads that were produced in 1960. Their records also indicate this design was phased out in the late 1960s. All forty warheads were dismantled and their uranium cores were used in a newer design warhead."

"Obviously their records are fucked up."

Blackman sat in his chair staring out the window. After a few minutes of silence, he finally turned to Reynolds. "I want you to ask the Russians if this particular warhead was sent to Cuba in 1962."

86

"They've just confirmed it was Russian, tactical, and early sixties vintage."

Dyan remained focused on her PC monitor.

"Dyan. Did you hear me?"

"Just a second." Her fingers raced across the keyboard. As she waited for the screen to answer her, she turned and looked at Jack.

"Did you hear what I said?"

"Yes. I heard you."

"You don't seem to be very excited about the news."

"Sorry. For me it's not anything I didn't already suspect. Thanks for confirming it though."

"Why does that not surprise me?" Jack looked down at Dyan. He could tell her mind was working on three things at once. He didn't doubt that she knew all about the details of the nuclear weapon, even though it was found just hours ago. He wondered how she did it. Where she got the energy. "For some-one who hasn't slept more than four hours a night since Monday, and . . . "

"I pulled an all-nighter Wednesday night."

"I was just going to say, and pulled an all-nighter Wednesday night, you look pretty damn good."

"Thank you." Dyan glanced back at the screen. "Come on, damn it. This thing is so slow today."

"If I didn't know your husband so well, I'd think that he'd think, with you spending so little time in your own bed, that you were having an affair."

Ignoring him, she stared at the now refreshed screen. Her fingers played with the keys again.

"I found him. He is in Sackets Harbor."

"Sackets Harbor, New York? Fifty miles away?"

"Yes. Look."

Since Monday's meeting with Iullia Zola, Dyan was obsessed with finding out how much of what she said was really true, no matter how outrageous it sounded. As Iullia explained, Williams's journal claimed he was actually her father, Aleksandr Popov. Indeed, her mother did die at childbirth, but contrary to what she was told by her adopting parents, both dead, her father was not killed in an automobile accident on November 25, 1962, when Iullia was just a year old. Yet, as he went on to explain in the journal, he had good reasons to keep his own life a secret from her.

Without the actual translated journal, something Dyan felt she needed to read in its entirety before coming to any firm conclusions, she spent the first few days reading Jack's notes and verifying, where she could, any statement Williams purported as fact. Some were easy. Like the coincidences he cited that somehow predicted his destiny. Birthdays, for instance. His, April 17, he claimed was the same as Nikita Khrushchev's. Iullia's, August 13, he claimed was the same as Fidel Castro. Dyan found these facts to be true. His claim that he met both leaders, their initial meetings facilitated by the birthday trivia, was impossible to verify.

Dyan was able to verify that Popov in fact worked for the

State Department up until what was thought to be his untimely accident. A linguist by training, fluent in Russian, Spanish, and French, his skills were in great demand during the dawn of the Cold War, when anything and everything spoken or printed by the Soviet Union was analyzed by the U.S. government. It appears information was important even before the information age.

Dyan found little to substantiate Williams's claim that he played a critical role during the October 1962 Cuban Missile Crisis, ferrying messages between the U.S. and the Soviet Union that were so sensitive, they were only allowed to be communicated in person. Although he possessed the linguistic skills to do so, why wouldn't the two leaders have just used the hotline? she wondered. She thought she found a hole in his story until she learned that the hotline, implemented for just such secret and sensitive communications, was not installed until after the October crisis, and as a direct result of it.

On Wednesday morning, as Iullia promised, Dyan finally had what she needed, a copy of the translated journal. She read the document, tallying each and every fact. By then she was able to verify over seventy-five percent of Williams's claims as true. For those remaining, although she could find nothing to support them, she also could find nothing to prove they were not true.

She started to establish a detailed action plan for proving or disproving the remaining issues when Jack interrupted her with the news of al Qaeda's ultimatum. If in fact al Qaeda was prepared to carry out such a threat, Dyan knew she needed to refocus all of her efforts on only one of the unsubstantiated claims. It was the most important part of the journal. The force that drove all of Williams's subsequent actions. But it was also the most unbelievable. Unless everything else in the journal was true, no one would believe it. Dyan still didn't. After all, who would believe that for the past forty years a nuclear warhead lay hidden just ninety miles off the coast of Florida, in Cuba.

It was a secret deal agreed to between the super powers to assure Cuba would never again be attacked by the U.S. A secret deal that ended the October 1962 nuclear standoff. A secret deal which to the rest of the world would make one man, the one with the most to lose if the weapon were ever used, a hero, and lead the other, who had no option but to back down anyway, to his downfall.

In the end only five people were entrusted with the secret, all others involved having been expendable. Popov, although in the expendable column, was spared by a president who was willing to only go so far to protect the secret. But in order to live a life free of fear, Popov would need to first die. Hence his fatal automobile accident and reincarnation as Richard Williams. His silence was forever assured by the promise that his daughter would be safe as long as he never tried to contact her.

Although this would all need to be proven in order to sub-stantiate the ultimate secret, al Qaeda's threat, with its forty-eight-hour deadline, had now changed Dyan's plan of attack. Instead of trying to prove the facts behind the secret, she made an assumption that the secret was fact. And if it was, she believed this was the muscle behind al Qaeda's threat. If that were the case, the nuclear weapon had been moved from Cuba to the U.S.

"The safest way to smuggle anything from Cuba to the U.S. is by boat. This boat," Dyan pointed to the PC monitor, "showed up on the video tapes at each of the three locations along the Intracoastal Waterway where the monitors went off earlier this month. I was able to finally pick off the boat's name. It was documented with the U.S. Coast Guard. I pulled the owner's financial records. Credit card receipts show he traveled to the Bahamas in January. What better place to rendezvous with a boat from Cuba? He's been making a leisurely journey up the coast, not drawing attention to himself, until he tripped the monitors. He tripped them because he had a nuclear warhead on his boat. He stopped off in New York City for a week. That gave him sufficient time to off-load the bomb. Then he continued his journey up the Hudson River, down the Erie Canal, and out into Lake Ontario. For the past two days he's made a half dozen charges on his credit card in and around Sackets Harbor, New York. One charge was at Liberty Yacht Marina. It looks like that is where he is right now. Liberty Yacht Marina is right here." Dyan pointed to the PC monitor, which displayed a map of Sackets Harbor.

"It's gotta be him."

"It's about five o'clock. Traffic is going to be a bitch, but there is no reason we shouldn't make it to Sackets by six-thirty. Give me ten minutes to get everyone together and brief them. I'll meet you in the parking garage at five-fifteen sharp," Jack said as he walked out the door of the office.

87

"What the hell is going on?"

Without hearing a customary knock first, Blackman was startled by the noise of his office door blasting open. But Cross's voice told him he should stay seated with his back toward the door, studying his PC screen.

"Give me a second." By now Blackman lost track of what he was reading on the screen, but stared at it anyway as he slowly counted to ten. Then he reached for the mouse and clicked it a few times, pretending he was interested in the changing screens. Finally he turned and looked at Cross. "David. Sorry, I didn't hear you knock. What can I do for you?"

"Don't play your fucking little games with me, Blackman. You're on thin ice as it is."

"David, I honestly don't know what you are talking about."

"You don't know what I'm talking about? Let me jog your memory. I'll start with the White House is curious as to why the Russian president called less than an hour ago demanding to know how the FBI knew the warhead found earlier today had once been in Cuba. Come to think of it, your president has the same fucking question."

Blackman counted again before responding.

"It's a theory one of our agents has as to how the weapon may have made its way into the country."

"A theory? And when did you find out about this theory?"

"Actually yesterday was the first I heard of it. It surfaced in another case. The whole premise is so outrageous . . . "

"So is finding a nuclear warhead in the middle of New York City. One you said wouldn't be there."

"What I said was we had no credible evidence to substantiate al Qaeda had a nuclear device."

"And you were wrong."

"And so was everyone else."

"What if that device had gone off?"

"Was the president prepared to recommend the evacuation of New York City?"

"If we knew . . . "

"No, David." Blackman held his arm straight in front of him with his palm facing Cross, like a traffic cop might signal a car to stop. "Don't play Monday morning quarterback with me. If someone had said we have no evidence, but it would be prudent to evacuate, what would the president have done?"

Cross stood silent with his face going red.

"You know as well as I do what he would have done. The whole country is running scared. Thousands are dying. Everyone has lost confidence in the government's ability to protect them. The president was not about to order seven million people to evacuate, close down Wall Street and thousands of other businesses, without credible evidence. The billions it would have cost to do so would pale in comparison to the continued loss of this administration's credibility. And if it had been a hoax, and nothing had happened at noon today, when would you have let everyone back into the city? Or would you have left it a ghost town forever?"

"But it wasn't a hoax. And this administration has still lost credibility over it. Probably more than if the goddamn bomb had gone off. At least then al Qaeda would have been blamed. Now we are being blamed for letting the bomb into the country, and al Qaeda is the hero for being compassionate. There is even growing public support to release bin Laden."

"How do you think the public would feel about its government if it found out one of its past presidents secretly agreed to let Cuba keep that nuclear warhead on its soil? That's right, David. So why don't you ask the president what he knows about that!"

"You're not implying . . . that's ridiculous."

"I thought the whole thing was ridiculous too, until shortly after noon today. But think about it. Let's just say for the sake of argument that in order to get Cuba to buy into the resolution of the missile crisis back in 1962, the U.S. and Russia agreed to let Cuba keep a nuclear warhead. A small tactical one. One that could be used to effectively stop any future invasion by the U.S. Of course it had to be kept secret because President Kennedy would never survive a re-election if he publicly supported such an agreement, even if it had averted nuclear conflagration. In order to preserve the secret, everyone who had a part in carrying it out had to be killed, except Khrushchev, Kennedy, and Castro. And probably Bobby Kennedy, too, because as important as it was to keep the secret, it was just as important to pass it on to the next president. Like the concept of mutually assured destruction, where neither side would launch the first strike against the other because of the destruction it would receive in return, the same concept on a smaller scale now applied to the U.S. and Cuba. The bomb was meant to frighten, not to be fired. But it would only work if the U.S. president knew any planned invasion would be met with that kind of a pulverizing response."

"Are you insinuating that this president . . . "

"No, I am not. The world has changed since 1962, and especially since 9/11. There is no doubt in my mind that if the president had known of this, he would have acted long ago to have that warhead removed. Unfortunately, the secret probably never got passed on. Jack was assassinated. If Bobby knew the secret, he saw no immediate need to pass it on, especially to President Johnson who would likely have used it to either discredit Jack or ruin Bobby's future chances for becoming president. Then of course we all know what happened."

For the next minute, neither man said a thing.

"I didn't believe it either when I first heard it. Even after we found the bomb earlier today, I still didn't believe it. In fact you were the one who finally convinced me it might be true."

Cross looked confused.

"The Russians. You said the Russians wanted to know how we knew the warhead had once been in Cuba. The probability of a nuclear warhead getting into this country is much greater when it comes from a place no one thought it ever would. We've been focused on Russia, Iran, North Korea, Pakistan — not Cuba. Once the Russians verified that warhead had been in Cuba, the theory became more believable."

The silence again ensued, only to be broken by the ringing of Cross's cell phone. He pulled it out of his suit coat pocket, turned his back to Blackman and answered it. A second later, Blackman's phone rang. He turned his back to Cross as he spoke. The two men ended their calls at the same time, turned and faced each other.

"Something has been bothering me all day today." Blackman spoke softly and calmly, then paused, tempting Cross to ask what. For once Cross was speechless. "Why did al Qaeda give up a nuclear weapon?" Blackman paused again. "We now know the answer to that question."

88

"Is that it?"

"That's it." Dyan lowered the binoculars and handed them back to Jack. "Do you see the wind sock?"

"I just noticed it."

The two of them were standing in the fifty-foot diameter gazebo perched on a hill overlooking the water at Sackets Harbor. It was a warm summer evening and the sun in the western sky to their left was just starting to dip below the roof line of the gazebo. At that angle it was illuminating the forty-foot motor yacht tied to the end of the middle dock of the small marina at the east end of the harbor.

The six of them, Jack, four other agents, and Dyan, drove in two separate cars from Syracuse. As Jack promised, they arrived in Sackets Harbor, a small town about fifty miles north of Syracuse on the eastern end of Lake Ontario, at precisely 6:30 P.M. Through the binoculars, Jack could see the four agents, dressed in casual summer clothing, kept in the office for situations like this, positioned around the large wooden building on the far side of the marina's docks.

"Someone just stepped out onto the rear deck of the boat.

Two people. A man and a woman. They have drinks in their hands. They just sat down."

"They are probably enjoying a cocktail before dinner."

"Is everyone in place?" Dyan heard Jack speak into his lapel microphone.

"How come I can't have one of those?" Dyan asked pointing to Jack's microphone.

"You're damn lucky I let you come with us to begin with."

"This is my case."

"And you are on administrative leave, remember? You stay right here." He handed her the binoculars. "I'm going over to the marina. I would rather apprehend them on land. So we'll wait to see if they leave the boat." A few minutes later Dyan saw Jack appear on the far side of the marina, then disappear.

An hour later, the couple, now on their third round of drinks, did not appear to look as if they would be leaving their boat any time soon. Dyan stood in the gazebo the entire time, looking as inconspicuous as possible, but also kept a close watch on the activities in the marina, especially those on the motor yacht. Her legs were the first part of her body to feel the effects of the past five days' sleep schedule. She eyed a bench near the water's edge just in front of the gazebo. She suddenly felt self-conscious about having been in the same location for the past hour. She wondered if people were getting suspicious. Moving to the bench was probably a good idea, she thought.

"God this feels good," she said as her legs and back melted into the seat. She gazed across the marina. The two suspects were still on the back of their boat.

"Did you move so you wouldn't look so obvious, or did you move because you were getting tired?"

"Yes." It was the only answer she could think of. She didn't see Jack sneak up behind her.

"It doesn't look like they are going to get off that boat any time soon, so I have another idea. Follow me."

A few minutes later Jack and Dyan were standing on the dock just feet from the motor yacht.

"Nice boat."

"Thank you."

"Do you travel very much with it?"

"Actually, we've been living aboard her. Spent the winter down south. Florida, the Keys, Bahamas. Regular snowbirds we were. Been traveling up the Intracoastal Waterway for the past two months."

"I told you this was big enough to live on," Dyan said to Jack, who was standing next to her.

"Oh most definitely," the woman on the boat spoke up.

"It's our dream to someday live on a boat, and whenever we can we like to talk to people who are doing it to see if they really enjoy it."

"Well why don't you come aboard and have a seat? We'd be glad to share our experiences with you."

"That's very nice of you. My name is Jack Nelson and this is my . . . wife, Dyan."

"Nice to meet you. My name is Dave. Dave Lawson. And this is my wife, Anne. Welcome aboard My Island."

89

"Those weren't alcoholic drinks you two were drinking on the back of that boat, were they?"

Jack, who was driving, turned and looked at the agent sitting in the back seat of the Taurus. "Iced tea, lemon, no sugar."

Dyan, who was sitting in the passenger seat, did not turn around. "I'm on administrative leave."

Within five minutes of boarding My Island, Jack and Dyan knew Dave and Anne Lawson were not the terrorists they were looking for. Dyan turned quiet as she wondered what she missed in her analysis. My Island was the boat's name she spied on the video. It was registered to a Dave Lawson. It was the boat that was nearby each time the monitors went off. This could not be a coincidence. What was she missing? she thought.

" . . . they were a very nice couple." Dave finally ended one of his long-winded stories.

"Except they seemed very nervous at times," Anne whispered.

"I think it was because they were new to boating. They didn't admit it, but you could tell the way he docked his boat. That's something you will see when you get one of these babies. It's not as easy as you think. But with practice, you'll do just fine."

Anne leaned toward Jack and Dyan and again whispered, "I always thought it was because of all that was going on."

Then Dave whispered, "We met them the day of the tunnel bombings."

"I think we all got a little more nervous that day," Dyan finally jumped into the conversation.

"No, I think it was because . . . well, you know. They were from Saudi Arabia."

They pulled into the federal building's underground parking garage just past eleven.

"Are you going home?" Jack asked Dyan.

"No. I've got to check out . . . "

"Dyan." Jack stood in front of her and put his hands on her shoulders. "You look exhausted. They found the bomb. There's no hurry any more. This can wait until the morning."

Dyan looked up at him. She knew he was right. She was exhausted. More tired than she felt in a long time. Though the word crept into her mind in the car, hepatitis, she never gave it another thought. She was just tired. That's all.

Her theory about Lawson and the My Island turned out to be nothing but a wild goose chase. It was the second time she was wrong in the past week. The first being that al Qaeda did not have a nuclear weapon. Still . . .

"No. I've got to check this out." She turned and started walking toward the elevators.

"You're going to disappoint your husband again."

"I'm not worried. He's used to it."

90

The ringing phone startled her. Actually, it scared the hell out of her. Who would be calling her at midnight? she thought.

Dyan spent the past hour re-reviewing the videos of My Island. She searched for a boat named Cocamo, but didn't find it, even though the Lawsons were certain the two boats traveled together from Norfolk to New York City.

The phone rang out again. It had to be her husband. Who else would be calling her?

"Dyan's escort service. Could I have your name please?"

"It's Blackman. Bill Blackman. But I must have the wrong number because I thought I was dialing the Syracuse Field Office of the FBI."

Dyan froze. She couldn't speak. She couldn't hang up.

"Thank you for not insulting my intelligence by hanging up. I guess you didn't understand when I sent you out on adminis-trative leave that it was a paid leave, did you? You are still going to get a paycheck. You didn't have to go out and get another job."

"I'm sorry, sir. I thought you were my husband calling."

"I'm glad your husband is so understanding of your new

career, but I hope you are not too attached to it because I'd like to offer you your old job back. That was the one working for the FBI, in case you don't remember. Although from what I understand it appears you never really left the FBI, did you Ms. Galloway? So my reinstating you probably doesn't mean anything to you, does it? Especially with your new career and all . . . are you still there?"

"Yes sir. I'm here."

"I'm sure someday, over a drink I hope, we will be able to sit back and smile over all this, but right now is not the time. I just got off the phone with Jack and he briefed me on what the two of you have been doing since I spoke with you on Thursday morning. He said you were checking out another potential lead. Have you found anything?"

"No. Nothing. The other boat doesn't show up on the tapes. But the videos I have show a very limited view of the area around the monitors. I'm sure there are other tapes we could pull. There must be hundreds of video cameras along that route that would verify what Lawson told us. It will probably take a few days to find out what's out there, and then pull the tapes. I'll get on it first thing in the morning."

"Dyan, we don't have a few days."

"Some of the recordings are digital. Those can be sent over the Internet. If I can locate some of those, I can have them reviewed by this evening."

"We don't have until this evening."

"I don't understand?"

"The Russians have verified that the bomb we found earlier today was one of those sent to Cuba during the 1962 Cuban Missile Crisis."

"Then Williams's journal . . . it's all true."

"The Russians claim all the warheads were returned."

"Well . . . they're mistaken."

"It's what their records show."

260

"Isn't there some way to double-check their records?"

"They have. They said that warhead was supposedly dismantled in the late sixties and the nuclear-grade material was used in a new class of weapons."

"Then how do they explain the one we found in the Empire State Building?"

"They can't. And, they aren't willing to comment anymore until their own people look at the weapon.

"They also mentioned the U.N. oversight that verified all of the warheads were removed, crated, and shipped back to the Soviet Union in 1962."

"You mean missiles."

"What?"

"Missiles. The U.N. verified all the missiles were dismantled and shipped back, not the warheads."

"Isn't that one in the same?"

"No. Since I met with Iullia Zola on Monday, I've done a little, actually a lot of research on the Cuban Missile Crisis. The Soviet Union sent forty-four medium range and intermediate range missiles to Cuba. But what most people don't know, and at the time we didn't know it either, almost a hundred smaller nuclear warheads were also on the island. Eighty on cruise missiles, six to be used on their Il-28 bombers, and twelve on short-range Luna rockets. The Luna warheads were very compact, less than a foot in diameter and just over two feet long, with a yield of two kilotons. That's about a tenth of the size of the Hiroshima bomb.

"The nuclear warheads for the medium and intermediate range missiles were stored on ships in the Cuban ports. But the smaller warheads were stored in bunkers. Our U-2 spy planes only photographed three-fourths of the missiles placed in Cuba and we never located any of the warheads. We had no idea what the Soviet Union had stored there. The U.N. verified the missiles were crated up and shipped back to the Soviet Union. But the most devastating part of the weapon system, the warhead, was never tracked. It would have been remarkably easy to move one of the Luna warheads to another location.

"Williams was right. A nuclear warhead was left behind. The Russians are mistaken."

"Williams might have been mistaken too."

"How can you say that? The Russians have already verified the serial number. It was one of the warheads sent to Cuba. Somehow, it got left behind. It corroborates Williams's scenario exactly."

"Dyan, a few hours ago al-Jazeera received another video from al Zawahiri. They claim they have another nuclear weapon. Unless we release bin Laden by 5:00 P.M. today, they are going to detonate it."

"A second nuclear warhead?"

"Yes, a second."

"What city?"

"That's what makes it interesting. All they say is, if we don't comply, one of our major cities will be wiped from the face of the earth."

91

"Do they or do they not have a second weapon?" Blackman was remarkably calm considering he hadn't slept in almost twenty-four hours. But what was even more remarkable was he hadn't blown up at Reynolds.

"Look, Ryan." Blackman glanced at his watch. "It's four-fifty in the morning. I have a meeting at the White House at six. A decision has to be made whether to evacuate forty-five million people from the fifty largest cities in the U.S. over the next twelve hours. And since we have so little time to do it in, the most critically ill in hospitals and nursing homes, along with police and whatever National Guardsmen we can mobilize, will be left behind. The impact on our economy is going to be staggering. Some liken it to the Great Depression. It is likely the final nail in the coffin for the current administration, and that's if we are lucky. It could mean the end of our way of life.

"The most important input for their decision needs to come from us. Do we think they have a second bomb?"

"I've been consistent all along, sir, in saying that I thought al Qaeda had a nuclear device."

"Ryan," Blackman's voice was noticeably louder, "I'm not

interested in your thoughts. I need facts. Credible evidence."

"Sir, everything points to it. That they have another one. But we still have nothing specific."

Blackman just stared at Reynolds. In the past two weeks he had lost all credibility in him. Why he didn't see his shortcomings before, he didn't know. But in this terrorist-driven environment, they were certainly apparent.

"I'd like your comments on this by 5:30 A.M." Blackman picked up the report from his desk, and handed it to Reynolds.

"What is it?"

"It's a theory which explains how a nuclear weapon could have gotten into this country. It surfaced in the past forty-eight hours. I've kept it from you because I was hoping you would come up with your own scenario. It's from Dyan Galloway."

"Galloway? I thought she was . . . "

"I reinstated her earlier today."

"Sir. This woman's theories change with the wind. Is she still saying al Qaeda doesn't have a nuclear device? It wouldn't surprise me if she was. She doesn't have the experience or the background to even be providing input in this area." Reynolds threw the report onto Blackman's desk.

Blackman picked up the report and handed it back to Reynolds. "I want your comments in thirty-five minutes." The ringing phone ended their conversation as Blackman turned his back to Reynolds.

"Blackman."

"The president would like to know what you are going to report."

"David, I think you know what I am going to say."

"Humor me."

"We have a credible scenario for how the first weapon got into the country. We have nothing to tell us there is a second one, although there very well could be."

"If there is, any leads on the location?"

"Nothing."

"You are making this very difficult for the president."

"Actually, al Qaeda is making it very difficult for forty-five million U.S. citizens, not just the president."

92

The sound was so familiar, yet Dyan could not place it. It didn't matter though. It made her feel good. Actually, it excited her. At least she felt like she was getting excited. She must be asleep. Dreaming. Yes, she thought. She was dreaming again.

There was the sound again. A voice. This time she recognized it. No wonder she was getting excited, she thought. What time is it? 4:59 . . . 4:59? Was it A.M. or P.M.? Suddenly, she felt herself shaking. She opened her eyes to see the brilliant white light all around her. Blinding her. "Nooooo!"

"Dyan." Jack pulled his hands back from Dyan's shoulder as she sprang from the chair. "It's okay. You were dreaming."

Dyan was on her feet now, staring at Jack. "What time is it?"

"It's five o'clock."

"A.M.?"

"Yes. Why? You didn't think you slept through the whole day, did you?"

Dyan fell back into her chair. "I feel terrible. I must look terrible." She ran her fingers through her hair like a comb. "What a grease pit. I could use a shower."

"Well lucky your husband was smart enough to think you

needed these." Jack handed a bag to Dyan.

"Oh my god . . . clean clothes. You gotta love that guy." Dyan stood up and reached to hug Jack, but before she could, her legs went limp and she collapsed.

"Dyan." Jack managed to hook his arms under hers, and lowered her back into the chair. "Are you okay?"

"I don't know. I feel weak. Just give me a second." She tried standing up again, but stopped and sat back down. She looked up at Jack. "If I didn't know any better, I'd think I was going to . . . "

Dyan turned, grabbed the waste paper basket, and "Argh, argh . . . " It was now the second day in a row that she threw up in the morning. She spit into the basket, then without raising her head, reached with her right hand and grabbed several tissues from the box on the back corner of the table. She wiped her mouth, then looked up at Jack. As soon as she saw the tears in Jack's eyes, she knew what he was thinking.

93

"He was dubbed the 'Pen Pal Correspondent.'"

"The what?"

"The 'Pen Pal Correspondent.'"

It was 5:15 A.M. Blackman had now been up for twenty-four hours. He guessed the young man sitting next to him at his hexagonal conference table was also on the same sleep schedule, though he was certain the twentysomething year old looked much better than he did.

When Blackman learned yesterday that the nuclear warhead was Russian, he requested a full background check on Aleksandr Popov. When the Russians later confirmed the warhead had been in Cuba, Blackman forgot about the request, moving onto more important issues. The young analyst assigned to the task did not. Given temporary but unlimited security clearance to pursue any and every government database in existence, he attacked the problem as if the fate of the world depended upon it. He completed his analysis at 5:05 A.M. and as previously instructed called Blackman, assuming he would get his voice-mail. Instead he got a face-to-face meeting with his boss's, boss's, boss's boss.

"He worked for the State Department, but starting in September 1961, he was temporarily reassigned to the Attorney General's Office, reporting directly to the Attorney General."

"Robert Kennedy?"

"Yes. It was the same time period President Kennedy started engaging in secret correspondence with Khrushchev. White House aides dubbed it 'Pen Pal Correspondence.' There was one courier who carried the messages back and forth between Washington and Moscow."

"Popov."

"Somehow he became a trusted friend to both Kennedy and Khrushchev. It was rumored that many of the most sensitive issues discussed by the two world leaders were never written down. Instead, Popov would memorize the message and pass it along verbally."

"So that is what could have happened during the Cuban Missile Crisis."

"That is correct. There is evidence that the correspondence between the two continued after October 1962. Then it came to an abrupt halt."

"When Popov apparently died."

"Yes. Shortly thereafter the hotline between Washington and Moscow was put into place."

"Did you find any evidence to support the new identity that was set up for Popov? Richard Williams."

"Nothing. It was all done without a trace. In my opinion, the only way for that to have happened was if it was carried out at the highest levels of government."

"Like the Attorney General's Office?"

"Yes sir."

94

*AL QAEDA THREATENS TO USE SECOND NUKE – 50
LARGEST CITIES TO BE EVACUATED*

*WASHINGTON, D.C., July 31 – The Department of Homeland
Security has ordered the evacuation of the 50 largest cities in the
U.S., to be completed by 5:00 P.M. EST today. The evacuation is in
response to the latest al Qaeda threat to "wipe from the face of the
earth" a major city in the U.S. unless Osama bin Laden is released.*

*The order comes less than twenty-four hours after the discovery of
a nuclear weapon on the 88th floor of the Empire State Building in
New York City. That bomb, originally part of a previous al Qaeda
threat, appears to have been voluntarily surrendered by them.
"The fact that they turned in the bomb would strongly indicate that
they have another," said one official who spoke on the condition of
anonymity. He also stated, "It shows how important it is to al
Qaeda to get their leader back."*

*The evacuation, which could eventually involve up to 45 million
people, is being coordinated by FEMA, the Federal Emergency
Management Agency.*

270

95

SYRACUSE HOST CITY FOR EVACUATION

SYRACUSE, NY, July 31 – Syracuse, as well as several other upstate New York cities, has been designated a host location for the evacuation of residents from New York City. Area schools, college dormitories, and larger buildings such as the OnCenter convention center and the county War Memorial, will house what is expected to be over 200,000 people evacuated in response to al Qaeda's threat to explode a nuclear weapon in one of America's major cities. The influx of evacuees will more than double the population of the city.

96

Jack pushed the doorbell button again. He could hear the muffled sound of the chimes from within the house. He looked at the number on the house, 3557. He looked at his notebook. 3557 Cumberland Lane. He was at the right place. He glanced at his watch. 12:32 P.M.

Dyan spent most of the night reviewing the video files for any sign of a boat named Cocamo. She found none. Earlier this morning she decided to try to identify who the owner of the boat might be. Although the Lawsons traveled with the Cocamo for several weeks, it was surprising how little they knew of the couple on board. Boat name, hailing port, first names, boat purchased in Florida in December, and a general physical description of the two people was about it.

For hours Dyan worked the data until she finally came up with a hit. Four central New York residents had registered boats in Florida in December. A Jones, a Rockland, a Stevens, and a Rahied. Mozat Rahied. He lived at 3557 Cumberland Lane in Baldwinsville, a town just northwest of the city of Syracuse, about a thirty-minute drive from the federal building.

"They're not home."

Jack was startled by the voice of the man standing in the driveway of the adjacent townhouse.

"Do you know when they might be back?" The man just stared at Jack without saying a word. "My name is Jack Nelson." He walked toward the man and held out his badge. "I'm with the FBI."

"I apologize. I wasn't being rude. It's just with all the crime, you never know . . . "

"No problem."

"The Rahieds are retired. They've been away on an extended trip since December. I don't know when they will be back."

"Dyan Galloway."

"It looks like you were right. It's got to be them."

"Did you talk to them?"

"No. The next-door neighbor says they've been away since December. Still not back in town."

"Well, they may not be back in town, but their boat is. It's docked at the Tri-Bridge Marina in Brewerton. According to the guy I just got off the phone with at the marina, they've been there for three days."

97

"I'm coming up behind you now. This isn't too obvious is it? Two identical silver Tauruses parked on the shoulder of Interstate 81."

"You can see the whole marina from here."

Oneida Lake, 26 miles long and 6 miles wide, was located in the center of New York State, about fifteen miles north of Syracuse. The lake and its connecting rivers were all part of the Erie Canal system. The canal crossed the entire state and enabled boaters to travel west as far as the Mississippi, and east to New York City. The Oneida River flowed into the western end of the lake, and Interstate 81 crossed the river at that point. The raised roadway provided the perfect vantage point for spying on the boats docked at the Tri-Bridge Marina, which bordered the interstate to the east.

Jack got out of his car, walked up to the car in front of his, opened the rear passenger door and got in. Ron Klien, the agent sitting in the front passenger seat, kept his eyes glued to the binoculars as he stared at the hundreds of boats in the marina below.

"There doesn't appear to be anyone onboard," Ron finally

spoke up in a soft-spoken voice.

"How long have you been here?"

"About fifteen minutes."

"Let me take a look."

"It's the third boat in from the end on that last dock in the very middle channel of the marina. There is an inflatable mounted on the back swim platform. You can't miss the name on the back."

"Okay. I see it now. Wow. Some boat." Jack stared for several minutes. "You stay here and keep an eye on things. If you see any movement, call me. I'm going down for a closer look."

"Can I help you?"

Although it was a gorgeous, sunny Saturday afternoon, the marina was almost deserted. "Fuckin' al Qaeda," Jack mumbled to himself. This was the third pass he made up and down the dock where Cocamo was tied up. Each pass, Jack walked a little closer and a little slower, trying to peer into the smoked glass windows of the yacht's cabin. At the sound of the voice he turned to see a gangly, long-haired, pimply-faced teenager standing about ten feet away. He wondered how the boy snuck up on him.

"Just admiring the boat."

"You from the FBI?"

Jack knew some people had the knack to pick out the fuzz, but he still wondered what gave him away. He was a six-foot-tall black man dressed like he was about to play eighteen holes, something he would normally be doing on a day such as this. Fuckin' al Qaeda, he thought again. So much for being inconspicuous.

"I was the one who took your call this morning."

Jack still looked confused.

"The woman from the FBI. Looking for the Cocamo. I was the one she talked to. So are they running drugs or something?"

"Why do you say that?"

"I was here when they came in on Wednesday evening. Filled 'em up. Twelve hundred dollars worth of diesel. Paid in cash. All hundreds. The guy was quiet, but the woman was nice. She told me they started their trip in Florida back in December. Big boat. Florida. Lots a cash. They had drug dealer written all over 'em. Now the FBI asking questions about 'em."

"Have you seen them around?"

"Not since yesterday morning. Thursday they were out all day on their boat. Yesterday morning I saw them walking around the marina. They were each carrying a small duffel bag. I saw a car pull into the parking area. A few minutes later the car was gone and so were they."

"Do you remember what the car looked like?" By now Jack had pulled out his small notebook and pen.

"A dark-colored SUV, I think. Na, I really don't remember."

"You are sure you haven't seen them since yesterday?"

"Hey, look around. Not much action for a Saturday in the summer. I guess everyone is home glued to their TV sets waiting for the big bang." The boy glanced at his watch. "Three more hours."

Jack looked at his watch. 2:03 P.M. He reached into his pocket and handed the boy his business card. "If you should see them again, would you mind giving me a call?"

"Be glad to. But I'm only on until six today. And I'm off tomorrow."

"That's fine. Thanks." Jack took one more look at the yacht then started to walk away.

"I think I know where they hid the drugs."

Jack stopped, turned around, and looked at the boy.

"It's almost too obvious. Can't you figure it out?" The boy pointed to the boat.

Jack walked to the edge of the dock and glanced at the boat.

"The inflatable . . . it doesn't have a motor. A yacht like this

276

with a top-of-the-line inflatable. Hydraulic swim platform to get it in and out of the water. That's a thirty-thousand dollar option on a boat like this. But what good is all that if the inflatable boat ain't got a motor?"

"Maybe they store it down below so it won't get stolen."

"Don't think so. Look at the back transom where the motor mounts. Not a scratch. It's never had a motor on it." Before Jack could get in a word, the boy jumped onto the swim platform. "I bet this is where they hide the drugs." He kneeled down and pointed to the large round tube that formed the side of the inflatable boat. "I noticed it when I was filling their tanks on Wednesday. The end cap on this tube was loose. Someone has cut the seal. See how it comes right off." The boy pulled on the cone shaped piece of plastic and it slid off. He then put his hand into the open end of the tube. "If they ever put this boat into the lake, this would have filled up with water and the whole thing would have sunk. But it makes a perfect place to hide a load of drugs."

Jack jumped onto the back of the swim platform, knelt down, and peered into the open tube. He reached in and ran his fingers along the inside bottom of the tube. His fingers confirmed what his eyes saw. There were deep scratches along the bottom of the tube, like someone had put a heavy object into it, scraping it along the bottom.

"Weird huh," the boy spoke up. "The other side is the same way."

98

"What do you make of it?"

It hadn't taken Ron Klien long to drive to the marina from his lookout perch on the interstate. He and Jack were now both peering into the open end of the tube on the inflatable boat.

"Somebody specially designed this insert to fit into the tube of this boat. It goes back about three feet. With this cap on, it makes it look like it's filled with air, like it's supposed to be."

"What about the scratches?"

"I agree with you. Looks like something heavy was pushed in here and caused all these scratches. This might be some paint that scratched off from whatever it was." Ron pointed to the gray marks on the interior of the tube.

"Get the lab guys down here. I want a sample of that."

Jack felt his cell phone vibrate in his left front pants pocket.

"Jack Nelson."

"Mozat Rahied used his credit card two hours ago when he checked into a hotel."

"You got agents on the way?"

"No."

"Why not?"

"Technically he is in another country. We can't touch him."

99

Jack grabbed the small plastic ice bucket from the cart and headed down the hall to the ice machine he passed when he got off the elevator just minutes ago. He pushed the large red button and the machine in front of him made a loud grinding noise as the ice cubes dropped into the bucket. Before he reached for the now overflowing bucket, he stripped off his golf shirt and tucked it into the back of his pants. He grabbed the bucket and headed back down the hall to where the cart was still standing.

"Excuse me." He knocked on the open door of the room where the cart was located. "Excuse me. Hello."

"Yes." A woman, he guessed not yet twenty, walked from inside the room toward the open door carrying a waste basket full of empty beer cans.

Jack pulled his stomach in as hard as he could, flexed his pecs, and held the overflowing ice bucket up in front of him. "I ran down to get a bucket of ice and I locked myself out of the room. Could you open the door for me? It's a few rooms down. One, nine, one, two."

The woman eyed Jack, then smiled at him. "I might be able to help you." She dumped the empty beer cans into the large plastic garbage bag hanging off the side of the cart and placed the waste basket on the floor. "This happens all the time. Which room?" she asked as she walked down the hall in front of Jack.

"One, nine, one, two."

She walked up to the door and slipped the plastic key card that dangled from the chain around her neck into the electronic lock on the door. A small green light flashed twice. She pushed down on the handle and opened the door.

"Thank you. I really appreciate this. You are a life saver." He squeezed into the doorway with his back facing away from her so she wouldn't see his shirt.

She smiled at him again. "The pleasure is all mine. Is there anything else I can do for you?"

It took Jack about an hour to drive from Tri-Bridge Marina to Verona, New York, located thirty miles east of Syracuse. He took the Thruway hoping to be able to speed his way there. Unfortunately the traffic in the east-bound lane of the interstate was heavy and kept him at less than eighty for most of the ride. At least he wasn't heading the other way. The west-bound lane was bumper-to-bumper, creeping along at less than fifty. Must be the New York City evacuees headed to Syracuse, he thought.

As he turned into the entrance to the hotel he felt as if he was entering another world. And technically, he was. Well, another nation anyway. The Turning Stone Resort, located in Verona, New York, was not part of New York State. In fact, it was not part of the United States. Turning Stone was located on the sovereign lands of the Oneida Indian Nation. The complex, which opened with a small casino in 1993, was now home to three championship golf courses, eleven restaurants, a convention center, and three hotels, including a brand new nineteen-story luxury hotel, the tallest building in the 150-mile stretch from Albany to Syracuse.

As Jack walked into the main lobby of the hotel complex, he still had no idea what his next step was going to be. He knew his FBI badge gave him less authority in the Indian territory than a Boy Scout on a street corner. Luckily Dyan was able to hack into the hotel's reservation system and find Rahied's room number. After knocking on the door several times, he put into action his hastily developed plan for entry.

Jack closed the door, took a deep breath, placed the bucket of ice on the small table next to the door, and reached for his shirt. He turned to face the room as he pulled the shirt over his head. It took a few seconds for his eyes to adjust to the bright blue sky shining through the wall of glass at the far end of the room. Once he stopped squinting, he couldn't believe what he saw.

100

Jack pulled the notebook out of his left back pants pocket. He opened it to the last page he had scribbled notes on. 1912 was the room number Dyan gave him. He walked over to the door, opened it, stepped out into the hall, and looked at the brass numbers on the wall. 1912. He felt relieved he was in the right room. He wondered how he would have talked the young lady into letting him into another.

He closed the door and walked to the other end of the room. "What the fuck?" He gazed around the room to make sure he wasn't missing something. "Kinky, real kinky." Standing next to the king-sized bed, in the space between it and the windows, were two tripods. Mounted on each was a video camera. Jack took a close look at each camera, wondering if anything had been recorded on them and how difficult it would be to rewind and watch them. He could only imagine what might be on them. Sex, obviously. Kinky, most likely. Why else would you bring all this equipment to a hotel room? He looked around again. A very fancy hotel room, he thought. And two cameras, no less. He glanced back at the cameras and wished he was more technologically orientated. He really wanted to see what was on the videos.

He walked around the room. One by one he opened all the drawers. They were all empty, except for the one with the Gideon Bible in it. The closet was full of empty hangers. Two small duffel bags were on the floor next to the dresser. He opened them. Clothes. Nothing out of the ordinary. "No props? They better be some actors, otherwise this is going to be one dull X-rated movie."

As he walked back toward the cameras, he noted the map on the top of the desk. A New York State road map. Then he saw it. A compass. Resting on top of the map. A small plastic one. One a hunter might use. "Idiots," Jack said aloud. Don't they know a compass like this doesn't work in a metal-covered car? And what the hell would you need a compass for anyway with all the signs along the road, he thought. "Idiots."

He turned and stared at the cameras. "What the hell am I missing?" Something is not right, he thought. He had to be in the wrong room.

Just as he reached for his phone, he felt it vibrate. "Jack Nelson."

"Hi, it's me."

"I was just going to call you. You need to double-check the room number. I don't think this is the right one. If I didn't know any better I'd think I'd stumbled into an X-rated porno set, not a bunch of terrorists."

"I just double-checked the reservation and room number. That's why I was calling you."

"One, nine, one, two is correct?"

"One, nine, one, two is correct."

"Then why were you calling me?"

"The reason why I had to double-check the reservation was about an hour ago the Rahieds' credit card was used here in Syracuse."

"Syracuse? Where?"

"They used it when they checked into the Marx hotel."

"The Marx hotel?"

"The one right next to Route 81."

"I know where it is. But why the hell are they getting a room there?"

"I don't know, but I checked and they reserved the rooms at both hotels at about the same time. Noon yesterday."

"Noon? So I guess that would rule out reserving rooms for someone evacuating New York City. At that time no one knew about the second bomb or the evacuation order."

"And why make them for friends in two different hotels, thirty miles apart? Plus they live here anyway. Why not have them stay at your house?"

"What the hell are they up to?"

"I don't know, but I double-checked everything. It's his name. It's his credit card."

"We've got to pick these guys up. Ron is at the marina in case they show up there. I'll wait here."

"You have no authority there."

"I'll have to wing it. If I'm lucky, maybe they don't know that. You need to get someone over to the Marx. Check out that room."

"I'll try but there's no one else around. This place is deserted except for me."

"Get the police to check it out if you have to."

"Will do."

101

"Look Ms. Galloway, in case you hadn't realized, we've got one huge traffic jam across the entire city. I've got every man in the department out on the street trying to deal with a couple hundred thousand very angry people, from New York City no less. I have no idea when I will be able to get someone to check it out, but don't count on it happening until later today. Much later."

Dyan spent the past hour trying to get someone to check out the room at the Marx hotel. Most of the FBI's Syracuse contingent were reassigned to New York City and Boston, the two closest cities where the bomb might be. The rest of the agents, like Klien, were already assigned priority details. With the influx of people into the city, the State Troopers, Sheriff's Department, and Syracuse City Police had their hands full.

She looked at her watch. 4:05 P.M. "Screw it. I'll drive there myself . . . even though I'm not a fuckin' field agent!" She stood up, grabbed her keys from the desk, then glanced out the window. Interstate 690 was like a parking lot. She walked closer to the window. The streets below were no better. "Damn, it's gonna take me forever to get there." As she stared out the window, a smile came over her face. It was a gorgeous summer afternoon, eighty-five degrees, without a cloud in the sky. The Marx hotel was two miles, three at most, she thought. She threw her keys on the desk. "I'll walk."

A minute later her phone started ringing. Dyan was already too far down the hall to hear it.

102

Jack unfolded the New York State map. Although he knew it was a five hour, 320 mile drive to New York City by car, he wanted to assure himself the straight line distance from there to Syracuse was sufficiently far, just in case the bomb was . . . "Fuckin' al Qaeda." As he ran his finger along the map from the city toward the center of the state, he noticed the heavy black line, probably made with a wide-pointed felt tip pen, that was drawn across the middle of the map. It extended from a point just north of the city of Utica on the east, through the center of Syracuse, ending to the west at the town of Camillus. At that end of the line there was an arrow, pointing west. The number 270 was written next to it in bold black numerals.

His eyes kept tracing up and down the black line reading off the cities and towns near it from east to west. Marcy, Oriskany, Oneida, Chittenango, Syracuse, Fairmont, Camillus. Then the number 270. It meant nothing to him. He looked up at the video cameras, then out the window, then back down at the map. Marcy, Oriskany, Oneida, Chittenango, Syracuse, Fairmont, Camillus, 270.

Then his heart started pounding. It wasn't Marcy, Oriskany,

Oneida, Chittenango, Syracuse, Fairmont, Camillus. The line went close to those points on the map, but it didn't go directly over them. He traced his finger along the line again. The only city or town the line passed directly over was Syracuse. He traced his finger back to the right. The only other thing the line passed directly over was a blue box with the number thirty-three. It was located between Oriskany and Oneida. Exit 33 on the Thruway. The Verona exit. The one he just used an hour ago. The one less than a mile from the Turning Stone Resort.

He traced his finger along the line to the left, and stopped at Syracuse. The line crossed at the intersection of Interstate 81 and Route 690, right in the very center of Syracuse, a block away from the Marx hotel.

Jack walked over to the desk and picked up the compass. He went back over to the edge of the bed and repositioned the map so the arrow was pointing directly out the window in the same direction the video cameras were facing. He placed the compass on top of the line drawn on the map and waited for the fluorescent-colored needle to come to a complete stop. Then he slowly turned the compass in a clockwise direction until the needle lined up with the "N" on the outside of the compass dial. His eyes then moved around the compass dial, counterclockwise, and stopped where the black line on the map extended out from under the compass. The line came out at the "W" point. The dial read 270. 270° due west.

Jack lifted his head and looked again at the two video cameras. He now knew what they were pointed at. He stood up on the bed and gazed off to the horizon. He thought he saw buildings against the skyline. He blinked. They were gone. He knelt back down on the bed, looked at the arrow on the map, then at the video cameras.

He grabbed his cell phone. "God damn it." He pushed the end button, then redial. "God damn it." With the influx of people into central New York, the local cell towers were overloaded. He pressed the redial button again. "Yes!"

"You have reached Dyan Galloway at the FBI Field Office . . . "

"Fuck. Where the hell is she?"

" . . . and you'll be connected to the operator."

"Dyan. I think I found out what the hell they are doing. Why they need two hotel rooms. I think the bomb is at the Marx hotel. The bastards are going to video tape the explosion from here. You need to get ahold of the nearest NEST team. Their headquarters is Andrews Air Force Base, but the closest team is probably in New York City. Get them up here. You also need to get someone to the Marx hotel. See if the bomb can be moved. Somewhere. I don't know where. Jamesville Quarry maybe? Any place away from people." He looked at his watch. "It's eight after four. You've got less than an hour. Call me as soon as you get this."

Jack closed his cell phone and stared at it. "Fuck . . . if I can't call out, how the hell is she gonna call me?"

103

Dyan sat on the bench in the small park at Columbus Circle. She guessed she was at least halfway to the Marx hotel, and even though she walked the past twenty minutes at no more than a leisurely stroll, she was exhausted.

"I might be tired, but I'm still glad I didn't drive," she whispered to herself. The normally empty Saturday afternoon streets were filled with crawling, mostly lost, out-of-town cars, each filled with as many people as seats would allow. With the county War Memorial Building and the OnCenter convention center, designated shelters for New York City evacuees, just two blocks away, it was no wonder the streets were clogged.

Throughout the afternoon, Dyan tuned in CNN to catch a glimpse of how the evacuations were going. Although it appeared the majority of the inhabitants in the fifty designated cities would be removed far enough from the effects of a potential nuclear explosion, the government was already being blamed for not protecting those left behind. With less than twenty-four hours to plan and evacuate over forty-five million people, the decision was made to leave behind those too sick to be moved. Insufficient transportation, mostly busses, in some locations meant thousands of poor families, with no means to escape, were also left behind. With little or no police or fire protection, rioting had already broken out, and the smoke rising above several cities looked as if bombs had already gone off there.

Dyan eyed the carloads of people wondering what their plan was if nothing happened this afternoon. What if no bomb goes off? Will they return home? What if al Qaeda puts out another twenty-four-hour ultimatum, then another, then another, then another? How long will these people wait it out? How long could al Qaeda hold them hostage?

She glanced down at her watch, then quickly stood up. Before she could take a step, everything around her started spinning, very slowly. Her vision blurred, then started fading black as she collapsed back down onto the bench. She lowered her head to her knees and took as deep a breath as her hunched-over body would allow.

"Why does this have to happen to me now?" she whispered. A tear dripped down the bridge of her nose, fell onto the concrete slab between her feet, then evaporated within seconds after it hit the hot surface. She slowly sat up and wiped the rest of the tears from her cheeks. She took another deep breath. She was getting that queasy feeling. "Not again?" She placed both hands, palms down, on her belly. "This is supposed to be the happiest time of my life." More tears dripped down her cheeks, but she did not reach up to wipe them away. Instead she stared at the carloads of people, rubbed her belly, and wondered what the world would be like when her baby arrived.

104

"Ron Klien."

"Ron, thank god."

"Jack. You all right?"

"Yes, I'm fine."

"You're breaking up. Where are you? Jack . . . you still there?"

"Are you still at the marina?"

"Yes. No sign of the Rahieds."

"I need to have you . . . "

"Jack, you're breaking up. I'm going to hang up and call you back."

"No!"

105

"My name is Jack Nelson." Jack flashed his ID at the man standing behind the black marble-topped counter. I'm with the FBI and . . . "

"Room nineteen ten. The elevators are to the right," the man interrupted. He must have recognized the confused look on Jack's face. "I gave a pass key to the other agent. The elevator doors must have closed just as you walked by."

Jack stood in front of the elevator and pushed the button again several times as if doing so would make the doors open sooner. He glanced at his watch. 4:54 P.M. "What the fuck do I think I'm doing?"

He still could not believe he made it back to Syracuse as fast as he did. He also couldn't believe he was standing where he was. Especially at five o'clock. Zero hour. "What the fuck do I think I'm gonna be able to do?" He pushed the button again. "Fuckin' elevator." The doors glided open.

He jumped in and pushed the button marked nineteen. The doors stayed open. "Come on." He pushed the button again, and again. They finally closed. 4:55 P.M. "Damn thing is so slow . . . come on!" The elevator was moving so slow Jack didn't even feel it coming to a stop. He was surprised when the doors opened in front of him.

He stepped out onto the floor. "Fuckin' figures." The Marx hotel was a nineteen-story round building. The sign on the wall across from the elevators indicated room 1910 was on the other side of the floor, farthest from the elevator. Jack started running to his left, down the curved hallway, glancing at each room number as he ran past them.

Room 1910. "Fuck." The door was locked closed. He started banging on it. "Open up. FBI." He rammed his shoulder against the door. It didn't budge. He reached down, lifted his right pant leg, and unbuckled the strap that held the Smith & Wesson 38 revolver in his ankle holster. He stepped back and aimed at the electronic lock.

106

"What time is it?"

Mozat glanced down at his watch, then back up at Ziara, who was standing next to the video cameras. "Four fifty-six. One minute later than the last time you asked me."

"Should we start recording soon?"

"We will, in one more minute. It makes no sense to start recording too early. We only have thirty minutes of space on each tape."

"It looks so peaceful. Like our country was once. Do you remember?"

Mozat walked over and put his arm around Ziara. "I do remember. And I also remember how the infidels destroyed everything we had. Killed our parents. I do this for Allah and Jihad, but I also do it for what they have done to us and our country."

"Will they know something has happened?" Ziara pointed down to the people, several hundred, looking like ants in the garden and parking lot below.

"At this distance I am told we still might feel the shock wave from the blast, along with a muffled sound off in the distance.

Within seconds a plume of black smoke will rise into the sky which should be visible from the ground below. It will not take them long to figure out what the mushroom-shaped cloud means."

"Praise be to Allah."

"Four fifty-seven. Now it is time to start the cameras."

107

Jack was about to pull the trigger when he noticed the crack of light coming from between the door and the jam that he didn't think was there a second ago. The crack got wider. The door was opening. He moved to the right, out of the direct path of the doorway, and raised his gun, pointing it chest-high at the very center of the door.

"FBI." The door was now half-way open. "Come out with your hands out in front of you."

The door stopped moving. The silence seemed to go on forever, but Jack's training told him it was only seconds. It was times like these when an FBI agent's patience usually made the difference between living or dying. As he held his arms out in front of him, tightly gripping the 38 revolver, his eyes focused in on his watch. Although he couldn't see the dial, he knew he only had minutes. To do what, he wasn't sure of yet. Then, seconds later, he had his plan. He'd shoot his way in. Maybe he could stop the bomb from going off. If not, it wouldn't make any difference anyway.

Jack squeezed his finger on the trigger.

"Jack, it's me."

"Dyan?" He loosened his finger from the trigger. The door opened and Dyan stepped into the opening. "What are you doing here? Didn't you get my message?"

"Jack. The bomb. It's here. We only have three minutes."

Dyan turned and went back into the room. Jack followed. Dyan pointed to the middle of the bed. It looked like a giant bullet, two feet long, and not quite six inches in diameter. It was painted gun metal gray. A digital timer, its red numbers flashing as every second ticked by, was taped with what appeared to be duct tape, close to the base of the weapon.

The red numbers counted down; 00:02:02, 00:02:01, 00:02:00, 00:01:59 . . .

Jack raised his gun and aimed at the timer.

"What are you doing?"

"I'm gonna try to stop it."

"But what if it doesn't work?"

"In two minutes it won't matter anyway."

"Wait." Dyan put her hand on Jack's out stretched arm. "Hold me."

Jack lowered his arm. "What?"

"Hold me." Dyan stepped over to him and put her arms around him. He wrapped his arms around her. She pressed her body against his and laid her head on his chest.

"I want you to know I fell in love with you the first time I saw you. I wish our life together could have been different."

"Dyan . . . "

"No, let me talk. No matter what happens in the next two minutes, I need for you to know something. Jack. I'm pregnant."

Jack pushed away and they both stared into each others eyes. Neither spoke. Neither had to. Their eyes spoke for them.

Jack reached for Dyan. They embraced in a long, gentle, but sensuous kiss. Jack shook as he started to cry. Dyan squeezed him even tighter. Still coupled, she reached up with her right hand and pulled his left forearm from her waist. He dropped it in response. She clutched his hand, placed it on her belly, then placed hers over his.

"Jack Nelson. There is no one else I would rather be with right now. You are the love of my life, the father of my child, and my husband forever."

Jack opened his eyes and blinked several times to try to clear the tears. He finally focused on the flashing red numbers.

00:00:07, 00:00:06, 00:00:05.

With Dyan still clutching him, he raised his right arm and aimed at the timer.

00:00:03, 00:00:02, 00:00:01.

His hand was shaking as he squeezed the trigger. "I love you," were the last words either of them heard before the deafening blast.

108

Mozat and Ziara stood next to each other in front of the window. His right arm was on her shoulder. His left hand was held out in front of them as they both stared at the second hand on his watch.

"Twenty seconds."

"We are about to witness both the beginning of the end, and the end of the beginning."

"Ten, nine, eight."

The loud noise startled them both. They turned in time to see the door to their room fly open.

"FBI. Get you hands up on your head." It took Ron Klien only seconds to position himself in the middle of the large room with his arms outstretched and pointing his nine millimeter revolver at Mozat and Ziara. "I said get you hands on your heads. NOW!"

Instead of complying, they both turned toward the window. "I am afraid you are too late young man." They both looked at the watch, then raised their heads and stared out the window.

109

"How sure are you he only had two?"

"David, you're a goddamn lawyer." Blackman took a deep breath, then lowered his voice. "You've read the report. There is no way he could have known about these details unless he was directly involved. Every fact was consistent with what we uncovered, except one of course, which he knew nothing about."

"And you believe him?"

"He's the only person alive that knows the whole truth, first hand."

"Why should we trust the bastard?"

"I don't think we have a choice."

"And why should he trust us?"

"Because he knows he doesn't have a choice."

"We have no proof he wasn't involved in selling the bombs to al Qaeda."

"Other than his word."

"His word!"

"And the fact he kept this whole thing a secret for over forty years. He had many opportunities before this to get rid of the warheads, and he didn't. He saw what we did to Afghanistan and Iraq. I think he was smart enough to know if we ever found out he was directly responsible for providing nuclear warheads to al Qaeda, that he'd be bombed to kingdom come. Plus if he had been involved, I believe he would have only sold one. He would have kept the second for what it was originally intended for. To protect him from attack."

"The bastard is a two-bit dictator."

"Who somehow has been able to stay in power while we've had eight presidents at the helm. He's the longest-reigning leader in the world today. David, Fidel Castro is no dummy."

The last forty-eight hours saw a whirlwind of activity by the administration to try to recover the public's confidence in its ability to fight the war with al Qaeda. Unfortunately, most of its victories were won behind the scenes and unbeknownst to the public at large, while al Qaeda's were clearly visible to the entire world.

The FBI was able to confirm by the paint samples found in the hidden compartments on the Cocamo's inflatable dingy that the nuclear warheads were stored there. The Cocamo was purchased by the Rahieds in December, and the yacht was finally identified on several videos as it cruised along the Intracoastal Waterway. The Rahieds spent several months in the Florida Keys and the Caribbean, which gave them ample opportunity to rendezvous with the party selling the weapons. Aleksandr Popov's journal provided the convincing story as to how the weapons got to, and remained in, Cuba. The only missing link was, how did the weapons, after staying secretly hidden in Cuba for over forty years, end up in al Qaeda's hands?

When the first weapon was discovered last Friday and confirmed to be one of the Russian warheads sent to Cuba in 1962, the Secretary of State was secretly dispatched to Cuba to meet with Castro. Fifteen minutes into their meeting, the Cuban president, red-faced and short of breath, and looking as if he was about to suffer a heart attack, requested a short recess. Two hours later he returned, obviously very upset, and listened to the rest of the Secretary's presentation. Without missing a beat and very matter-of-factly, Castro confirmed the existence of two warheads.

During the 1962 Cuban Missile Crisis, 158 nuclear warheads were on Cuban soil. It was then that Castro first saw the real power these weapons commanded. The two superpowers were on the brink of war, in which Cuba would likely be the first to be annihilated, yet neither side fired a weapon. Castro was convinced war was averted because each side had nuclear weapons, and now some of those weapons were located ninety miles from U.S. soil. Their possession, not their use, was enough to stop a war from starting. This he felt would be his guarantee against a future U.S. attack. Once his Army surrounded one of the bunkers where the warheads were being stored, he put on his best madman routine for both Khrushchev and Kennedy, which was enough to convince them to agree to his demands.

Two of the smallest tactical warheads would be secretly left behind. They were hidden in a vault at his Presidential Palace. Anyone who helped carry out the plan, including the two Cuban Army Generals who made the physical transfer of the weapons, were to be eliminated. That would leave four people with knowledge of the secret. The Kennedy brothers, Khrushchev, and him. He was unaware of Kennedy's pardoning of a fifth, Popov.

Following 9/11, Castro waited for communications from the U.S. government regarding the warheads. He knew with the current war on terror, the U.S. could no longer tolerate the weapons under his control. He indicated he was looking forward to negotiating an economic trade agreement in exchange for releasing the weapons. When the U.S. did not come forward, it confirmed his long-held suspicion that knowledge of the secret had vanished with the untimely deaths of the Kennedy brothers. It was a suspicion he could never approach the U.S. government with directly.

With his advancing age, Castro did not want the same fate to befall him. He shared the secret with his brother Raul, and his close advisor José del Garro. He left the meeting earlier to confirm the warheads were missing, which they were, to confront his brother Raul who he believed knew nothing of the missing weapons, which he did not, and to find del Garro, who he then found out had been missing for several days. He now suspected del Garro as the traitor. Fearing U.S. retaliation, he pledged complete cooperation.

The meeting with Castro confirmed the al Qaeda threat of having a second bomb was real, and led the administration to order the largest evacuation in human history, even though they realized some would be left behind. Although the decision was in the best interest of the public, leaving the sick and poor behind further eroded the public's confidence that its government could protect it.

Now, forty-eight hours later, the administration was fearful of the second shoe dropping, one that could topple it. With bin Laden still in custody, what if al Qaeda had a third nuclear warhead? Everyone was waiting for the next ultimatum to surface.

"Why did al Qaeda give up that first warhead?" Blackman waited, but Cross did not respond. "They knew they could terrorize us just as much, and maybe even more, if they could prove to the American public they had a nuclear weapon. And what better way to prove it than to turn it over to us. They hoped we'd panic, which we did. They hoped we'd believe them if they said they had more, which we did. They hoped their second threat would result in enough public pressure to release bin Laden. Think what that would have done for their cause. But they also knew that if they ever exploded the bomb, we'd never release bin Laden. They understood the true power of a nuclear warhead. It's not the destructive power of the bomb itself, but the threat of using it. That philosophy is what kept the Cold War cold, it's what kept the Cuban Missile Crisis a crisis, and it's what Castro thought had protected him all these years. If you can use the weapon correctly, you never have to use it.

"I am convinced Castro is telling the truth. I am convinced al Qaeda only had two weapons. I am convinced they gave up the first one to make us believe they had more where that came from. They used the second one to reinforce their claim. Now they have no more warheads. Their tactic now is to try to terrorize us with words."

"It appears to me it is working."

"Only if we let it."

EPILOGUE

Things were different. Her place was changed. It was more peaceful, more calming. Like floating on a puffy white cloud. She could not remember the yesterdays or think about the tomorrows. Her only thoughts were of the now. Of being here. And although it changed, in many ways it was also the same. She wondered . . . could this be heaven?

The sounds drifted into her thoughts. Had they always been there? Was it only now that her mind was letting her hear them? Was it a voice? It had been so long since she heard a voice. A real voice. Yes, it was a voice. But the voice spoke words she could not understand. Yet her mind seemed to. She knew because her body leaked warm wetness.

Then suddenly the voice changed. The words cried out, louder and louder. The cloud she was on shook. The warmth left her. Then there was silence. She knew she was still in that place, but how could it be heaven? There was no crying in heaven, was there? Not hearing an answer, she drifted off to sleep.

"Honey."

She immediately recognized the calming voice, but

remained frozen, lying on her side in the bed, her back towards him.

"Honey. There's a hungry little boy here who is patiently waiting for his breakfast."

Dyan opened her eyes. 4:06 A.M. "You can set your clock by him." She rolled onto her back and turned her head. Jack was laying on his side with his head propped up on his arm. Sitting, with his back against Jack's chest was the smiling four-month-old. "One of these mornings I've gotta get a picture of this. You look so cute." She rolled onto her side and gently poked at the baby's stomach.

"What about me?"

Dyan looked at Jack. "You're cute too." She leaned over and gave him a kiss. "But he's cuter."

"I can live with that." He picked up the baby and laid him down next to Dyan. The little boy waved his arms and legs, knowing what came next.

"Did you get ahold of Blackman?" At the sound of Jack's voice the baby turned his head.

"What? You can't eat and listen at the same time?" The baby turned his head toward Dyan and within a second was back eating his breakfast. Dyan looked up at Jack. "Men."

"You mean him, right?"

"Both of you."

"So, did you get ahold of him?"

"Yes, he called me back yesterday."

"And?"

"And what?"

"What did he say?"

"He said he thought I was doing the right thing."

"And what do you think?"

Dyan looked up at Jack again. "The news must have traveled fast. An hour later I got a call from the president."

"The president of what?"

"Funny. He said he heard I was leaving the Bureau and thanked me for all that I had done. He also thought I was making the right decision."

"And what do you think?"

"He said he thought I had done more to fight terrorism than any person he knew. That if it wasn't for me, he probably would not be sitting in the Oval Office today."

"And you don't believe him?"

"Thousands of people died . . . "

"The hepatitis virus was spread a month before you found out what they were doing. I'll say it again, before YOU found out what they were doing. Think how many more would have died if it hadn't been for you."

"What about you?"

"What about me?"

"I may have found the bomb that day, but you stopped it from going off."

"But YOU found it. Dyan, the president is right. You took down al Qaeda." Jack gently knocked on the bed's wooden headboard with his fist. "No terrorist attacks in a year. No evidence of any more sleeper cells. No more bombs. Our form of government survived. The war may never be over, but it looks like we survived some of the worst of it."

There was a long period of silence as they both watched the baby.

"You never answered my question."

"What question?"

"How do YOU feel about leaving the Bureau?"

Dyan looked down at the baby. His mouth was still on her breast, but he had stopped sucking. His eyes were closed. She looked up into Jack's eyes. They both smiled.

"I KNOW I made the right decision."